William Hutton

# Twelve Thousand Miles over Land and Sea

Wanderings in Europe

William Hutton

**Twelve Thousand Miles over Land and Sea**
*Wanderings in Europe*

ISBN/EAN: 9783337194185

Printed in Europe, USA, Canada, Australia, Japan

Cover: Foto ©Andreas Hilbeck / pixelio.de

More available books at **www.hansebooks.com**

# TWELVE THOUSAND MILES

OVER

# LAND AND SEA;

OR,

# WANDERINGS IN EUROPE.

BY

## REV. WILLIAM HUTTON,

PASTOR OF GREENWICH STREET PRESBYTERIAN CHURCH, PHILADELPHIA.

PHILADELPHIA:
GRANT, FAIRES & RODGERS, PRINTERS,
52 & 54 NORTH SIXTH STREET.
1878.

TO

MY ALMA MATER,

WITH HEARTY WISHES

FOR THE CONTINUED PROSPERITY OF

# HAMILTON COLLEGE,

THESE "WANDERINGS IN EUROPE" ARE

MOST GRATEFULLY DEDICATED

BY THE AUTHOR.

"I SAT me down to build a boat
 And set it on the sea afloat:
 I wrought it with a loving will,
 Putting to task my utmost skill:
 I gave its form the highest grace
 My hand and eye knew how to trace,
 And beautified its every part
 According to my native art.
 I set the mast, and spread the sail
 To catch the softliest-breathing gale,
 And then I sent it forth to go
 Whichever way the wind might blow.
 Who knows?   It may be lost at sea,
 Or come with treasure back to me."

*MacKellar.*

# LIST OF ILLUSTRATIONS.

# PREFACE.

"A thing of beauty is a joy forever"; and so is an excursion to the "Old World." It can never be forgotten. It opens up a "new world" of thought and imagination. It is both a stimulus and tonic. It strengthens the body, invigorates the mind, and cultivates the taste. The scenery is so charming, and the customs and costumes are so peculiar, that the tourist is being continually surprised and delighted. And this is true of both city and country. The farmhouses, fences, trees, birds, flowers, and garb of plodding peasants are quite unlike to those of his native land. And the cities and towns, with narrow, crooked streets, old, many-cornered buildings, and ivy-covered walls, contrast strikingly with American cities now "springing up." Then, the means and methods of locomotion, the peculiarly constructed railroad cars, dog and donkey wagons, present scenes amusing and grotesque. The castles, ivied ruins, monuments, museums, libraries, art galleries, exhibition palaces, royal parks, stately cathedrals, charm by their beauty, inspire by their grandeur, and instruct by their treasures of knowledge and of art.

Having been appointed a delegate, in 1874, to the General Assembly of the Irish Presbyterian Church, we were permitted, after the duties of that office were discharged, to wander over "land and sea." These "wanderings" extended through Ireland, Scotland, England, Wales, Belgium, Germany, Switzerland, Italy, and France. Purchasing the best guide books, maps, and time tables, and selecting the routes that seemed most pleasant, we traveled alone. By this method perfect freedom was enjoyed. We were neither consigned to hotel keepers, omnibus drivers, or muleteers, nor conducted hastily through art galleries, libraries, and cathedrals, by impatient guides. Some 400 miles were traveled on foot. The poets conducted us to many a shining lake, shady bower, and sparkling stream; and our pages are adorned with quite a number of selections from their writings.

Sketches of these wanderings—published in several religious journals—were widely read, and favorably received; lectures were also prepared, descriptive of the places visited, and scenes witnessed. Friends —lay and clerical—suggested that the "notes" and "sketches" be put in permanent form, and generously subscribed for a large number of "copies." This modest little volume presents itself in response to these friendly solicitations. The writer, young, and inexperienced at book-making, pleads for that kindly indulgence usually granted the "first literary venture."

WILLIAM HUTTON.

*Philadelphia, March,* 1878.

# CONTENTS.

# WANDERINGS IN EUROPE.

## CHAPTER I.

### TEN DAYS UPON THE DEEP.

WEDNESDAY, May 20th, dawns with a sky clear and cloudless. The harbor of New York presents a beautiful scene as the mists rise from the waters and disappear at the presence of the sun. Huge ferry-boats float hither and thither freighted with hundreds of men and women going to their accustomed toil. Lively little tugs steam merrily seaward in quest of some wind-forsaken ship, or other hapless craft, that may require aid. The stately ocean steamer moves slowly to her mooring, as if wearied by her journey over the sea. Sturdy laborers unburden the richly-freighted ships that lie along the wharves. The sailors have climbed the masts, and are busy in the rigging preparing

to meet the winds that so wildly sweep the sea.
Away in the distance the white-winged boat glides
gracefully over the shining waters.    Here and
there the shrill sound of the steam-whistle—the
boatmen's salutation—startles the stillness of the
morning, and awakens the echoes along the neighboring shore.    As the hour of 9 approaches, the
scene at the Cunard wharves, Jersey City, is lively
and exciting.    Heavily laden express wagons
thunder through the gates, and drop their costly
burdens near the waiting ship.    Omnibus, coach
and cab crowded with sea-bound passengers, whirl
in eager haste to the appointed place.    Hundreds
of men and women exchanging hurried glances,
move upon the decks, or stand upon the wharf.
But the last bell has rung, the parting moment
come, and friends must bid adieu—some never
more to meet!  How touching is that scene—
hands are closely clasped, loved ones are embraced,
the kiss of affection is impressed, sobs give ut-
terance to feeling, and eyes are dimmed with tears.
All aboard!    And the steamer is in motion.
Slowly she swings into the current, and her prow
is pointed towards the sea.    The wharf is fairly
white with handkerchiefs wildly waving, and
many parting kisses are flung from tiny fingers.

Steadily and gracefully our ship moves over
the waveless waters, and at 11.30 we have passed

beyond the " Narrows," and the pilot is dismissed.

The city and its gleaming spires have disappeared; the " Highlands " have sunk beneath the sea, and at 4 o'clock the sandy shore of Long Island passes slowly out of sight.

Our gallant captain stands upon the "bridge," and puts the men in motion. His method is peculiar. A whistle, and the sailors rush upon the deck; a second whistle, and up the ladders they go—nimble-footed fellows—like a troop of squirrels; a third whistle, and they swing off and begin to unfurl the sails. But to give unity and effect to their labors they unite in singing. And just here we have one of those strange, weird, sailor songs, so often the precursor of fearful blasts, and the accompaniment of wild surgings by the sea. How mournfully it sounds, and what a feeling of sadness it excites! As we listen, a sense of loneliness steals through the soul. We become conscious of the situation. We realize, that "out on an ocean all boundless we ride," and that we are not " homeward bound." Home and friends, green fields and fragrant flowers, are behind us, while around and beneath is the ever-changing, billowy, treacherous sea! The eye sweeps the horizon without discovering an object. The land upon which we so recently gazed, has strangely and suddenly disappeared. The sea and the sky are all that we behold.

And even now the sky is overcast, and the scudding clouds herald the coming storm. But how grand the sea ; how strange and varied its motion !

Look at those swelling waves with snowy crests, chasing each other past the plunging steamer. How they whirl and leap, like schoolboys at play !

How buoyant, joyous, free, seem these briny billows. They submit to no restraint. The captain's voice and the seaman's song are alike unheeded. Onward they rush impelled by the rising wind. We wonder not that so many of the young are attracted by the sea. Its very movements inspire. Its wide expanse, varying hue, and changeful voice, charm, fascinate.

> " Roll on, thou deep, dark-blue ocean—roll !
>     Ten thousand fleets sweep over thee in vain ;
>   Man marks the earth with ruin—his control
>     Stops with the shore ; "
> "Thou glorious mirror, where the Almighty's form
>     Glasses itself in tempests ; in all time,
>   Calm or convulsed,—in breeze, or gale, or storm,
>     Icing the pole, or in the torrid clime,
>   Dark-heaving ; boundless, endless, and sublime,
>     The image of eternity—the throne
>   Of the Invisible."

The last sad refrain has been sung by the sailors ; the sails are all set, and the stiffening wind has stretched the canvas to its utmost tension.

Our noble vessel, the Abyssinia, is one of the largest and staunchest ships of the Cunard line— 370 feet long, 42 feet wide, and 35 feet deep. The ship's force numbers one hundred and thirty-seven men, and some half a dozen women.

These are divided into three departments. The sailing department has 50 men ; the engineer's department, 43 men, and the steward's 44 men and some half a dozen women. Each of these departments is thoroughly organized; every man is at his post, and every man expected to do his duty. The discipline is excellent. The men are kept constantly busy sweeping and swabbing the decks, burnishing the brass, and trimming the sail.

The steward's department is quite popular, and admirably managed. The table is well furnished ; the waiters prompt and courteous. We have fresh (?) strawberries a thousand miles from land ! They are as rosy and red as if they had just dropt blushing from the bushes.

There are a large number of passengers on board. All the cabins are full—even the steward's rooms are occupied.

Among them are Americans from north and south, east and west; Canadians, English, Scotch, French, and a few Irish gentlemen, "all of the olden time." Various trades and professions have representatives—bankers, merchants, doctors, clergymen of different denominations, and sundry politicians. A number of ladies are going abroad; some to improve their health, others to enlarge their experience, complete their education, or—kind fortune favoring—to change their name!

In the steerage, quite a number of stalwart men and sturdy women have taken passage. With some of these the trip is one of pleasure. They cross the sea to visit friends and cheer the hearts of aged parents. But with others how different! They have been unfortunate. No work could be obtained; no friendly hand was outstretched, and homeward they return hoping for better days in the sea-girt isle. And yet they are not utterly dejected. They are humorous and witty. Nor has the old fiddler lost his cunning. With what skill he draws that magic bow!—and how the trembling strings give expression to the feelings of his heart. How in the twilight hour he stirs the *soles* of his nervous auditors by his lively music; or, by a sudden change, moistens the eye of the sympathetic listener, by his tender and plaintive melodies!

During the first two days the decks are crowded; the merry laugh is heard; the steward's bell is responded to with delight; and the abundant food

is eaten in quantities that would startle the econo-
mic proprietor of any modern boarding-house.
But by the whirling waves, and rocking ship, the
scene is changed.  The decks are deserted ; the
laughing has suddenly ceased, and the recently
joyous company is sullen and silent.  The few who
appear at the summons of the steward, look, apparently, with unmingled disgust at the food he
has provided.  Here and there, along the ship's
side, some suffering passenger casts wistful eyes at
the hissing waters, and leans tenderly downward
as if soliciting the sympathy of the sea.  Cries,
strange and startling, are heard in the cabins.
The excited stewardess rushes along the narrow
aisles as if the safety of the ship depended upon
the celerity of her movements.

The doctor, quick-footed, tramps "fore and
aft," giving gentle hints, suggesting methods of
treatment, and adding the required prescription.
Our ship has suddenly become a floating hospital.
Everybody, and every object, seems to be at the
point of dissolution and disintegration.  The expressions of dissatisfaction at the unsteadiness of
the ship are frequent and emphatic.  Some even
wish for the wings of the storm, that they might
fly homeward and be at rest.  The experience is
decidedly *bitter*.  Not a few would willingly
forego the pleasures promised in the future, in

order to be released from the pain experienced in the present.

But the sky suddenly brightens, the wind blows less violently, and the sea grows calm. And what a change in the expressions and movements of the passengers! The decks are crowded; the dining-room becomes a centre of attraction, and laughter is heard in the cabins. The recently staggering ship, impelled by wind and steam, moves over the less turbulent waves with surprising steadiness.

We are now acclimated and prepared to enjoy the situation. True, it is novel, and yet it is de-lightful. The manner in which time is spent differs with the taste of the individual. But a change of method is induced by the position in which we are placed. Several old friends were left on shore and new ones must be found to take their places. Business is at home, and so are the daily papers. Shopping must be dispensed with, and so must pastoral visitation. And yet how quickly time flies, and with what joy we meditate upon our isolation !

We do not forget absent friends, and yet we feel glad at the temporary separation. Peace, quiet, restfulness is ours. Hurry, anxiety, excitement, dwell not here. What a blessed relief from all things human ! The postman does not trouble us. That benevolent book-agent, whose unfathomable

valise holds specimen copies of all the recent pub--
lications, no longer annoys by his irresistible im-
portunities. Those hoary-headed beggars, whose
mournful tales have moved the bread from the
pantry to their pockets, are absent. The nimble-
footed newsboy does not startle with the shrill cry
of "Murder in the fifth ward!" "Terrible accident!" "Fire and great loss of life!" "Drown-
ing in the Delaware!" From such unwelcome
news the bounding billows separate us. The daily
papers come not with their chapter of accidents;
the "latest scandal," and the bitter declamations
of partizan politicians. We are in blissful ignorance of human affairs. And "when ignorance is
bliss 'tis folly to be wise."

Three objects impress us; the sea, the sky, the
ship. With the sky we hold communication.
Daily, at noon, the captain has a message from the
sun. It is brief and to the point. It informs us
of our exact location, and of the distance traveled
since the previous noon. This is all the news we
have from abroad, and more we do not want.
"Plenty to eat and nothing to do." What a
happy lot is ours! Yes, truly; plenty to eat.
Coffee comes at 7 o'clock; breakfast at 8.30;
lunch at 12; dinner at 4; tea at 7.30, and supper
at 9 o'clock. How time flies in discussing the
merits of these English dishes! When the tables

are deserted, the decks present a lively scene. Here and there are groups engaged in brilliant conversation. Some of the quiet ones sit in comfortable chairs reading the last novel, or looking over a guide-book, arrange their future excursions.

Sometimes the scenes are positively amusing. Here are venerable women conducted to their chairs. Suddenly the ship gives a lurch, and a procession of chairs, with fearfully frightened occupants, marches in " double quick " to the side of the vessel. A rebounding wave returns the fugitives, and they are made secure, to their evident satisfaction, by being fastened with a rope. At certain hours the " fashionables promenade." The captain, a gallant tar, usually leads the procession. With swaying forms and bending limbs, up and down the deck they march in zigzag lines. Many a merry laugh is indulged in at the expense of some hapless fellow-passenger. Opportunities are frequently afforded for the exhibition, both of agility and strength; and many gentle courtesies are accepted and responded to, during these afternoon excursions.

There are occasional excitements created by the nearness of some ship, or in exchanging signals with some distant steamer. One evening, just before dark, a rush was made to the forecastle, while the cry, "ship ahead!" rang up and down the steamer. The vessel was slowly moving under sail, across our bows, to leeward.

The rapid motion of the steamer brought us speedily within speaking distance, and were it not for the immediate command of the captain to put the helm " hard to port," we would have run her down in a few minutes. We came so near, that a slight mistake by the wheelsman, would have led to the most disastrous consequences. On another occasion a ship approaches us from the north, swinging gracefully on the pliant wave. She comes so close that we could distinguish the faces upon the deck, and our hearts beat fast and strong, when thus brought face to face with fellow-travelers upon the wide and restless waters.

Sad and startling was the news this morning. One of our passengers has disappeared,—never-more to be seen! Judge Doolittle, of Utica, came on deck at 9 o'clock last evening, and has not since been seen. It is supposed that in a state of mental depression, or melancholy, he cast himself into the sea. Sad news to be flashed back to waiting and anxious friends.

The Queen's birthday is duly celebrated by passengers and crew. At early morn the British flag is sent flying to the mast-head in honor of the Queen. A sumptuous dinner is provided;

speeches made; national airs sung,—including "God save the Queen" and the "Star Spangled Banner."

"A grand concert!" Such is the notice that greets the eye, both in the cabin and on the deck. The object is a worthy one—the Sailors' Orphan Home, at Liverpool. The state-room is crowded—quite a brilliant audience. Minister Schenck—our minister returning to the Court of St. James—presides, and introduces the performers. A French "prima donna" and the leader of a New York orchestra, are the "special attractions."

We have some good "fiddling" and "trilling," with a few real good old English songs that "bring down the house," or, rather stagger the steamer. The captain, as jolly a tar as ever guided a ship, sings in true sailor fashion, "I'm afloat, I'm afloat, and the rover is free."

A collection is taken up remarkable both for the amount, and the material; one hundred and eighty dollars is put upon the plates, all in silver and gold, except one representative of the depreciated greenback.

The Sabbath day comes, bringing a clear sky and a quiet sea. A service is held in the morning at which both passengers and crew are present. The captain reads the Episcopal service ; responses loud and hearty being made by the officers and crew. A sermon is preached by a venerable divine, a New York city pastor.

The situation, and the surroundings, are adverted to by the preacher, who secures undivided attention by the soundness of his doctrine, and the appropriateness of his theme.

The most delightful evening spent on shipboard, is this evening of the Sabbath.

A goodly number of the passengers, male and female, stand upon the deck, and unite in singing some sweet and familiar hymns. The sea is like glass; the stars sparkle in the sky, and the moon is full. The ship glides so smoothly that we are quite unconscious of motion. And here, under the canopy of the starry heavens, and upon the bosom of the deep, shut out from all the world, we join with heart and voice in singing " Nearer my God to thee," and " Jesus lover of my soul." As the words, " safe into the haven guide," are repeated, hearts are touched and eyes are tearful. We feel that God is here, listening in the silence of this twilight hour, to the songs His children are singing, and the prayers they are offering in song.

But the tenth day has arrived. For nine long days we have looked upon the sea and sky, and now we wish for land. Our vessel has averaged about three hundred miles a day, and land is promised before the setting sun.  As the day advances the land excitement increases.  The sea has changed its color and the waves have changed their form.  " Kerry Coast lies off to the left," says one.  " Yes," replies an old woman of evident Irish extraction, who had been sick during the voyage, " an' one sight off the auld counthry will cure me!"  Everybody is on deck at 5 p. m.  Eyes, aided by opera-glasses and telescopes, are peering into the mists that have settled along the Irish coast.  The steerage passengers crowd the forecastle.  Suddenly a giant rock looms up grandly in the sea.  Land! land! is rung out in merry shouts.  Slowly and beautifully the Kerry mountains make their appearance, and the Irish coast, for scores of miles, bursts upon the sight!  What an excitement among the steerage passengers.  How some of them fairly leap for joy!  Laughter and tears are mingled, as those lofty mountains and green fields appear beyond the swelling flood.

We sweep along the coast with bright eyes and happy hearts.

> " All the storms will soon be over,
> Then we'll anchor in the harbor."

We pass Valentia Bay, where the ocean cable is landed.  On a broad rock, high above the waves, stands the signal station, to which our captain reports, by sending to the mast-head, the colors of the

Abyssinia. The sun has now set, and lights are blazing along the coast. It looks as if Will-o-the-wisp, with lighted torch, went bounding from head-land to headland all the way to Cork. Mizen Head, Cape Clear, and old Kinsale, are passed in succession; and at 11 P. M. we enter the harbor of Cork.

A lighter is waiting, some miles from the shore, to receive both passengers and mail. Parting words are spoken; cheers given for the noble Abyssinia, and we are steaming up to Queenstown at the hour of twelve.

Less than a score of cabin passengers land at this point. And these are tourists, intending to visit places of interest in Ireland; six of them—a company of ladies—going direct to Killarney. But we are ashore, and rushed immediately into the custom-house. Here, valises, trunks, and satchels are carefully examined by her majesty's faithful officers. What a diligent search for "see-gars." And what surprise is manifested when we declare that there was no such contraband material in our possession, and that we were not even partial to the weed. "The gintleman may pass along," exclaims the disappointed smoker. So we "pass along" to the "Queen's hotel," and there enjoy the solid comforts of a bed that seems to be moving, but is really motionless.

# CHAPTER II.



QUEENSTOWN is built on the side of a hill that slopes gradually down to the sea. It was formerly called " Cove," but received its present name upon the visit of her Britannic Majesty, in 1849. From the heights above the town the scenery is quite picturesque. Yonder is Spike Island. It is a convict depot, and some two thousand men are employed in excavating and building. Close by is Rocky Island, having a powder magazine cut in the solid rock, containing some ten thousand barrels of powder. What a splendid prize for the Fenians. And how easily they might get—well—blown up!

This harbor of Cork, that stretches away before us to the sea, is one of the finest in the world. It is capable of affording shelter to the entire British navy. Here, the celebrated Drake found refuge, when closely pursued by the Spanish fleet.

24

And Crosshaven creek, into which he sailed and where safety was found, is known to the local mariner as " Drake's pool." The city of Cork is eleven miles distant, and we are off to the home of the " Corkonian." What charming scenery ! The harbor so magnificent; the winding river Lee; the groves and villas; the sparkling lawns and lovely green fields, are a feast for eyes wearied with the monotony of the sea.

What freshness and beauty all around us! What sweetness in the bird songs ! What fragrant odors on the breeze ! With the clear sky, balmy air, and beautiful scenery, we are delighted. What a pleasant introduction to this saintly isle, on this May morning !

But here is Cork, the southern capital. And here comes Mr. " Corkonian," an excellent specimen. What an excellent subject for an artist. How he bows, and whines, and pleads for the privilege of " carryin' yere satchel." We demur, pleading as an excuse, the need of proper exercise. He responds: " Och in sure, a jintlemun the likes of you sur, wouldn't tire yerselves. Plase, sur, I'll be afther takin' you to wheresomever you might be goin, and unsasin' blessins on yer sowl ! " Of course we relent, relax our hold upon our baggage, which is quickly seized by this oily boy of Cork. Then follow questions about "Ameriky"

in rapid succession, that fairly surprise us.  As
we proceed, we are fully enlightened regarding
the woes and wants of "ould Ireland."  The repressive policy of the British government; the
system of absenteeism by which Ireland is impoverished ; the unhappy relation subsisting between
landlord and tenant; the course that should be
pursued in order to restore harmony, and bring
about an era of good feeling ; these and kindred
topics, are discussed with a logic and an eloquence
that would win fame for a learned professor.
Not since college days, when studying *Bowen*,
have we been so instructed in political economy.
Now and then we cast a suspicious eye upon this
philosophic individual, somewhat perplexed in
harmonizing his extensive knowledge and his
shabby appearance.  He has a shrewd cast of
countenance, and occasionally his eyes twinkle
merrily.  His " brogue " is the genuine southern
type, and the repetition of complimentary phrases,
with a peculiar modulation, indicate that he has
kissed the " blarney stone."  But that pale face
and these well-patched garments, reveal his poverty.  Indeed, the discrepancy between the man and
the garments, excites the suspicion that they were
ever made to his measure.  If so, then surely the tailor
lost his reckoning.  Our sympathy is excited by
his tales of suffering, and after he has conducted

us here and there, pointing out the objects of interest, we propose some compensation. A multitude of pennies carried in our pockets over the sea, are kindly offered, and as kindly refused. The amount is considerable, and yet this hungry mortal has no regard for "coppers,"—"he always likes a bit o' silver sur." We yield the point and give him both, receiving in return, such an Irish blessing!

After conversing with this "Corkonian," we concluded that Gray was correct in his elegy, when he asserted the possibility of highly gifted men dying without proper recognition.

Indeed, upon the marble slab that will mark the last resting place of this rustic philosopher, might well be inscribed the words—

> "Perhaps in this neglected spot, is laid
>     Some heart once pregnant with celestial fire;
>  Hands that the rod of empire might have sway'd,
>     Or wak'd to ecstasy the living lyre.
>  But knowledge to *his* eyes her ample page,
>     Rich with the spoils of time, did ne'er unroll;
>  Chill penury repress'd *his* noble rage,
>     And froze the genial current of the soul."

Cork is a city of considerable size. Its population is estimated at between seventy and eighty thousand. It is well built, and quite attractive. The principal streets are wide and well paved, but not remarkable for cleanliness. The city is governed by a mayor, sixteen aldermen, and forty-eight councillors. It returns two members to the British parliament. History informs us that St. Fionn Bar, an anchorite, founded a monastery in Cork in the beginning of the seventh century; and that his seminary was attended by 700 scholars. It is related that Cromwell caused the church bells to be cast into cannon, during his residence in this city. Here William Penn was converted to Quakerism, by the preaching of Thomas Loe; and not far distant is the grave of Wolfe, author of the lines beginning, "Not a drum was heard—not a funeral note." It was in Cork that the celebrated Father Mathew began his career as a preacher of "total abstinence." He was supplied with funds by a brother-in-law, who was—strange to say—a distiller. The effect of "Mathew's" preaching upon the brother-in-law's distillery was very decisive. The distillery ceased its flow of liquid fire, and the brother-in-law became a bankrupt! The Roman Catholic Church of the Holy Trinity, a beautiful Gothic edifice, was founded by this reformer.

And in St. Patrick street, the people of Cork have erected a "handsome" statue of this most successful temperance advocate.

It would seem that the influence of good St.

Fionn Bar is still felt in this southern city, for no less than eight educational institutions of a scientific character are here located. The Queen's college, built of limestone, in Gothic style, is an imposing edifice, and occupies a conspicuous position. The " Royal Cork institution " has an extensive library, and some interesting manuscripts in the Irish language. The museum has a number of stones inscribed with the letters used by the Druids previous to the introduction of Christianity. Among other objects of interest, the Shandon Church, with its storeyed steeple of red-stone and limestone, is worthy of mention. This church has a steeple 120 feet high, and a good chime of bells. It is a fortunate circumstance that Cromwell is no longer a resident of Cork, else the heart of Rev. Mr. Mahony would not have been so tenderly touched by the chiming of those bells, nor would his poetic genius be made immortal by chiming down the ages the following musical measures:

> " With deep affection
> And recollection
> I often think on
> Those Shandon bells,
> Whose sound so wild would
> In the days of childhood,
> Fling around my cradle
> Their magic spells.

> " I have heard bells chiming
>     Full many a clime in,
>     Tolling sublime in
>         Cathedral shrine ;
>     While at a glib rate
>     Brass tongues would vibrate,
>     But all their music
>         Spoke nought like thine."

But lest the reader of Irish extraction should regard Cork, because of these educational facilities and poetic and historic memories, as a good place in which to live—a paradise of plenty—we would point to the *Work-house*, the largest in the country, and to the nearly forty pawnbroking establishments in the city.

These two, and we might say twin institutions, reveal the poverty of the people.

Blarney Castle is not far distant from Cork, and we are off to kiss the " Blarney stone." Upon purchasing our ticket and stepping into the cars, we at once perceive that this " train " is a foreign institution. The cars—about the size of the American—are built in compartments. Each compartment accommodates some eight or ten persons, who sit face to face. Between these compartments or divisions, there is no communication. The doors open each side, and are locked by the "guard" before the departure of the train from each successive station. While passing from station to

station, the passenger is practically a prisoner, and
wholly at the mercy of his fellow-travellers. A
projecting board, running the entire length of the
train, furnishes a foot-path for the "guard."
And along this narrow pathway the conductor
moves briskly and rapidly to examine tickets, ad-
mit and release passengers. While the cars are
in motion, the guard usually occupies a small compartment, or "caboose," at the end of the train,
from which he communicates with the engineer.
Of course the thought of being locked up, and limited in our range of vision, is at the outstart un-
satisfactory. Then the fear of being carried beyond the proper station is not soothing to the
nerves of a tourist, bent upon improving every
mile, and every minute. And occasionally we hear
passengers shout lustily, and see them swing their
arms threatingly at the guard, who seemed forget-
ful of their release, until the train had well-nigh
started.

We have, years ago, read thrilling narratives of
hand-to-hand encounters between passengers; and
of the brutal treatment the weak received at the
hands of the strong, when the thundering of the
cars drowned the cry for help, and the distance
between the stations afforded opportunity for the
commission of crime.

But if there be a dark side, there is also a bright

one; and we sit fearless and contented in this Irish conveyance. We are happily alone, and the car is locked. Solitary confinement in a foreign land! Well, that pea-nut man cannot enter; neither can the youth with gum-drops. Then that pestilent vendor of trashy novels is excluded. So is the man who spoils our "nap," and excites our cupidity, by screaming out "prize from ten cents to twenty dollars in each package of superior candy!" All these disturbers of the traveller's peace are here happily unknown, and we are ready to shout for joy.

The road, over which we are carried at a high rate of speed, is well built. The bridges are solid, and the stations neat. All necessary precaution is taken to avoid accident.

The track is fenced in with wire-ropes; signal stations are erected at suitable distances; carriage roads pass over, or under, the railroad by means of bridges, and thus speed and safety is secured.

The "guard" is a novelty. He wears an official robe shining with buttons; is generally bland; has a charming "brogue"—a genuine son of the soil.

At each station we find a policeman. He is dressed in a close-fitting blue suit, girt with a broad banded leather belt and brass buckle; his head closely shaven, and shielded by a little round cap strapped tightly under the chin. The atmosphere is fresh and fragrant, and the prospect most delightful. The cottages of the peasantry are built of stone, one story high, whitewashed, neatly thatched, and surrounded by the omnipresent "potato-patch," the camping ground of the goose, and the dormitory of the porker.

The fields are very small, seldom containing more than two or three acres, and frequently not more than one. The fences are clay, overgrown with grass, and crowned with the white-blossomed hawthorn, or yellow-flowered furze.

*Blarney Castle*, so celebrated in Irish song, was built in the fifteenth century, by Cormac Mc-Carthy. It was a massive structure, and prior to the use of gunpowder, must have been impregnable. The lower portion of the edifice, and the tower, 120 feet in height, still remain. We are admitted to the grounds by a woman, who, conscious of the dignity of her position, points with pride to the majestic pile, and dilates with marvelous fluency upon the beauty of the scenery. And the grounds surrounding the castle are certainly beautiful. In former days they were adorned with statues, grottoes, bridges, and various kinds of rustic ornament. But since the time,

"The muses shed a tear,
When the cruel auctioneer,
With his hammer in his hand to sweet Blarney came,"
2

some of the stately trees have been cut down, and
the statues have disappeared.    But nevertheless—

> "The groves of Blarney,
>     They look so charming,
> Down by the purling
> Of sweet, silent stream,"

that we forget the glory of the past in the beauty
of the present.    We enter the castle.    Here is the
dark and dismal chamber where prisoners were
confined.    And this is the banquetting hall.    Above
us rises the tower, from the summit of which a
magnificent view of the surrounding country is
obtained.    And yonder is the famous *Blarney
stone*.    Who has not heard of its magic power?
And what son of Erin, or what tourist, has failed
to kiss it when the opportunity has been afforded?
And have we not turned aside to visit the building for this very purpose?    For—

> "There is a stone there
>     That whoever kisses,
> Oh! he never misses
> To grow eloquent."

This "real stone" is difficult of approach.    It
is clasped by iron bands to a projecting buttress,
at a considerable distance from the ground.    We
must climb to a considerable height, and then
holding on to the bars reach down and bring the

Blarney Castle

lips in contact with this magic stone. With breast pressing the hard rock, head and shoulders projecting over the battlements, heels pointing skyward, the feat is performed.

A stout German just arrived upon the scene, and exceedingly anxious to acquire smooth and winning speech, attempts to do likewise. But whether, owing to the weight of his head, or the pressure of his heels, the sinewless arms are unequal to the task, and the disappointed Teuton retires in disgust. Why this stone is so famous, or how such effects came to be ascribed to it, cannot be easily explained. There are various theories, but none satisfactory.

It is said that the smooth, fluent, persuasive speech, with which the people of this locality have always been gifted, was traceable to the magical power of this particular stone. Such is the tradition of the elders. Such appears to be the belief of this singularly loquacious guardian of the premises.

And no tourist of slow speech, or limited vocabulary, can afford to be skeptical, when by the exercise of faith, and the expenditure of a few shillings, such advantages may be gained. How many tourists in the past have had their tongues loosed by the magic "touch," we cannot affirm, no record being kept by the institution.

Having paid the janitrix the usual admission fee, and receiving in return blessings and commendations, numerous and varied, we sauntered along the " gravel walks there for speculation and conversation," admiring the natural beauty of the locality and musing upon the changes that had taken place since the days of the famous McCarthy's.

Resuming our wanderings, we proceed to the Lakes of Killarney. The country is somewhat wild and boggy; this is particularly so as we near the lakes. Arriving at the depot, we select our hotel, and are driven thither in a truly novel conveyance, an Irish jaunting car. The passensengers sit sidewise, back to back, the feet reaching towards the ground, but resting upon a footboard. The driver occupies a seat in front, sometimes on a plane with the passengers, and sometimes slighly elevated. The passengers while sitting in this "backward" position, do not press upon each other, as there is some space between them, and this space is frequently occupied by children. Jaunting cars roll through the streets, having two or three adults on each side, and two or three good-sized children thrown in between; the whole party being pulled along by a little Irish pony. In clear weather this mode of traveling is exceedingly pleasant, allowing an uninterrupted view of the country, and frequent changes of position.

The "Lake Hotel" has been selected, and we are met at the door by the portly matron, who keeps the establishment. Our hostess is a genuine Irish "lady." She is bland, witty, and has a charming "brogue." She politely informs us, that the house is full of guests, from all parts of the world, but that a "gintleman" from "Ameriky" is always welcome. Being thus kindly assured, we hang up our hat, and feel perfectly at home. The house is admirably located, the table well furnished, and the charges by no means extortionate.

The population of Killarney numbers some 5000, including the beggars. The laziest-looking set of loungers we have yet seen, are here. Many of these shiftless fellows prey upon the unsuspecting visitors. A few act as guides, and demand the largest fee for the simplest service; others beg, and their importunity is such, that the only escape is by yielding to their demand, and giving them "a few coppers." Killarney has several benevolent institutions; a dispensary, a fever-hospital, an almshouse, and lunatic asylum. There is also a nunnery, with a school attached, in which 400 girls are instructed by the nuns. But we proceed to a tour of the country and the lakes. A jaunting car is engaged and we are off at a gallop.

Here is the Cathedral, a stately edifice of recent construction. A writing upon one of the pillars appeals to our sympathy and reminds us of the departed. It is as follows: "Of your charity, pray for the soul of Mary Catharine O'Sullivan, who died April 19th, 1873, in the 65th year of her age.—Jesus mercy, Mary help."

Several requests of a similar character are posted in various parts of the building. Reference is made to the decease of Thomas, Earl of Kinmare, —from which we infer that the deceased nobleman was in Communion with the Roman Catholic Church. In the churchyard is a monument,—a monolith of Peter-head marble,—to the memory of an Irish Chief Justice.

From the Cathedral we ascend to the venerable *ruins of Aghadoe.* These consist of portions of an ancient castle, church and tower. Antiquarians declare that the architecture points back to the sixth century. Both in the ruins and the cemetery, there are some very quaint carvings and sculptures. Here, at the head of a grave stands a crucifix in stone; and yonder is a virgin and child roughly chiseled out of the rock. These specimens of rude Irish art, are two and a-half feet wide, and the strange inscriptions intimate that they belong to the sixth or seventh centuries.

These ruins lead our thoughts back through the ages. They indicate the antiquity of the country. They also teach us the fleeting character of human glory, and lordly power. In these ancient castles dwelt martial chiefs who went forth to battle, a thousand years ago. And here are the slowly decaying walls of churches and monasteries, where in centuries gone by canons, monks, and friars, clad in holy vestments, chanted their evening prayers in slow and solemn measures. And yonder are battlements and towers, ivy-covered and slowly crumbling, where haughty chieftains walked in pride, and shook the shining spear, or hurled the deadly weapon. And all have passed away: silence reigns supreme!

The outlook from these ruins is simply magnificent. The tourist who does not visit Aghadoe, can form no conception of the beauty and grandeur of the scene. In the distance to the right is "Tomies" Mountain, 2400 feet high; a little further along the "Purple" Mountain, lifts its head to an altitude of 2700 feet. In front, away off in the distance is "Tore" Mountain, nearly 2000 feet and the "Stoompa," 2300 feet, above the level of the sea. Beneath us in the valley and partly encircled by these mountains, lies Lough Leane, the largest and the loveliest of the lakes of Killarney. Innumerable islands, covered with hoary ruins, sparkle upon its shining waters. Its shores, fringed with groves, verdant lawns, and castle ruins, charm the eye with a scene of varied beauty.

Camillan and Cloghereen Woods; Kenmare and
Muckross Demesne add their coloring to the picture,
making it the most beautiful we have ever seen.
Those black mountains, vivid green shores, and
shining waters can never, from memory be effaced.

From Aghadoe we proceed to the "Purple"
mountains. Here is the residence of Lady Headley,
and yonder the house of M. Jas. O'Connell, brother
of the famous "Daniel." The isolation or seclu-
sion of these "lordly" mansions is quite noticeable.
They are usually surrounded by high stone walls,
or impenetrable thorny hedges. A gateway carefully guarded, admits to the premises. The entire
arrangements point back to feudal times, and
reveal an impassable gulf, separating landlord and
tenant,—the aristocracy, and—well,—the Fenian
democracy. At the entrance to the *Gap of Dunloe*
stands a cottage, once occupied by the famous Irish
beauty—Kate Kearney.—Her charms inspired the
local bard to write:

> "O did you ever hear of Kate Kearney,
>   Who lives on the banks of Killarney?
>   From the glance of her eye
>   Shun danger, and fly,
>   For fatal is the glance of Kate Kearney."

We are met and welcomed by Kate's grand-
daughter, who now keeps this way-side inn. At

this point the carriage road terminates, and the bridle path begins.

A number of tourists are enjoying the hospitalities, so freely offered and urgently pressed. This kind woman has great sympathy for "Gintlemin such as yese, thravilin' in the hate uv the day." She bids us be "sated," while she runs, not to kill a kid, but to "fetch a little dhrop of the crather." Quickly two bottles are presented, one containing "mountain dew," or "potteen," and the other "goat's milk." Our temperance principles are put to the test, but (to their credit be it spoken), come off victorious. Failing to dispose of these inspiring beverages, she next presents her photograph, urging, as a reason why we should become the happy possessor, her relationship to "Kate" of romantic memory. Fearing lest such a "souvenir" should excite jealousy in our little family circle, we politely decline the purchase, and compliment her upon those illustrious ancestors, of whom we had heard and sung in boyhood's happy days.

Before passing through the gap of Dunloe, an amusing incident occurs. A partnership had been formed early in the day with another gentleman, for the purpose of lessening the expenses in connection with the jaunting car, and also of resisting the demands of those burly beggars that infest the

2*

mountain path. Two horsemen, wild mountaineers, come galloping up and offer their fiery chargers to carry us over the mountain.

We decline,—preferring to walk,—our friend however will ride, and there is now a dispute. Which horse shall he choose? Each rider prefers the claims of his favorite animal; and all the fine points, from head to hoof, of these rival steeds are referred to, dilated upon, and urged with such wit and argument, as provokes the loudest laughter.

Finally the contestants submit to the decision of our companion. He will hire, and pay liberally for the horse that gallops the fastest. Then we have a race. Away down the road they start, and up they come sweeping around the curves at a tremendous pace. The ignorant spectator might suppose that life itself depended upon the result, such spurring, whipping, and yelling to win the prize! Neck and neck they come, with flashing feet and flying tail. One of the horses runs ahead of the other, and is rewarded by having placed upon his back a respectable-looking gentleman weighing over 200 lbs. avoirdupois.

The Gap of Dunloe is exceedingly wild. The narrow pathway winds along, now beneath over-hanging cliffs and anon in the shadow of bold precipitous mountains.

A quickly flowing stream traverses the gap,

forming in its onward march five small lakes, called the "Cameen" lakes. Of these lakes, one is justly celebrated as the receptacle of the last Irish snake. Purple Mountain, so called because of the purple-coloured shale covering the summit, rises 2300 feet above this lake. From the top of this mountain, that sainted Presbyterian, Patrick, sent the last of those venomous reptiles down into the "Black" Lough. "An' in sure isn't there the thrack," exclaims our guide, pointing out a seeming pathway in the mountain side, "along fwitch they come." We argue the case, but without effect. Our guide, and a half dozen men and women, who have met us on the way, each one carrying a bottle of Irish whiskey and a bottle of goat's milk, believe it as sincerely and as firmly as they believe in their own existence. Certainly the mountain is high enough to witness such a spectacle, and the "Lough" black enough to hide such venomous reptiles.

From this point we have an excellent view of Macgillicuddy's Reeks, said to be the loftiest mountains in Ireland. The valley at the base of the "Reeks" is called "Coom-a-Dhuv," or, the black valley.

The scene is bleak, barren, desolate. There are no trees, fields, crops,—nothing but a wild moor stretching away for miles, and terminating in those dismal " Reeks." The contrast between the Lakes of Killarney, just over the " Purple " Mountain, and this " Coom-a-Dhuv," is most remarkable.

But the boatmen await our arrival at the lower lakes, and we hasten on to meet them. We are followed down the mountain by groups of mendicant merchants, — their stock in trade consisting of stout woolen hose and strong Irish whiskey.

They beg, and insist upon having some compensation for accompanying us. When this is denied, or but feebly responded to, their smiles are changed to frowns, and their flattery to abuse. Dear reader, beware of them. And if you ever visit the Gap of Dunloe, or climb to the " Black Lough," to drop a tear upon the grave of the last Irish snake, be sure to go in company with a man that weighs 200 pounds, and wields a rousing " shillelah."

Arriving at Lord Brandon's Cottage, we embark in a nice little row-boat. At the oars are two sturdy men. The name of one is Michael Sullivan,—a descendant doubtless of the famous Kerry chieftain of that name. We float joyously over the " upper lake."

It is only two and a half miles long, and three quarters of a mile wide. Twelve islands sparkle upon its bosom. The shores are rocky, and wild

mountains cast their shadows upon the surface;
—but the islands are beautiful.

Here is " Arbutus Island," so called because
covered with that verdant shrub,—a perfect gem.
The Eagle's Nest lifts its head 700 feet above the
river, and the echo is remarkable. Mountain an-
swers mountain, repeating the echo many times,
and with great distinctness.

Middle Lake is much larger than the Upper
Lake, the scenery less wild, and in some respects
more beautiful.

Lough Leane is the largest of the lakes of Killarney. It is five miles long and three miles wide.
Thirty islands sparkle on its surface. Some of the
finest ruins in the country render these islands specially attractive. Here is *Ross Castle*, to the summit of which we climb. The view from those
ivy-clad and crumbling walls is charming.

It was built ages ago by one of the O'Do-
naghues, and was the last of the Munster Castles
to surrender to the English. This occurred in
1652. *Muckross Abbey* ruins, situated on the
margin of the lake, consist of an abbey and
church. The abbey was founded in 1440, and
some portions are still in a good state of preserva-
tion. In the church, there are many tombs, inscribed with the names of Irish chiefs and heroes,
—O'Sullivan, McCarthy, and O'Donaghue Mor

—who in ancient times owned the soil, and led their clans to battle. Our boatmen are quite familiar with the history of the "saintly isle." Their stories are amusing. The traditions respecting Irish kings, and the legends pertaining to saintly characters, are alluded to, and dwelt upon, with a gayety or gravity, becoming the subject of remark. Now and then snatches of Irish melodies awaken the echoes, and give too swift wings to these happy hours.

Of all the islands, *Innisfallen* is the most beautiful. The historical associations are exceedingly interesting. Here are hoary ruins pointing backward more than 1,200 years! The abbey is said to have been founded by St. Finion in the year 600. In this abbey were prepared the celebrated "Annals of Innisfallen." This work consists of portions of the Old Testament, a compend of universal history down to the fifth century, and an interesting history of Ireland to the beginning of the fourteenth century. The original copy, written some 600 years ago, is now in the Bodleian Library, Oxford University. No complete translation of this work has ever been published.

The island, with its verdant lawns, flowering shrubs, and stately trees, its ivy-mantled ruins, and historic associations, is the most beautiful of those sparkling gems that shine upon the bosom of the lovely Lough Leane.

The calmness and beauty of this "fairy-isle" tempts us to linger, but time forbids. For years we have longed to look upon this moon-lit scene, and now must bid it a fond farewell.

"Sweet Innisfallen, fare thee well,
    May calm and sunshine long be thine,
How fair thou art, let others tell,
    While but to feel how fair be mine.

"Sweet Innisfallen, long shall dwell
    In memory's dream that sunny smile,
Which o'er thee on that evening fell,
    When first I saw thy fairy isle."

# CHAPTER III.

## WANDERING THROUGH IRELAND — KILLARNEY TO DUBLIN.

FROM Killarney, our rambles extend to the western part of Ireland. Tipperary—whose citizens are so skilled in the use of the "blackthorn"—is visited : and so is Kilkenny, famous for its peaceable cats. And here is the old town of Athlone : and not far distant is Lishoy, the early home of Oliver Goldsmith. It is now known by the name of Auburn, and is the reputed scene of the "Deserted Village." Some features corresponding to the descriptions in the poem still remain :—

"The never-failing brook, the busy mill"

may yet be seen; and so can the

"Decent church that topp'd the neighbouring hill."

The ruins of the parsonage attract the tourist's eye, and point to the lines descriptive of the site :—

48

> " Near yonder copse, where once the garden smiled,
>    And still where many a garden flower grows wild,
>    There where a few torn shrubs the place disclose,
>    The village preacher's modest mansion rose."

Whether Lishoy be "sweet Auburn, loveliest village of the plain," or not, we are pleased to know that tourists turn aside from the beaten path, to visit the early home of this much admired Irish essayist, novelist and poet.

The ocean now rolls before us; and the scenery along this Galway coast is both wild and beautiful. Large islands possessing remarkable ruins lie like huge breakwaters between the ocean and the bay. These Arran Islands figure quite conspicuously in legend and song. The pagan Irish believed, that the Paradise they prayed for could be seen from this rocky coast. These isles of the west were to them the isles of the blest. Mr. O'Flaherty—an excellent authority—declares that an enchanted island often appeared and disappeared to the west of Arran. The ancient Irish believed it to be :—

> " That Eden, where the immortal brave
>    Dwell in a land serene,—
>    Whose bowers beyond the shining wave,
>    At sunset oft are seen."

From Galway to Westport, the scenery is probably the wildest, and the people perhaps the most unlettered and superstitious, in all Ireland. This will be believed when we call the region Connemara, and the province, Connaught.

Westport, a good-sized town, is honored in being the home of an Irish nobleman,—the Marquis of Sligo. The noble lord occupies a mansion which, for size and surroundings, might well be termed a castle. The demesne is beautiful. We are freely admitted, and admire the lawns, trees, and splendid edifice, and the forest that partly covers this 350 acre inclosure. Some four miles distant, *Croach Patrick* lifts its head 2,500 feet high, and looks down upon " Clew Bay," one of the most remarkable bays in the United Kingdom. This mountain is visited at certain seasons by large numbers of devotees from all parts of Ireland. Up the sloping sides they clamber, performing "Stations," as they ascend.

It is the Irishman's Mecca ; and an excellent place to go on a summer excursion. If this sacred mount could be transferred to the shores of New Jersey, great would be the excitement among the stockholders of Camp Meeting grounds.

The proprietor could easily execute a lease upon " his own terms ;" and ecclesiastical speculators would derive a " handsome profit " from the investment.

*Castlebar* is the county town of Mayo. Here the Earl of Lucan has his summer residence and model farm. His lordship owns the land on which the town is built, and quite an extent of the country surrounding. Oxen are fattened on the products of the farm, and shipped for sale to English markets. Dairying is also conducted on a large scale, and the Castlebar brands of butter bring the highest prices in the London markets. This stock-raising, and butter-making, may not be regarded as " noble " employment ; but this " Peer of the Realm " enters the lists against all competitors. His lordship is a gallant soldier. He commanded the British cavalry forces during the Crimean war, and ordered that fatal " charge of the Light Brigade," having received his instructions from Lord Raglan, the general-in-chief. The Earl of Cardigan, a fiery Scotchman, and brother-in-law of Lord Lucan, amazed at the " order," took his place at the head of his " brigade," exclaiming, " Here goes the last of the Cardigans ! " A blunder had been committed, but by whom ?

> " Forward the Light-Brigade !
>   Charge for the guns !" he said :
>     Into the valley of death
>       Rode the six hundred.
>   " Forward the Light-Brigade !"
>     Was there a man dismayed ?
>     Not tho' the soldier knew
>       Some one had blundered."

That fatal charge led to such bitterness of feeling between Raglan and Lucan, that the latter was recalled by the Queen. A dozen miles from Castlebar, there are two exceedingly romantic lakes, Lough Conn and Lough Cullin. Bordering the lakes are high mountains, green meadows, forests of oak and ash, tracts of blooming purple heather, clusters of shining cottages, and the stately mansions and sparkling lawns of country barons. By invitation of a witty and intelligent young Irish gentleman, we enjoy an excursion in a jaunting car around those lakes on a lovely summer's afternoon. To these shining shores English tourists frequently come for the purpose of fishing. In these waters perch, pike, trout and salmon sport, and many a "speckled beauty" of large size and fine flavor has rewarded the skill of the fisherman. Game, feathered and four-footed, abound in the woods. Pontoon should be visited. Americans, we are informed, seldom wander in this direction, but those who come are delighted.

Large tracts of land in this part of Ireland have, in years past, been laid waste by the tyranny of landlords. During those dark years—'43 to '48—when the crops failed, and the tenantry were unable to pay the rent, thousands were "ejected" from their homes, and those homes razed to the ground, by the despotism of the owners of the soil.

The darkest chapters in Irish history, are those descriptive of the cruelty and oppression practised upon the peasantry of the western part of Ireland, during those mournful years of famine. To-day we may travel scores of miles without seeing a house. Twenty-five years ago, along these sloping hillsides and blooming valleys, there were large and populous villages. But those villages fell before the onward march of the detested "crow-bar-brigade." The fiat went forth from the local sovereigns, and the impoverished tenantry were forcibly ejected from the homes of their ancestors, and compelled to bid adieu for ever to the land of their forefathers. Thousands went to England and Scotland, but the larger portion emigrated to America. Here and there in our travels we meet with a "son of the sod," who has returned either for the purpose of visiting some relatives, or of purchasing a little farm, and remaining to die in "auld Ireland."

These tracts of depopulated country are now pasture lands. Flocks and herds graze upon the former sites of happy villages. Fences that marked the boundaries of farms have been levelled; the old and stately trees that shaded the homestead have been cut down; the roads that united neighbouring villages have been upturned with the plow; the clusters of shining cottages have fallen before the "crowbar;" and thousands of the "ejected" inhabitants are scattered to the ends of the earth.

We look in vain along these hillsides and through these valleys for a house; and we listen for the sound of the human voice, but the silence is like that of death; we search over those broad acres for some happy group of joyous children, but none can be found. What a change in a land, fertile and beautiful! Flocks and herds owned by Irish landlords or English and Scottish tenants, roam over the broad acres, usurping the place of men.

> "Sweet was the sound, when oft at evening close,
>   Up yonder hill the village murmur rose;
>   But now the sounds of population fail,
>   No cheerful murmurs fluctuate in the gale,
>   No busy steps the grass-grown footway tread,
>   But all the blooming flush of life is fled.
>   Amidst thy bowers the tyrant hand is seen,
>   And desolation saddens all the green."

Some of these landlords having sown the wind, are now reaping the whirlwind. So cruel, merciless, and tyrannous, has been their treatment of the impoverished inhabitants, that acts of violence have been resorted to, and many of these land-owners have been compelled to leave the country. They now reside either in England or on the Continent. There stands the lordly mansion, surrounded by beautiful groves and lovely lawns, but it is empty, and the owner fears to return, lest the bullet or the dagger should speedily avenge the injuries inflicted upon a helpless people.

The rents are collected by "agents," and the affairs of the "absentee" managed by these much despised officials. Recent legislation, however, has been more favorable to the interests of the tenantry. In case of ejectment, or forced removal at the termination of a lease, compensation is awarded for improvements made. But the relation between landlord and tenant is not the happiest. Religious animosities add fuel to the flame. And the ineradicable hatred of English rule, renders fruitless the conciliatory measures of those humane " proprietors," who are known to be favorable to the "powers that be." But harsh and severe as the English rule may have been in the past, and repressive and unjust as doubtless much of the present legislation may be, still it would be an evil day for the island were the British forces to be withdrawn, and Ireland henceforth to be governed by the " Fenians." The Irish people are patriotic, but not united. Even the men elected to the British Parliament, for the very purpose of securing national emancipation, quarrel in the presence of their enemies, much after the fashion of the Kilkenny cats. This country, with soil so fertile, scenery so varied and beautiful, climate so genial and healthful, should be prosperous and happy. There are certain features of this western country, and customs of these witty people, that are worthy of a passing notice.

The farm-houses are not widely separated, as in America. Farmers are "next-door neighbours." Clusters of shining cottages reveal the homes of the peasantry. These villages frequently occupy a commanding position, and the outlook from some of them is quite picturesque. At the close of the day, the old men gather in groups, and discuss the growth of crops, or the election of a new "mimber of parleement." The young men and maidens need not walk miles to see each other and talk about future prospects; here they meet at a moment's notice! This village life is exceedingly social. It is said by those who ought to know, that many of the young men of New England, wearied with the monotony of farm-life, forsake their homes and repair to neighboring towns or distant cities. The farm-houses are too far apart, and the young people crave for society, companionship. Thus the farms are left uncultivated, while the factories are overcrowded. The young Irish farmers are subjected to no such inconveniences. Scores of people meet both in going to and returning from their daily toil. And when the labors of the day are ended, they gather in joyous crowds along the sloping hills, and various innocent amusements give wings to the happy twilight hours.

> " How often have I bless'd the coming day,
>   When toil remitting lent its turn to play,
>   And all the village train from labor free,
>   Led up their sports beneath the spreading tree !
>   While many a pastime circled in the shade,
>   The young contending, while the old surveyed;
>   And many a gambol frolicked o'er the ground,
>   And sleights of art and feats of strength went round,
>   And still, as each repeated pleasure tired,
>   Succeeding sports the mirthful band inspired."

But the spectacle of cattle leaving the pasture, and entering the dwelling of their owners, there to abide during the night, is certainly both novel and amusing.  But this is the case.  Cows and calves and peasants do really occupy the same building. The houses are one story high, a loft being added. The hens come home to roost upon one of the beams of the "loft."  The cows come home from pasture and occupy that part of the house under the "loft," usually at the end of the building.

The cattle are securely tied to posts, and they stand up, lie down, or ruminate, just as they please; while the chanticleer by his vigorous crowing, informs the sleeper that the day is about
3

to dawn. And no inconvenience is experienced. Neither sounds nor smells annoy in the least these people of simple tastes. In alluding to this family relationship, and the intimacy existing between the man and the brute, and expressing some surprise at the novel spectacle, the response made by a witty Irishman was decidedly amusing. "Yis sur, and sure you ought to visit the place where the pig sits on the chair, and looks out uv the windy." I should like to visit that village but time forbids.

The style of dress, both of men and women, is also striking. The materials are largely of home make. Flax is grown and manufactured. The old spinning wheel hums all day long, driven by the pliant foot of the old lady of seventy summers. Wool is raised, and flannels and frieze are woven and dyed, to suit both taste and temperature. The women like bright colors. The red is the most popular. Most garments are shapely, and somewhat "fancy." Low shoes, woolen hose, knee breeches with brass buttons, dark-blue frieze coat,—swallow-tail pattern, white or colored vest, necktie of brilliant hue, and black hat, give these Irishmen an attractive appearance. A blackthorn or "shillelah" steadies the movement, and gives promise of action. And such "action," inspired by a "dhrop of the crathur," may be frequently witnessed at the close of the market, or during the progress of a "fair."

The scenes by the wayside are occasionally amusing. Donkeys are numerous. This animal is the poor man's burden bearer. Here they come in troops, laden with peat. Yonder they march with large and heavy sacks upon their backs.

And here is a little fellow carrying on his back a sack of oats, behind which is seated a good-sized Irish woman smoking a pipe! There is a suspicious looking movement in the eye of this donkey, as if he were meditating a sudden lurch, or other strategical movement to relieve himself of the oppressive burden. And such flank movements are by no means rare. "The baste will prefer a good batin to carryin' a heavy load,"—this is the testimony of the drivers. And such is the testimony of both men and women, who have found themselves suddenly sprawling upon the ground, while the delighted donkey was galloping in the distance, and braying loudly as if laughing at the fun.

We are much interested in the flowers and the birds. In the mountains, the blooming purple heather is a pretty sight. Along the roads, the daisies and the buttercups are everywhere seen. The starlike daisies greet us from every hill side and valley.

> "I see thee glittering from afar:—
>   And then thou art a pretty star;
>   Not quite so fair as many are
>       In heaven above thee !
>   Yet like a star with glittering crest,
>   Self-poised in air, thou seem'st to rest ;
>   May peace come never to his nest,
>       Who shall reprove thee !"

And what numbers of butterflies on brilliant wing fly past, or whirl about, as if inviting us to a chase.

> "Oh pleasant, pleasant were the days,
>   The time when in our childish plays,
>   My sister Emmeline and I
>   Together chased the butterfly !
>   A very hunter did I rush,
>   Upon the prey : with leaps and springs
>   I follow'd on from brake to bush ;"—

The bird songs too, sound strangely. Here is the cuckoo, a very strange bird indeed. It builds no nest. Whether this arises from sheer laziness, want of skill, or lack of parental instinct, we cannot affirm. With unblushing effrontery, it lays its eggs in the nests of other birds, showing very little taste in the manner of its selection. Like some beings higher up in the scale of existence, it appropriates the labors of others without even saying, —"by your leave." It is a cheat, a fraud : and yet as cheats and frauds of pleasing exterior, and charming voice, are admired and even courted by reason of these superficial accomplishments, so we forget the failings of this bird, as we look upon its plumage, and listen to its song.

> "O blithe new comer! I have heard,
>  I hear thee and rejoice:
>  O cuckoo! shall I call thee bird,
>  Or but a wandering voice?
>  While I am lying in the grass,
>  Thy loud notes smite my ear?
>  From hill to hill it seems to pass,
>  At once far off and near!
>  The same whom in my school-boy days
>  I listen'd to: that cry
>  Which made me look a thousand ways,
>  In bush, and tree, and sky."

And yet there are birds of more joyous wing and varied song than the cuckoo. The cuckoo simply repeats its own name while, if possible, hiding in the thick foliage; but the sky lark takes a loftier flight, climbing into the air, until sometimes lost to sight. Then the song of the skylark is exhilarating. This little dark-brown bird pours forth its music with the most passionate earnestness. Upward it mounts, fluttering and flashing in the sunlight, singing with an enthusiasm that is inspiring,—so wild and free, and full of joy! How we love to lie upon the grass and watch it in its upward flight. How we would

love to soar to those sunny heights, where it
makes the air musical with its melody!

> "Up with me! up with me, into the clouds!
>     For thy song, Lark, is strong;
> Up with me, up with me into the clouds!
>         Singing, singing,
> With all the heavens about thee ringing.
>     Lift me, guide me till I find
> That spot that seems so to thy mind!
>
> I have walk'd through wilderness dreary,
>     And to-day my heart is weary;
>     Had I now the wings of a fairy,
>         Up to thee would I fly.
> There is madness about thee, and joy divine
>         In that song of thine;
> Up with me, up with me, high and high,
> To thy banquetting place in the sky!
>         Joyous as morning,
>     Thou art laughing and scorning;"—

Our travels are now through "Fairy Land."
The people believe in the existence of fairies. A
mountain in the distance is declared to be the
home in this section of these mysterious beings.
What and who they are, and where they came
from, are questions frequently discussed with great
seriousness by the ancient of the land. Some
believe they are evil spirits released for a season,
and placed upon probation.

That they have power over man and beast is firmly believed. Peculiar forms of disease that afflict both man and beast, are ascribed directly to their agency, and strange stories are told of their doings and misdoings. Certain individuals are supposed to be familiar with their movements, and to influence their action. These are usually old women. These old women are herb gatherers, and compounders of strange mixtures. They prescribe for man and beast, and marvelous are the stories told of the healing properties of their decoctions.

Then the ghost stories related by some of these villagers are startling; and the houses said to be haunted are pointed out with strange gestures and suspicious looks. These things are believed sincerely by the ignorant, and their words and acts prove the sincerity of their belief. But of course they are deluded. No intelligent man or woman believes in fairies, or ghosts, or haunted houses. Poets find in them excellent material and pleasant company: and travelers may, after a long march, be amused and even refreshed by the "yarns" spun by boozy benighted bogtrotters. But the fairies are creations of fancy, and the ghosts are the creatures of fear. The sketch of peasant life in the west of Ireland would indeed be imperfect without an allusion to the subject. Let us be slow, however, in casting stones at these simple-minded people. How many horse-shoes are still nailed over the doors: how many leather shoes are still hurled after the newly wedded couple: how many wishes are breathed upon the first sight of the new moon: how many calling themselves respectable, gather around the table turner and spirit-rapper, to hear from the dead—and this, too, in enlightened and Christianized America!

In some villages we meet with individuals who speak only the Gaelic or Irish language; but by all we are treated kindly, and questioned closely about " Ameriky."

Sitting one afternoon upon a 'cliff that overlooked meadows, rivers, lakes, woods and cultivated fields. we were quickly surrounded by some twenty of both sexes. One old woman, in broken English, inquired diligently about her daughter who lived in Philadelphia. She solemnly charged us to inform that naughty girl, that her mother was anxiously awaiting a message, and a " triflin' sum o' money." We promised compliance, suggesting, however, the difficulty in a large city of recognizing that particular individual. But the old woman replied, "In sure it's *my* dawther I want ye to spake to in Phillydelphy." That was sufficient. We hope to meet " her dawther" some fine Thursday afternoon parading on Chestnut street, when she shall be reproved for her negligence, and urged to transmit with all despatch that "thriflin' sum o' money." The hospitality of these people is proverbial. After answering a number of questions, and imparting some required information, a woman suggested the propriety of providing refreshments. Several pressing invitations to come to the village, were extended and politely refused. Then the command was given to go to the nearest house and procure some "pratees and eggs, and a mug o' milk for the jintlemun from Ameryky." In order to avoid swallowing what we did not relish, we bade them good-bye and pressed on in our journey. Then came blessings upon the stranger. " God be wi' ye sur." " God bliss ye and take ye home safely." Such were the repeated utterances of old and young.

These parting blessings, and pious greetings, are exceedingly beautiful and impressive. In meeting a traveler, he always salutes you with the words, " God save you, sur." Upon entering a field, " God bless you," are the words with which you are greeted by every laborer; and in these fields women work side by side with men, from dewy morn till dusky eve. Indeed, if we were to judge these people by the language used in salutations and farewells, we should regard them as both orthodox and pious.

It is true, that relics of paganism still exist in

their festivals and bonfires; and yet they appear to be devout worshippers, after the manner of the Roman Catholic Church. They are regular in their attendance upon the services of that Church. Distance does not afford an excuse for absence. They walk miles over the mountains and through the valleys, that they may kneel before the altar on the Sabbath day. And this trait of character we admire. Roman Catholics, in their promptness and regularity at church services, are examples to certain classes of Protestants. How many Protestants lounge lazily at home on God's holy day, or plead a very short distance, or a seeming change of weather, as an excuse for non-attendance upon the services in the house of God. Would that in the matter of church attendance, they were like unto those whom they affect to despise!

But we must leave this blooming wilderness, and repair to the capital. The distance is about one hundred miles, and we travel by rail. Along the iron pathway are the mansions of some of Ireland's proudest and wealthiest noblemen: the seat of the Earl of Mayo: the home of Lord Cloncurry: the beautiful residence of the Duke of Leicester, approached by smooth winding pathways, and surrounded by velvety lawns, and groves of elm, ash and oak. The "guard" unlocks our prison door, and cries out "Dooblin!"

# CHAPTER IV.

## DUBLIN TO DERRY.

DUBLIN, the capital of Ireland, situated on the river Liffey, by which it is divided into nearly two equal parts, is certainly a beautiful city. The approaches to it, remind the traveler of that charming city of the West—Philadelphia. The population is 245,000, and the number of houses 25,000. The principal thoroughfares are very wide,—in some parts as wide as Broad street, Philadelphia. The side-walks paved with smooth flags, and the streets with stone, are kept quite clean. The houses are uniformly high, and built of brick and stone. Some of the stores on the great promenades are magnificent structures. The city, to-day, is thronged with people; the aristocracy are out in carriage and on foot, making quite a display. The contrasts in the shape and color of garments, and in the methods of locomotion are quite striking. Here marches the blue-jacketed policeman, and there the red-coated soldier. A horseman rides through the street on prancing steed; his dangling sword, nodding plume, and martial movement, attract the attention of the crowd, and excite considerable enthusiasm. Tram-cars crowded with excursionists, roll in every direction; carriages of strange shape, occupied by Irish nobility, and driven by liveried coachmen, sweep along the fashionable promenades; jaunting cars, drawn by spirited ponies, fly over the bridges, and swing around the "green;" and handsome men and women move gracefully in pairs, exchanging happy smiles. The appearance of the people pleases us: and we are delighted in listening to their conversation,—so soft and sweet are the tones of the voice. We have never heard the English language spoken with more ease and fluency than by the educated citizens of Dublin.

There are a few objects worthy of special note, as we wander through the streets and suburbs of this ancient city. Yonder is the house in which the poet Moore was born. It is a three-story brick, and now used as a "corner grocery." This tall aristocratic mansion is noted as the birthplace of the great Duke of Wellington. It took a Dublin Irishman to conquer Napoleon. In 1817, the citizens of Dublin in appreciation of the Duke's genius and services, erected the " Wellington Testimonial," in Phœnix Park. This memorial cost

$100.000. Here is the "Bank of Ireland," a magnificent building costing $500,000. This was formerly used as the "Parliament House." We are admitted to the old "House of Lords." The furniture is the same as when the room was occupied by those lordly representatives—even the old tapestry still decorates the walls. Trinity College, a notable and ancient institution of learning, is visited with much interest. It was founded by the authority of Pope John XXII. in the fourteenth century. Bronze statues of Burke and Goldsmith—both of whom were graduates of this institution—stand at the entrance. The buildings are conveniently grouped, and attractive, and thirteen hundred students are in attendance. The library building is 270 feet long, and contains over 200,000 volumes. In this library are a number of very valuable manuscripts,—one of them being a Latin copy of the Gospels, and attributed to St. Columba, who lived in the sixth century.

Christ's Church Cathedral, dates back to the 11th century, and here in ancient times was kept St. Patrick's staff, and other objects of pious regard. In this cathedral, the Church liturgy was first read in Ireland, in the English tongue. There are many monuments erected to the memory of distinguished men. Some of these are very beautiful.

The Cathedral of St. Patrick occupies the site of an ancient structure erected by St. Patrick. And the well at which that venerable man baptized his converts is enclosed in the present building. The janitor leads us up one of the aisles, uncovers the well, and offers a glass of water. And is this the identical well at which St. Patrick baptized his converts, fourteen hundred years ago? "Yes, sur, sure of it." We taste the water and make no reply. It may be, and doubtless is, the identical well. The Cathedral is cruciform, consisting of nave, transept and choir. It has recently been "restored" by Sir B. L. Guinness—the Dublin brewer—at an expense of $900,000! The pulpit cost $5,000, and was erected by Mr. Guinness as a memorial of a deceased friend. There are a few monuments erected to the memory of distinguished men. This marble slab marks the resting place of Jonathan Swift, who was once dean of the Cathedral. The music "furnished" by the choir, is said to be "very fine." The principal singer receives the modest salary of $2,500 a year! And this too, in poor "auld Ireland!"

The Castle of Dublin is worthy of a visit. Here reigns and rules the Lord-Lieutenant. He is the representative of Her Majesty, and assisted by a "privy council," governs the island. The various apartments are spacious, elegantly furnished, and beautifully decorated. The vice-regal chapel is a gem. It is most elaborately ornamented with oak carvings, and beautified with the emblazoned "arms" of the successive vice-roys.

Brilliant were the receptions, and costly the banquets in this castle, during the reign of the polished Chesterfield as Lord-Lieutenant. Here assembled the chivalry and beauty of the Emerald Isle. Here walked in triumph Miss Ambrose, "the matchless beauty" of the court. And here too, the Misses Gunnings, declared to be the "handsomest women alive," won the admiration of the assembled courtiers.

Phœnix Park affords the citizens ample playground. It covers an area of 1,750 acres, and is adorned with statues and monuments.

Dublin is not distinguished for its commerce. In former days the manufacture of "poplin" was a leading industry; but at the present time, only 200 looms are at work upon this Irish fabric. The wages paid mechanics and laboring men, vary from 75 cents to $1.50 per day.

We enjoy a Sabbath in this ancient city. Quiet prevails, the churches are crowded, and but few cases of drunkenness are observed. In the Presbyterian churches the singing is good, and the preaching excellent. The sermons are not written, but "notes" are used. The preachers wear a gown, which makes us doubtful, for a while, of the "ecclesiastical connections" of the incumbent; but the absence of organs and responses, and the presence of Francis Rouse, afford inspiring assurance of the character of the place.

The Sabbath-schools are not quite so well attended, nor are the services as "interesting" as in America. Thorough home instruction, is an article of faith with Irish Presbyterians. The training of the young is not handed over exclusively to the Sabbath-school teacher; hence perhaps the slim attendance upon the services of the school. But the sanctuary is magnified: parents and children walk hand in hand to the house of God: whole families may be seen sitting side by side; and thus the children early learn to respect and reverence the place of prayer. Parents appear to exercise some authority over their children, and children —even of large growth—seem to yield a willing obedience.

But we climb the "Nelson Monument," 121 feet high, and take a last view of the Irish metropolis. What a wide and magnificent prospect! The city lies at our feet encircled by green fields and waving woods; and the bay shimmers in the distance, flecked with tiny sail, that move phantom-like over its shining waters. Few cities have given to the world greater men. Here Wellington, Burke,

Moore, and Grattan, first beheld the light of day.
And in yonder venerable University were educated those, who, in the centuries past, adorned
the various professions, shaped the policy of kings,
and roused the nations by their lofty and impassioned eloquence.

Belfast is distant from Dublin 112 miles, and
for 50 miles the railroad skirts the Irish sea. The
view of land and water is charming. Yonder are
the Skerry Islands, to which St. Patrick fled when
pursued by the Druids. Here is the village of
Balbriggan, famous as the birth place of the " Balbriggan hose." And this is the town of Drogheda,
and yonder the " Boyne waters!" This is the
scene of one of the most memorable and eventful
battles in Irish history. On July 1st, 1690, William, Prince of Orange, met and defeated James
II., in the " battle of the Boyne." Throughout this
region, the soil is well cultivated, the houses neat,
and the surroundings attractive. The smoothly
shaven lawns are white with bleaching linen, and
the whir and hum of spindles, and the crowds of
keen-eyed merchants, tell the traveller that he has
reached Belfast.

This city is the commercial metropolis of Ireland. The situation and surroundings are pleasing
to the eye ; and the business activity of the people,
the neatness of the dwellings, and cleanness of the

streets, make a favorable impression upon the tourist. Northeastward, is the Belfast lake—a beautiful sheet of water—twelve miles long and five broad, over which the shipping pass to the sea. Northward, Cave Hill rises to a height of 1,200 feet, from the summit of which a commanding view may be had of the lake, the ocean, the greater part of County Down, and the western coast of Scotland.

At the base of this hill is the magnificent residence of the Marquis of Donegal, the owner of the soil. To the south and east, the fields stretch away into the dim distance, revealing in the waving grass and ripening grain, every shade of green.

In 1871, Belfast had a population of 175,000. Of this number 119,000 were Protestant; and of the latter 61,000 were Presbyterians. This denomination constitutes over one-third of the entire population. The principal streets are wide, well paved, and quite clean. The stores are large, well stocked with the "finest linen,"—the fancy display in the windows equalling anything of the kind we have heretofore seen. There are quite a number of handsome private residences; some magnificent public buildings—colleges, hospitals, museums—built in different styles of architecture, on sites beautiful and commanding. The Queen's

College, is an imposing edifice, 600 feet long, and pleasantly located.

The people of Belfast are bright, active, intelligent. Such healthy-looking men and women we have never before seen. Here are faces round as the full moon, and ruddy as the sunset. And then the tones of the voice are so musical. What music when three thousand unite, as in the Ulster Hall, in singing some familiar and dearly-loved psalm or paraphrase !

The industries are numerous. Shipbuilding is conducted on quite a large scale. Some of the best boats of the "White Star Line" were launched from the yard on Queen's Island.

The linen trade, however, engages the attention, and furnishes employment to the larger portion of the population. It is to the manufacture and sale of linen, that Belfast is indebted for the wealth it possesses, and the influence it wields. There are a number of mills,—some of them employing as many as 3,000 operatives. All the flax handled is not grown in Ireland, nor is the Irish flax regarded as the superior article.

Flax is imported from Russia, Belgium and France. Some manufacturers prefer the French, while others regard the Belgic, as the better material.

We are conducted through one of the largest

mills, and witness the various processes of scutch-
ing, carding, spinning, warping and weaving.
Around us whir and hum over 30,000 spindles,
while 2,000 operatives,—men, women and girls,
—watch and guide the flying machinery, pack and
press the newly-made fabric, and pile it on waiting wagons, that bear it to the merchant's store.
The men receive from seven to nine dollars, and
the women and girls from two to three dollars per
week.

The quantity of thread and linen stored in some
of these warehouses is very large. A merchant
who kindly conducts us through his vast establishment, states that in taking stock recently, "he
figured up for fun," the quantity of yarn on hand,
and found that it would encircle the globe 107
times!

There are schools organized in connection with
some of these factories. Rooms are furnished with
desks, benches and books. Maps hang upon the
walls. Teachers are appointed and paid by the
company. And in these schools the "half-timers"
are educated without charge. These "half-timers"
are the young of both sexes, who are only employed, or permitted to labor, a certain number of
hours each day. The remaining hours are spent
in these "factory schools," and thus mental training, and physical toil, go hand in hand.

But the great event of the week is the meeting of the General Assembly. Belfast is the stronghold of Presbyterianism; and the assembling of the ministers and elders of this orthodox church, in this orthodox town, excites quite an interest among both rich and poor, old and young.

The church in which the Assembly meets is St. Enoch's, a recently erected edifice, capable of seating over two thousand people. The internal arrangements are novel. There are two galleries, and there are two platforms. Upon each platform stands a pulpit, the higher platform being nearly on a plane with the upper gallery.

The members of the Assembly, and delegates from foreign bodies, occupy seats on the first floor. The galleries are "reserved,"—an admission fee being charged, varying from six to twelve cents.

The Irish General Assembly is not a representative body, ministerially. There are some six hundred ministers in connection with the church, and they are all supposed to be present at every annual meeting. Each church is represented by one elder. The moderator is elected, not by calling the entire roll of members, but by calling the roll of Presbyteries. Presbyteries vote, through some individual member, for the candidate put in nomination. The nominee having the majority of Presbyterial votes, is declared moderator. This officer is thus practically elected at the Presbyterial meetings held prior to the meeting of the Assembly, and is not voted for directly by that body.

To those not familiar with such time-saving ecclesiastical machinery, the results are both surprising and amusing. The echo of the last Presbyterial vote has scarcely died away among the rafters, before the newly-elected moderator steps upon the platform *gowned* and *banded*, and proceeds to deliver a discourse of immense length, and of great philosophic and theologic pretensions! He knew all about the "coming man," and prepared himself accordingly. And while the voting was in progress, he was decking himself in an adjacent room with the robes of office. In the transacting of business, there is an amusing admixture of the grave and the gay, the humorous and the solemn, the noisy and disorderly, and the profoundly meditative and prayerful.

During the discussion of some exciting topic, the moderation and self-restraint of some of the members are severely tested. The "Sustentation" scheme excites a lively debate. If there be any subject upon which an Irish preacher can talk with force and fervor, it is "Sustentation." And the result is manifest to all. Never have we seen a better "sustained" set of theologians. Such theological limbs, bodies, and heads, are only seen in Ireland. There is a considerable amount of muscular Christianity, in this ancient and venerable body.

Then, these preachers are splendid debaters,—so keen, logical, fluent, impassioned, brilliant! And how mercilessly they handle an opponent! Never shall we forget the scene witnessed during the discussion of the "organ question." There was very little harmony in the body, while the use of the "harmonium" was the subject of debate. Some of the brethren had, during the previous year, introduced that harmless and helpful instrument to their choirs. The young people were delighted. Some of the old people were offended. The matter was brought to the attention of Presbytery, and now came before the General Assembly. What excitement among those venerable men! Yonder is an old patriot so opposed to organs, that he persists in occupying the platform, while two co-presbyters are endeavoring to lead him off. No, never! until by facts and figures, dates and deliverances, he "shuts the mouths of these patent worshipping machines!" And yet, when the meeting is adjourned, there is no more genial, jovial, warmhearted set of men on earth. All that occurred during the heat of discussion is forgiven and forgotten, and they gather round the well-laden table of some generous host, and give

swift wings to the hours, by their amusing anec-
dotes, quick flashes of wit, and merry peals of
laughter.

Apart from the stated meetings of the Assembly,
there were several pleasant gatherings of the members, and invited guests. Prominent among these,
were the breakfasts at Ulster hall. These breakfasts are provided by the Presbyterian ladies of
Belfast, for the members of Assembly, their wives
and daughters, and the deputations from foreign
bodies.

The Hall is an immense structure, and most
beaufully decorated for the occasion. The flags of
those nations having delegates in attendance,
are gracefully suspended from the galleries, and
among them the "stars and stripes."

Sixty tables, each fifty feet long, groan under the
most tempting viands,—every conceivable luxury.
Flowers of various hue, and tastefully arranged,
grow out of tiny vases, making the air odorous
with perfume. Hundreds of sweet-voiced, rosy
cheeked maidens, flit hither and thither anticipat-
ing some want, or, tempting the bashful guest with
a sugar-coated morsel. One thousand guests are
seated,—the delegates from abroad being honored
with conspicuous positions at the Moderator's
table. The arrangements are admirable, and the
success complete. Some of the brethren are called

upon for speeches; and such mirth-provoking, and laughter-exciting addresses, can only be heard at an Irish feast. And is laughter an enemy to good digestion? By no means. Who are the dyspeptics? Are they those who at the table enjoy "the feast of reason, and the flow of soul?" Certainly not. They are the solemn eaters; the men and women who go to, and return from the table, as if that were to be their last earthly meal. They eat in silence, and the penalty is paid in suffering. Not so apparently with these Irishmen. They "laugh and grow fat."

A breakfast is provided by the ladies forming the " Total Abstinence Society," and the Assembly invited. All are welcome, *provided* they be "total abstainers." Being duly qualified, we proceed to the lecture-room of Dr. Cook's old church on May Street. We are surprised and delighted, at the number of ministers and elders present,—headed by the gentlemanly Moderator. Temperance is becoming popular, among both the ministry, and laity, of the Irish Presbyterian Church. Multitudes are total abstainers. And during the discussions in the General Assembly, quite an advanced position was taken by many of the leading members, and some very able speeches made in advocacy of the doctrine. The whiskey-bottle, and the punch-bowl, are gradually disappearing; and even the wine-cup, is seldom seen upon the table. Drinking is a dangerous custom. And the scenes of drunkenness, witnessed in these Irish towns, are heart-rending. Little children clad in torn garments, leading drunken fathers and mothers along the highways! Oh, what misery, and wretchedness, and woe, the cup brings to thousands of Irish homes!

A grand Sabbath-school meeting, is held annually during the sessions of the Assembly. Three of the largest churches are selected, and the entire Sabbath-school force of Belfast, teachers and scholars, march from their respective schools to the places appointed.

These thousands of teachers and scholars, marching through the streets of a Sabbath afternooon, with Bible in hand, was a spectacle not soon to be forgotten. Nor were they all clad in purple, and "fine linen." Many of these boys and girls, belonging to the mission schools, were bare-footed, and wore soiled and tattered garments. Over three thousand assembled at Dr. Cook's old church on May Street, and were addressed by delegates from Scotland, France, and America.

The reception given by the General Assembly to the various deputations from abroad, is hearty and enthusiastic. Never have we listened to such thundering applause so long continued. Matteo

Prochet, from the Italian Church, Pastor Lorriaux, of Paris, Dr. Donald Frazer, of London, representing the English Presbyterian Church, and Professor Blaikie, of Edinburgh, are heard in succession. But it should be stated, that the most respectful, and yet the most enthusiastic reception, is accorded the delegates from the great Presbyterian Church of the United States. The response by Dr. William Johnstone, of Belfast, is witty, eloquent, brilliant.

The Irish people, rich and poor, Protestant and Roman Catholic, love America. This fact is daily impressed upon us, as we wander from place to place. In the meanest hovel, and among the poorest and most ignorant peasantry in the wilds of Connaught, expressions of love for, and interest in, the country beyond the sea, were frequent and emphatic. And in this city of Belfast, men of culture, learning, and wealth, are most enthusiastic admirers of America and its institutions. Hence, whenever the American delegates appear upon the platform, the house is crowded, and the reception given is most hearty and inspiring.

But our duties as a delegate being discharged, and the Assembly having adjourned, other places must be visited.

The "Giants' Causeway," some forty or fifty miles distant, invites us, and we wander thither. This excursion is most enjoyable. The railroad skirts the northwest shore of Belfast Lough, affording a charming view of the harbor, Cave Hill, and the home of the Marquis of Donegal; then winding around the "Hill," it runs through well tilled fields, with here and there a cluster of shining cottages shielded by shady trees, until Antrim is reached. At this point the traveller catches a glimpse of Lough Neagh, the largest lake in the United Kingdom.

Strange stories are told respecting its origin, and the petrifying properties of its waters.

The formation of the lake, is ascribed to the carelessness of a woman ! Poor creatures, for what mischief, do the legends and traditions of the past hold them responsible !

And yet, this carelessness was pardonable. In the year 65 (long, long ago), she went to the well to draw water. This well must remain covered; else it will overflow, and ruin the land. The woman, hearing the cries of her infant child, hastened away, forgetting to cover this sacred fountain. And lo ! it rises and overflows, until 98,000 acres, are submerged, and the largest lake in Great Britain, shines before the eyes of the frightened inhabitants !

Fishermen of keen sight, and brilliant imagination, have discovered beneath its silvery waves, the ruins of ancient castles. And Moore has published the discovery, in the following lines :—

> "On Lough Neagh's banks, as the fisherman strays,
>   When the clear soft eve's declining,
> He sees the round towers of other days
>   In the wave, beneath him shining.
>
> Thus shall memory often, in dreams sublime,
>   Catch a glimpse of the days that are over,
> Thus sighing, look through the waves of time.
>   For the long faded glories they cover."

Ballymena, a town of six thousand inhabitants, and one of the largest flax and linen markets in Ireland, and Coleraine, situated on the beautiful river Ban, are both visited. The latter is an ancient town, dating back to the sixth century, and famous for the manufacture of a fine quality of linen, known as " Coleraines." Portrush is reached, and we are in sight of the " Causeway." At Portrush, the celebrated Adam Clarke was born, in 1762. He was apprenticed to a linen manufacturer, but being of studious habits, and finding that employment uncongenial, he changed his occupation and became a school master. He taught school in this town ; and an obelisk erected to his memory, occupies a conspicuous position in this northern sea-port.

The Giant's Causeway is along the coast, eight

miles distant, and we are off in a jaunting car. The day is bright, and a fresh wind blowing. Driven shoreward by the pressure of the blast, the white-capped waves leap like racers over the "Skerries," and dash with fury against the rock-bound coast.

"A coorse day on the wather," mutters our coachman, and we readily concur. All along the shore, the white limestone rocks are carved into the most fantastic shapes, by the action of the billows.

Here is the "Giant's Head," and "Spy glass," "Fin Mac-Coule's Nose," the "Devil's Punch Bowl," and the three "Sugar Loaves."

But by far the most interesting object before reaching the Causeway, is "Dunluce Castle." The ruins are exceedingly picturesque. The castle stands one hundred feet above the sea, on a perpendicular rock. The outer walls of the castle are built upon the edge of the rock, and seem but a continuation of it. The entire surface of the rock is covered by the ruins, and the only connection with the main land, is by a wall about eighteen inches broad. In ancient times this castle, thus situated, must have been well-nigh impregnable. It was erected, fought for, and occupied, centuries ago, by the Lords of Ulster. Here, the brave MacQuillians, and the lion-hearted MacDonalds, measured lances, and the triumphant chief marched in pride around the sea-girt walls. But how changed the scene to-day! The warrior has disappeared; the noise of battle and the voice of song have ceased; while through the deserted halls, the wind plaintively wails, as if over the desolation time has wrought.

The Giant's Causeway is certainly a wonderful place. It is quite unique in the spectacle which it presents. There are two objects, or classes of objects, that challenge our attention. The first, is the "Headland;" and the second, the "Causeway" proper. The Headland rises to a height of 370 feet, and, at some points, reveals thirteen different strata.

The shape assumed by, and the relative position of the strata, form the striking feature. At about twelve feet from the summit, the rock is formed into ranges of pillars, or columns. These pillars are in a vertical position, each pillar being sixty feet high. This range of pillars rests on a bed of coarse rock, sixty feet thick. Beneath this rocky entablature, is a second range of pillars, each forty-five feet high, resting upon a coarse unshapen strata :—and thus to the surface of the sea.

The "*Amphitheatre*," is very striking. The headland assumes an exact semi-circular form. Around the upper part, runs a row of columns, each column being eighty feet high.   Then follows a projection of rock.   Beneath this rocky projection, is another row of pillars, each sixty feet high. Then comes another rocky projection, or bench for the giants,—and thus down to the sea, forming a beautiful harbor.

The "*Giant's Organ*" is forty-five feet high, and composed of a number of pillars, long and short, arranged like the strings of a harp. On this instrument, the giants played for the amusement of their guests!   The clear metallic ring of these rocks, tempts the "guide" to propound his theory of the objects, and uses, of these strange formations. He walks up, strikes one of the "strings" of this wonderful harp, and then inquires if we hear the music!   We respond in the affirmative.   Then he replies, what must have been the tender, and pathetic modulations, when the giant's fingers moved among those strings !

The headland is also remarkable for the color of the strata. The entire cliff appears as if painted. Here are various shades of green, vermilion rock, red ochre, intermingled with lichens, ferns and rock plants ; and the whole surface, from the shining waters to the grassy summit, is sprinkled with blooming sea daisies.

The "Causeway," is composed of a number of pillars, forming a pathway into the sea.   There are over forty thousand of these columns! They are regular in shape, and fit together as closely as if cut and adjusted by some skilful hand. Our guide points out columns having three, four, five, six, eight, and nine sides and angles. But strange to state, that of these forty thousand pillars, but *one* is triangular, and only *three*, are possessed of nine sides!

Here is a wishing-chair. The seat is an octagon,—a stone having eight sides ; three other stones, different in shape, form the back ; and the feet rest upon another, unlike either of the preceding.

Now, how can we account for these strange and beautiful formations? There are two theories,— the geological, and the mythical. Geologists tell us, that these pillars are composed of about one-half flinty earth, one-quarter iron, and one-quarter clay and lime. They are plutonic in their origin. They are formed by a fusion of the above elements into one mass, which in cooling, has cracked or crystallized, into the strange shapes already described. At what period in the world's history, this fusion and crystallization took place, we are not informed.

The mythical theory, is somewhat amusing. Fin Mac Coul, was champion of Ireland. A Scottish giant offered to fight "Fin," for the "belt," and the "championship." Fin, like a

4*

good Irishman, accepted the challenge.   But how could these "sporting gentlemen" be brought together?   The surging sea separated them.   Fin applied to the King, for permission to build a highway to Scotland.   The King granted permission; the Causeway was built, and the Scotchman was beaten!   Here is a well, right by the sea. The waters are fresh, and sweet, as a mountain spring.   An old Irish gentleman—a descendant, doubtless, of Mr. McCoul—sits by the well, and kindly invites the tourist to drink of the sparkling waters.   The charge is a sixpence, but the beverage is refreshing.

But here comes the mendicant merchants, with photographs, and "specimens" boxed up, and ready for shipment.   And the rush, and the roar, to make the first sale!   "Irish Diamond!" shouts one; "Malachite!" thunders another; "Jasper!" roars a long, mean-looking fellow; while a toothless old woman presses to the front with a bundle of photographs, in one of which, her venerable self, is the most conspicuous object.

There is no escape.   We are completely surrounded.   "The whole box for a shilling!" screams a little fellow, who has come down from the highest heading with the swiftness of an eagle. We apologize for appearing among them, and exciting this rivalry in the sale of needless articles;

but no excuse will be accepted by these blatant, bullying beggars. And to escape from this motley crowd, we make a few purchases, and rush on to Londonderry.

This city has a population of 25,000, and is beautifully located on the banks of the river Foyle. The ground on which the city is built, is sloping, and the summit of this sloping hill is crowned by the Protestant Cathedral. The city was fortified with walls, which still remain, encircling the old town. The walls are one mile in length, and from fifteen to thirty feet wide. They furnish a fine parade and promenade ground, and afford a magnificent view of the surrounding country. The newly-built portion of the town, communicates with the "ancient city" through seven gates, and over some of these archways, are stone effigies of historic characters.

The religious history of the locality is quite interesting. An abbey was founded in Londonderry, in the early part of the sixth century, by Columbkille. The present Cathedral, occupies the site of this ancient abbey. Columbkille, was born in the county Donegal, and was a most enterprising and successful missionary. One hundred monasteries in Ireland, owed their origin to this Presbyterian Evangelist. These monasteries, were missionary colleges, established in connection with churches : and thus learning, and religion, walked hand in hand, in those far distant ages. The population of Derry is largely Protestant. The handsome structure of the " McGee College," occupies a conspicuous position on the left bank of the river. This edifice cost $100,000, and was the gift of a Dublin lady to the Presbyterian Church. The Roman Catholics have erected a "Cathedral," on a commanding site, overlooking the river. Our guide informs us, that these poor people have been collecting money for this purpose, during the past thirty-six years. Penny by penny, shilling by shilling, for thirty-six years !

Can we fail to admire such persistence, in the midst of such poverty ? Is not this the secret of their success in church erection ? Every member gives—it may be but a trifle—and gives continually. What vast sums of money are contributed by the poor Irish servant girls in America, for the support of the Roman Catholic Church ! How noble edifices, and magnificent cathedrals, rise along our fashionable promenades, stone upon stone being laid, and pinnacle after pinnacle reared, by the contributions of these so-called menials ! How many of the Protestants who hire them, might learn a lesson of loyalty to their own church, from the example thus set before them ! How much there is of dead orthodoxy !

The siege of Derry, was a memorable event. In December, 1688, there was an uprising against the Protestants. The "apprentice boys" closed the gates against the invading army, and the town was besieged. The siege lasted 105 days, during which time, the citizens suffered most intensely. Tallow, hides, and the flesh of dogs, were eaten to sustain life. Twenty-three hundred of the inhabitants died of famine, or by violence.

The besieged, were inspired by the Rev. George Walker, who prophesied coming deliverance, and gallantly defended the city. In 1828, a monument was erected to the memory of this patriot. It is a handsome Doric column, 120 feet high, surmounted by a statue, and stands upon those immortal "walls." Here also, close to the monument, is " Roaring Meg"—the cannon that " won the day." And here, stands six of the thirteen sycamore trees, planted by the thirteen apprentice boys, who dared to close the gates against Lord Antrim's men. Nor have the patriots all pa-sed away. We are greeted by one, eighty years of age, a most venerable and intelligent old Irishman. He is thoroughly familiar with the history of the siege, the localities famed for conflicts, the old houses used as prisons, and everything pertaining to the past and the present of the city. He presses us to go around the walls "just once more," and with descriptions of men and events, in chaste language and fervid eloquence, delights and charms us, until late in the afternoon. Begging to be excused from further explorations, and assuring him of our high regard for his knowledge, patriotism, and eloquence, the old man, assuming an attitude erect, defiant, lifts his right hand, and pointing in the direction of a neighboring valley, repeats, with distinctness and emphasis,—

" When Lord Antrim's men came down yon glen,
　　With drums and trumpets gay,
　The apprentice boys, they heard the noise,
　　And then prepared for play!"

A bright shilling is placed in his hand, and lo, in a twinkling, he has disappeared!

Before bidding adieu to the Emerald Isle, a few facts may be stated respecting the cost of living, and of travelling, and the social habits of the people.

The railroad rates are, for like accommodation, about the same as in America,—perhaps a trifle cheaper. The hotel charges are reasonable, but the statements of a hotel-keeper are liable to be misunderstood, or to deceive. He will inform you that lodging is, perhaps, two shillings. In the morning, on the bill, it appears to be nearly four shillings. Sundry items not previously named now appear, such as "attendance," "blacking boots," etc. Then, in hiring a conveyance, you agree to pay so much, and suppose that to be the sum total of the expense. But on returning, the driver claims, and insists upon receiving, an additional sum, equal in some cases to one third of the original charges.

In the hotels, the bar-tenders are generally women. Women sit down with men, and drink, without any apparent loss of self-respect. Women walk together to the " tavern," call for their whiskey, drink it, and pass along without being criticised. At fairs and markets, men and women march through the streets singing ballads, and selling the printed songs at a half-penny apiece. When a young couple discover that " life, without the other, would be a desert drear,'' the parents come together for the purpose of " match-making." So many cows, sheep, pigs, goats, are demanded as a dowry. If the demands are regarded as excessive, or the parents of the bride are unable to comply, then follows a discussion, in which the advantages of the " union," and the pedigree of the family, are skilfully presented.

These discussions are exceedingly interesting. The high contracting parties hold adjourned meetings ; and many a *spirited* debate is held over the gift of an additional sheep, or the claim to an extra porker.

When the dowry is settled, and the union consummated, then comes what is euphoniously termed the "dragging home." The bride and groom, mounted upon the same steed, and accompanied by a score or more couples on horseback, dash along the highways,—usually in the evening,—to their future home.

The character of an Irish "wake," is pretty well understood. When the corpse is "laid out," candles are lighted, and pipes and tobacco placed either on the corpse, or close beside it. The whiskey bottle stands upon the table. As each friend of the departed arrives, the party stand around the deceased, and give expression to loud and bitter lamentations. Then, games, mystical and mirth-provoking, are indulged in by both sexes, old and young. Singing, and sighing, alternate in strange succession; and story-telling hastens the dawn, when these laughing and sobbing mourners suddenly disappear. These customs, it is true, prevail among the peasantry, and are limited to certain localities.

# CHAPTER V.

## SCOTLAND—THE LAND OF BURNS.

BIDDING farewell to Ireland, and embarking on the steamer "Rose," we set sail for Greenock, Scotland. The wind being favorable, our vessel sweeps along at a high rate of speed. The sail over Lough Foyle is quite enjoyable. On the left, rise the wild mountains of Donegal, and on the right, the bold "Headland" of the Giant's Causeway is quite conspicuous. We are now jolted by the chopping sea of the North Channel. Rathlin Island is passed. The Mull of Cantire is rounded, and yonder is Ayr, and the land of Burns!

> "'Twas in that season, when a simple bard,
> Unknown and poor, simplicity's reward,
> Ae night, within the ancient burgh of Ayr,
> By whim inspired, or haply prest wi' care,
> He left his bed, and took his wayward route,
> And down by Simpson's wheel'd the left about;
> The drowsy Dungeon-clock had number'd two,
> And Wallace tower had sworn the fact was true;
> The tide-swollen Firth, with sullen, sounding roar,
> Through the still night dash'd hoarse along the shore."

Next comes Arran Isle, the property of the Duke of Hamilton. We enter the Firth of Clyde, and pass the Island of Bute. On our left is Mount Stuart, the home of the Marquis of Bute, and Dunoon Castle, owned by the Duke of Argyle.

On our right, on gently sloping ground, is Greenock, where our feet first touch Scottish soil.

This is a lively town of 60,000 inhabitants. The principal industries, are ship building, and sugar refining.

There is a very fine promenade and carriage way along the river, and some very handsome residences on the esplanade. The houses are four and five stories high, and divided into " flats," for the accommodation of families. The cemetery is located above the town, and is the finest we have seen thus far in our travels. The lots, are neatly enclosed with closely cut boxwood, and silver holly. Where the lots are large, the yew tree frequently marks the resting-place of the dead.

The view from this cemetery is magnificent. The mountains of Dumbartonshire, and Argyleshire, are in full view; and the entrance to the Gare Loch, and the Long Loch, comes within range of the eye.

There is one grave in Greenock, visited by every tourist. This is in the burying-ground of the old West Kirk, and is that of Burns' Highland Mary

A winding path, leads to this much frequented spot. In 1842, a monument was erected, and on the upper part are chiseled medallion portraits of the lovers,—the right hands being clasped.  On the lower part are engraved the following lines, from Burns' poem—"To Mary in Heaven: "

"Oh Mary! dear departed shade!
    Where is thy place of blissful rest?
See'st thou thy lover lowly laid?
    Hear'st thou the groans that rend his breast?"

This Scottish maiden seems to have won the poet's heart, and her memory is perpetuated in several of Burns' most beautiful poems :

" Ye banks and braes, and streams around
    The Castle o' Montgomery,
Green be your woods, and fair your flowers,
    Your waters never drumlie!
Here simmer first unfaulds her robes,
    And there they langest tarry :
For there I took the last fareweel
    O' my sweet Highland Mary.

But oh, fell death's untimely frost,
    That nipt my flower sae early !
Now green's the sod, and cauld's the clay,
    That wraps my Highland Mary !
And mouldering now in silent dust
    That heart that lo'ed me dearly !
But still within my bosom's core
    Shall live my Highland Mary!

A slow and solemn procession, is marching along the hill-side, to the city of the dead.  In that company of mourners, not a female form can be seen. This surprises us, being in such marked contrast with Irish funerals, where women are always among the chief mourners.  But a Scotch cousin informs us, that women never attend funerals.  The male relatives, only, follow the dead to their last resting-place.

This may be an improvement upon the Irish and American custom, or it may not.  Fewer carriages will be required, and a saving in expense effected.  And this alone, is a decided improvement.  Why should a poor laboring man be compelled to provide carriages, for all the women who are desirous of going on a burial excursion ?  And why should not the men, whose duty it is to attend, provide carriages at their own expense? How many poor men and women, are burdened, for months and years, with debts incurred in the burial of a friend !

A reform in funeral customs, is certainly desirable in certain places.  Funerals are too expensive. There are too many flowers : too many carriages : too many tearless mourners : too much pomp and parade.  In the burial of the dead, publicity is sought after, when secrecy should be observed.  And then, these Sabbath processions to the grave !  How

lacking in sympathy, how indifferent to the sor-
rows of the bereaved, are those surging crowds that
surround the home of the deceased, or struggle for
admittance at the gates of the cemetery ?  Surely,
it must be a trying ordeal, for a sensitive mourner
to be subjected to the rude gaze of a gaping and
unfeeling multitude, while following the silent
form of a loved one to its last resting-place. Sometimes, Sabbath funerals may be a necessity.  But
the exclamation of a popular Philadelphia undertaker, who had for years witnessed the scenes just
described, is worthy of being noted.  " O, I never
want to be carried to the grave on a Sunday !"

It is customary in Greenock, and in the great
manufacturing cities of Scotland, to quit work  on
Saturday at 12 o'clock.  This enables the laboring
men and their families, to make excursions to  the
fields, the mountains, or the lakes.  It affords a
rest, fresh air, and prepares the wearied laborer for
the proper observance of the Sabbath. This being
Saturday afternoon, silence reigns in the ship-
yards, and the great manufacturing establishments
are closed.  Steamboats, crowded with happy excursionists, are chasing each other over the Clyde,
and up the Gare Loch, and the Long Loch.  Family groups are scattered along the hillsides,
plucking the wild flowers, and breathing the
scented air.  Truly, this is a pleasant way of pre-

paring for the Sabbath. Might not a similar course be adopted by our great American establishments, without injury to the employer, and with profit to the employed ?

Paisley, is a prosperous town, on the route to Glasgow. The Abbey Church was founded in 1163, by Walter Stuart, ancestor of the royal family of Scotland. In a small chapel, at the south side, is the tomb of Marjory, daughter of Robert Bruce, and wife of Walter Stuart. In Paisley, Wilson, the American ornithologist, was born ; and Prof. Wilson (Christopher North) was a native of this city.

Glasgow, situated on the Clyde, and by it divided into two unequal parts, is the commercial metropolis of Scotland. In wealth and population, it ranks as the third city in the United Kingdom. Over 500,000 people dwell within the city limits. Glasgow is famous for its manufacturing establishments. Ship-building is a leading industry. The Clyde, from Greenock to Glasgow —some twenty miles—is a continuous ship-yard. There are more steam and sailing craft sent from these yards, than from all the other British ports combined. There are numerous linen, woolen, and cotton factories. Iron ware, pottery, machinery, and chemicals, are manufactured on a large scale. The St. Rollox chemical works, are said to be the largest in the world.

The streets of Glasgow—most of them—are wide, stone-paved, quite clean, and lined with solid structures, four and six stories high. The building material is a light-colored, fine-grained, sandstone. In the recently erected edifices, there is very little sameness, no lack of variety in the style of architecture. It is difficult, at first sight, to determine what may be the character of a building,—whether store, factory, bank, church, or fortification. Argyle Street is the principal street of Glasgow. It runs east and west, and is three miles long. The stores on Argyle, and Buchanan streets, are splendid edifices.

George Square, a quadrangle of imposing structures, is the finest in the city. It is ornamented with several costly monuments.

Here are effigies in marble or bronze, of Queen Victoria, Prince Albert, Sir Walter Scott, Sir John Moore, and Lord Clyde. Scott's monument stands in the centre of the square, and is quite conspicuous.

It consists of a high square pedestal, and a fluted Doric column eighty feet high, surmounted by a colossal standing statue. It was the first monument erected to the Scottish Bard.

The University of Glasgow crowns Gilmour Hill. The buildings form a rectangle 600 feet long, and 300 feet broad, and cost over two million dollars. The Botanic Garden, is not far distant from the University, and its beautiful grounds, and choice collection of plants, make it a popular resort both for citizens and students.

The Necropolis, or city of the dead, covers a steep, rugged eminence, 225 feet high, on the east side of Molindinar ravine. It is approached through an ornate portal, and along a handsome one-arched bridge, called the " Bridge of Sighs." Winding, flower-bordered paths, climb to the summit, which is crowned by a lofty monument, erected to the memory of Knox.

The Cathedral, founded in 1133, is a Gothic edifice, 319 feet long, 63 feet wide, 90 feet high, and crowned with a spire 225 feet in height. The choir is 97 feet long, and has pews and other sittings in the old cathedral style. The lady chapel has exquisitely carved, early-pointed windows, and contains a monument to Archbishop Law. The crypt is 125 feet in length, and exhibits such varieties and combinations of structure, as to render it, in the estimation of critics, the masterpiece of architecture in Scotland. The Cathedral has 80 stained glass windows. A number of these were executed at the royal glass-painting establishment in Munich. The subjects represent Old and New Testament history, and are arranged in chronological order. It is said that the display of stained glass in this Cathedral is greater, and more brilliant than in any other edifice in Great Britain.

The Established Presbyterian Church holds service in the choir, at eleven and two o'clock every Sabbath. The greater part of the adjoining yard, is paved with tombstones. On the north side of the Cathedral, is a simple monument to the memory of the *nine Covenanters*, who suffered at the " Cross " of Glasgow, " for their testimony to the Covenants."

The inscription on this monument, reads as follows :

> " Years '66 and '84
> Did their souls home into glore,
> Whose bodies here interred ly,
> Then sacrificed to tyranny.—
> To Covenants Reformation
> Cause they adhered in their station,
> These nine with others in this yard,
> Whose heads and bodies were not spar'd,
> Their testimonies foes to bury ;
> Caus'd beat the drums then in great fury ;—
> They'll know at resurrection day,
> To murder saints was no sweet play."

Here is another specimen of the antique :

> " Heir ur Bureit Sr Waltir,
> Sr Thomas. Sr Jhohe, and Sr Mathiew.
> By Lineal descent to Utheris Barons
> and Knights of the Hoys of Minto
> w. t. thair wyffis, Bairnis, and Bretherein."

5

These monuments remind us that Glasgow, is a Presbyterian City. What numbers of Presbyterian Church edifices tower along the highways! There are one hundred and eighty of these structures, within the limits of the city. And some of these churches are costly and magnificent.

The Sabbath day, is carefully observed in this city. Services are usually held at eleven o'clock, A. M., and two o'clock, P. M. And never have we seen such crowds of people, old and young, marching to the house of God. Here they come, filling, not only the sidewalks, but the streets! The entire city seems to be in commotion, at the hours named. Cleanly clad, Bible in hand, in hundreds and in thousands, they press up to the gates of Zion. How beautiful is the sight!

> " From scenes like these old Scotia's grandeur springs,
> That makes her lov'd at home, rever'd abroad. "

We worship in the morning with Dr. Bonar's congregation. The doctor is a thorough Scotchman, and most excellent preacher. There was more scripture in that morning's sermon, than in any dozen sermons to which we have yet listened. It was a rare treat, to listen to his exposition of the word of God.

The pews have narrow desks, on which are placed a Bible and psalm-book, for *each indi-*

*ridual.* While the Scriptures are being read, or the sermon preached, every worshipper has a Bible in hand ; and both reading, and reference, are closely scanned. The singing is not quite so good as the preaching. While the benediction is being pronounced, the people are seated, and remain for a few moments motionless, as if engaged in silent prayer. All notices of services are read after the benediction ; and in some churches the collection is taken up in the vestibule, after the congregation is dismissed. In the afternoon, we attend the Barony Free Church, of which Mr. Wells is pastor. The sermon is excellent. The preacher uses no manuscript, shows a thorough familiarity with the Scriptures, is quite earnest, and, occasionally, truly eloquent. This church, bordering on the " Wynds," is one of the most successful of the Glasgow missionary enterprises, and is doing a noble work among the poorer classes of the vicinity.

A thousand children attend its Sabbath-school. Some of these boys and girls are poorly clad, and many of them are noisy, quarrelsome, and well-nigh ungovernable.

The hymns sung at the opening of the school are familiar : "Safe in the arms of Jesus," and " Lord, I hear of showers of blessings." The old " Tron " school, and the " Wynd " schools, are visited. Here are gathered the waifs, swept in from the " Wynds." And such a crowd of boys! Along these streets, through these narrow and filthy lanes, and up these winding, stony stairways, did Chalmers walk, his great heart fired with the love of Jesus, and of perishing man. And nothing less potent, than the purest love for God, can sustain the Christian worker amid such surroundings.

We have seen the darkest, foulest, spots in Philadelphia and New York, but nothing to compare with these " Wynds." Here, humanity is thoroughly imbruted. Men, whose bloated or shrivelled forms reveal the mastery of vice, stagger along, swearing as they go; women, shoeless, sit in long lines on the curb-stone, muttering imprecations upon some hapless wretch; their garments filthy, hair dishevelled, features distorted, modesty, self-respect, shame, all gone! God pity them!

And why this poverty, wretchedness, and degradation? Why these staggering men, and demoralized women? Why these haggard looks, pallid faces, and blood-shot eyes? Why these ragged, unwashed and starving children? And why these ceaseless strifes, and horrid oaths. And the answer comes from a thousand desolate homes, and ten thousand broken hearts—Rum!

To-day, amid these sickening sights, and disagreeable sounds, we find the Christian men and women of Glasgow, toiling nobly for the uplifting of these wretched mortals. Here they are in the mission Sabbath-schools, with Bible in hand, pointing to God as the only help, and to Jesus Christ as the great deliverer. Success to them in their noble work!

The houses in Glasgow are, like those of Greenock, divided into "flats." These flats, consist of three or four rooms on the same floor. One of these rooms, is used as a kitchen, another, as a sitting-room and dining-room, and a third, as a sleeping-room. When the family is large, two flats are rented. And the rent is quite reasonable. A suit of rooms,—three or four,—in a good location, may be rented for seventy-five dollars a year. For every flat there is a bell, and the name of the occupant, is painted upon the bell-pull at the front-door. By this arrangement, the proper party is reached, and no other tenant is disturbed.

The street scenes are sometimes amusing. Here is a sturdy Highlander with his bag-pipe, out of which he is squeezing some lively Scottish airs. A young athlete, handsomely dressed in Highland costume, dances along the pavement, keeping time to the music. He leaps, bends, whirls, and gyrates up and down the street, with marvelous agility. Is this a Highland fling, or a Scotch hornpipe? It is certainly a success. Just see the crowds of men and women! If one of Darwin's ancestors were on exhibition, the excitement could not be more intense. But this is better than a monkey-show,—financially,—for see the pence, how they fly from lofty windows, and jingle merrily upon the side-walk!

Then these "cannie Scots," will listen to a song. Singing in the streets, and selling the printed songs, is quite popular. Some of these songs, illustrate life on the "flats,"—just described.

Women in Scotland, living in the same house, will have their "little misunderstandings." And it sometimes happens, that "outsiders" hear of it; and occasionally, a local poet attempts to create harmony out of the discord. The following song by a Scottish bard, is an effort in this direction, which we trust will escape the notice of the ladies referred to:

> "Says Mistress Bell to Mistress Todd,
>     'Ye'd better clean the stairs!
>   Ye've missed your turn for mony a week,
>     The neighbours a' did theirs.'
>   Says Mistress Todd to Mistress Bell,
>     'Aw tell ye Mistress Bell,
>   Ye'd better mind yer ain affairs,
>     And clean the stairs yersel.'
>
>   Says Mistress Todd, 'When it suits me
>     To think that it's my turn;
>   Ye've a vast o' cheek ta order me,
>     There's not a woman born

That keeps a cleaner house than me,
  And mark ye, Mistress Bell,
If ye'd only do the same as me,
  Ye'd gang and clean yersel.'

Says Mistress Bell, 'Ye clarty fash,
  Wha was't that stole the beef?'
'What do ye say?' cries Mistress Todd,
'Do ye mean that aw'm a thief?'
Says Mistress Todd. 'Ye greet skyet-gob,
  Ye'd better haud yer jaw,
The very clothes upon yer back
  Belangs the wife below!'
*Chorus:*  O, what tungs i' the row upon the stairs,
  Clittering, clattering, scandal and clash
    I' the row upon the stairs."

But all Scottish women, are not modelled after the pattern of Mistress Bell, or Mistress Todd. There are a number of very useful, and inoffensive females, scattered through the country. But as is frequently the case in other lands, they are not always fully appreciated. Their skill, thrift, and good house-wife qualities, lack recognition.

They are willing to make others happy. They are craving for wider fields of usefulness. Their breathings after fellowship with some appreciative swain, are very tender, and cannot fail to awaken a loving response. One of these neglected ones, thus appeals:

"Noo I'm a braw lassie, wi' guid claes an' plenty,
  A wee pickle siller an' a',

Baith weel-faurt and sonsie, and rosey and dainty,
    Will nane o' ye tak' me awa'?

I can shape, I can shew, an' am real guid at spinnin',
    I'll keep ye aye cosy an' braw,
I'll clean up yer hoose, I'll attend t' yer linen,
    An' darn yer stockins an' a'.

I'll no fash my head wi' political matters,
    Like ladies that make me think shame;
But let them come to me wi' clavers and clatters,
    I'll tell them their place is at hame.

I'm maistly gane oot o' my senses wi' anger,
    I may speak till the day that I dee,
But I see that's needless t' stand any langer,
    There's naebody here wanting me."

*Chorus:* "For it's noo high time I was married ye see,
        I would like to be settled in life;
    I think a bit laddie could hardly dae better
        Than tak' me, and mak' me his wife."

The following song is sung, by the women, with
great energy:

"I can wash, I can bake, I can brew, I can spin,
    And when I gang to kirk, oh! don't I cut a shine,
    But there's naething in this worl' wad mak' me ha' sae
        cheery
    As if I had a young man jist tae ca' me dearie."

This young woman has many admirable qualities, which young men should carefully consider.
But how vain is the lassie! She "cuts a shine,"
in church! What a singular weakness, for so excellent a worker.

Now why should the fringes, and flounces, the flowers, and feathers, be carefully preserved for exhibition in the kirk? Are not the wearers distracted in thinking about them; and are not the worshippers distracted in looking at them? Are not other maidens, whose circumstances will not permit them to "shine," tempted to remain at home, and not attend the kirk? And will not the prudent "laddies," avoid these "shining lassies," fearing the future expense? "Cutting a shine" in church, is a naughty habit.

From Glasgow to Edinburgh, over the mountains and the lakes, is 111 miles. We reach Loch Lomond. This is regarded as the finest of the Scottish lakes. It is 23 miles long, and in some places 5 miles broad. The depth is from 20, to 100, fathoms. Studded with sparkling islands, and surrounded by wild rugged mountains, its shining shores have witnessed many a bloody encounter between the warlike Highland clans. How often has the lofty "Ben Lomond," looked down upon the struggles of contending chiefs!

Having secured a pleasant position, on a lively little steamer, we float away towards the north, among

> "Those emerald isles, which calmly sleep
> On the blue bosom of the deep."

Here is the beautiful isle of Inch Murrin,—the property of the Duke of Montrose. It is the largest of Loch Lomond's islands, and furnishes an ample play-ground for the swift-footed deer. Rounding the wooded promontory of Ross, we reach Rowardennan. Ben Lomond towers above us 3,200 feet. The distance from the lake to the summit is four miles; and the view from this mountain, is said to be one of the finest in Scotland. The lake now becomes quite narrow, and the mountains on either side grow wild and romantic. Yonder, on the bushy banks, at the base of the hill, is Rob Roy's Prison. How the very name, suggests Clannish strife, and deadly combat!

> " Yes, slender aid from fancy's glass
> It needs, as round these shores we pass,
> 'Mid glen and thicket dark, to scan
> The wild Mac Gregor's savage clan."

At Inversnaid, passengers for Loch Katrine are landed. This is the scene of Wordsworth's exquisite poem,—"To a Highland Girl."

> " Sweet Highland girl, a very shower
> Of beauty is thy earthly dower!
> Twice seven consenting years have shed
> Their utmost beauty on thy head;
> What hand but would a garland cull
> For thee, who art so beautiful?

Oh, happy pleasure here to dwell
Beside thee in some heathy dell :
Adopt your homely ways and dress,
A shepherd, thou a shepherdess !
Nor am I loath, though pleased at heart,
Sweet Highland girl ! from thee to part ;
For I, methinks, till I grow old,
As fair before me shall behold,
As I do now, the cabin small,
The lake, the bay, the waterfall :
And thee the spirit of them all !"

A four-horse chariot, carries us over the moor, from Inversnaid to the banks of Loch Katrine. The scenery is exceedingly wild. Flocks of sheep roam over the hills, and no sound greets the ear, except the bleating of some fleecy wanderer,—

" Away on the mountain wild and bare,
Away from the tender shepherd's care."

We touch the shores of Loch Katrine at Stronachlachar. This beautiful sheet of water, and the mountains surrounding it, have been immortalized by Scott, in the " Lady of the Lake." The uses to which it is put to-day, are much more practical than poetical. Its waters are conducted over the mountains, and through the glens, all the way to Glasgow. And in that populous centre, they quench the thirst, cook the food, and wash the faces of half a million of Scots.

The scenery around the eastern shore is magnificent, and, in some features at least, corresponds with the description of the poet :

> " The broom's tough roots his ladder made,
>     The hazel saplings lent their aid ;
>     And thus an airy point he won
>     Where, gleaming with the setting sun,
>     One burnished sheet of living gold,
>     Loch Katrine lay beneath him rolled ;
>     In all her length far winding lay,
>     With promontory, creek, and bay,
>     And islands that, empurpled bright,
>     Floated amid the livelier light ;
>     And mountains, that like giants stand,
>     To sentinel enchanted land.
>     High on the south, huge Ben-venue
>     Down to the lake in masses threw
>     Crags, knolls, and mounds, confusedly hurled
>     The fragments of an earlier world ;
>     A wildering forest feathered o'er
>     His ruined sides and summit hoar.
>     While on the north, through middle air,
>     Ben-an heaved high his forehead bare."

This summer's day on the lake, will long be remembered. The sky is bright ; the wind blows gently over the silvery waters ; the islands charm by their beauty ; and the mountains loom up so grand !

> " The summer dawn's reflected hue
>     To purple changed Loch Katrine blue ;

> Mildly and soft the western breeze
> Just kissed the lake, just stirred the trees.
> The grey mist left the mountain side,
> The torrent showed its glistening pride ;
> Invisible in flecked sky,
> The lark sent down her revelry ;
> The blackbird and the speckled thrush
> Good-morrow gave from brake and bush."

This little island on our left, is historic,—at least in poetry.  But there are no skiffs to-day, skimming the shining waters; and no beauteous form, guiding the tiny craft.  We are not quite so fortunate as the huntsman, who, after the sound of his magic horn, looked wonderingly as,—

> " From underneath an aged oak,
>     That slanted from the islet rock,
>     A Damsel, guider of its way,
>     A little skiff shot to the bay,
>     That round the promontory steep
>     Led its deep line in graceful sweep,
>     Eddying, in almost viewless wave,
>     The weeping willow twig to lave,
>     And kiss, with whispering sound and slow,
>     The beach of pebbles bright as snow.
>     The boat had touch'd the silver strand,
>     Just as the hunter left his stand,
>     And stood concealed amid the brake,
>     To view this Lady of the Lake.
>     And ne'er did Grecian chisel trace
>     A Nymph, a Naiad, or a Grace,
>     Of finer form, or lovelier face !

What though no rule of courtly grace
To measured mood had trained her pace—
A foot more light, a step more true,
Ne'er from the heath-flower dashed the dew ;
What though upon her speech there hung
The accents of the mountain tongue—
Those silver sounds, so soft, so dear,
The listener held his breath to hear."

# CHAPTER VI.



A FOUR-HORSE stage is in waiting, and we ride through the wild Trossachs, to Callandar. This is the scene of the chase. It was here

> "The wild quarry shunned the shock,
> And turned him from the the opposing rock !
> Then, dashing down a darksome glen,
> Soon lost to hound or hunter's ken,
> In the deep Trossach's wildest nook,
> His solitary refuge took."

And in this rocky, woody wilderness, the Knight of Snowdoun,—James Fitz-James,—"lost his gallant gray."

"See," says the driver, "it was just at this point"

> "Close on the hounds the hunter came,
> To cheer them on the vanished game ;
> But, stumbling in the rugged dell,
> The gallant horse exhausted fell.
> The impatient rider strove in vain
> To rouse him with the spur and rein,

> For the good steed, his labors o'er,
> Stretched his stiff limbs to rise no more."

Here is Loch Achray, where in quietness and beauty,

> "The rocks—the bosky thickets sleep,
> So stilly in thy bosom deep."

A short distance from the Loch, we pass the Highland huts of Duncraggan, and the entrance to the deer-forest of Glenfinlas. Along these hillsides, and through these valleys, the bold and brave Roderick-Dhu, walked at the head of the Clan-Alpine. Here he whistled and the warriors, quick-footed, hastened to their chief.

> "He whistled shrill,
> And he was answered from the hill;
> Wild was the scream of the curlew,
> From crag to crag the signal flew.
> Instant, through copse and heath, arose
> Bonnets, and spears, and bended bows:
> On right, on left, above, below,
> Sprang up at once the lurking foe;
> From shingles grey their lances start,
> The bracken-bush sends forth the dart,
> The rushes and the willow-wand
> Are bristling into axe and brand,
> And every tuft of broom gives life
> To plaided warriors armed for strife.
> That whistle garrisoned the glen
> At once with full five hundred men.

Passing Loch Venachar, we look down upon Coilantogle Ford, where Roderick challenged Fitz-James, to single combat.

> "See here, all vantageless I stand,
>     Armed like thyself with single brand;
>     For this is Coilantogle Ford,
>     And thou must keep thee with thy sword."

Both were brave warriors. The struggle was severe. Blood flowed freely. Gael and Saxon, never fought before, or since, more gallantly,—if the testimony of Sir Walter is to be credited.

> "Like adder darting from his coil,
>     Like wolf that dashes through the toil,
>     Like mountain-cat who guards her young,
>     Full at Fitz-James's throat he sprung,
>     Received, but reck'd not of a wound,
>     And locked his arms his foeman round.
>     They tug, they strain!—down, down they go,
>     The Gael above, Fitz-James below!
>     The chieftain's gripe his throat compressed,
>     His knee was planted in his breast;
>     His clotted locks he backward threw,
>     Across his brow his hand he drew,
>     From blood and mist to clear his sight,
>     Then gleam'd aloft his dagger bright!"

From Callandar to Stirling, we go by rail. The scenery along the Teith, and at Doune, and Dunblane, is both picturesque and beautiful.

Stirling is famous for its castle, its church, and the bloody battle fought in the immediate vicinity. A narrow and winding street, leads to the Franciscan Church, erected by James IV. in 1494. In the choir, James VI. was crowned, on which occasion John Knox preached the coronation sermon. Ebenezer Erskine, the founder of the "Secession Church of Scotland," was one of its ministers. Here we find a copy of the "breeches" bible, of 1585. Genesis iii. 7 reads: "And they sewed fig leaves together, and made themselves breeches." Some historic mansions are pointed out, by a Scottish guide, 84 years of age. Argyle Lodge, where Prince Charles was entertained by the Marquis, is the most conspicuous. Passing through a narrow entrance, we reach the Palace and Castle; sit in the black oak chair used by James I. and VI., and rest our note-book on the black oak table, the first used by Knox, at the communion service.

The Castle is built upon a green trap rock, 310 feet above the level of the plain. And the view from these lofty battlements, is beautiful and grand. Beneath us are the green fields, where the tournament was held; and from this spot,—"The Ladies' Look-out,"—proud matrons looked down upon the friendly contests of rival Scottish chiefs. Here, Queen Mary stood, 300 years ago, when

> "The castle gates were open flung,
>   The quivering draw-bridge rocked and rung,
>   And echoed loud the flinty street
>   Beneath the coursers' clattering feet,
>   As slowly down the deep descent
>   Fair Scotland's King and nobles went.
>   Now in the Castle-park, drew out
>   Their chequered bands, the joyous rout,
>   There morricers, with bell at heel,
>   And blade in hand, their mazes wheel,
>   Their bugles challenge all that will,
>   In archery to prove their skill.
>   Now clear the ring! for, hand to hand,
>   The manly wrestlers take their stand,
>   The vale with loud applauses rang,
>   The Ladies' Rock sent back the clang."

Yonder, crowning a cliff nearly 600 feet high, stands Wallace's monument.  The tower is 220 feet high, and surmounted by an open crown. This site was well chosen, being in the vicinity of Stirling Bridge, the scene of Wallace's first victory over the English, in 1297.  The river Forth, fringed with poplar, ash, and willow, and winding through green meadows, and fields of ripening grain, forms thirteen beautiful curves, as it rolls past Stirling Castle!  Then, the Vale of Menteith on the west, the Campsie on the south, the Ochil Hills on the north, and Bannockburn— memorable as the scene of a bloody battle fought in 1314, by Edward II. of England and Robert the Bruce of Scotland—all may be seen from these Castle walls.

The cemetery, adjoining the Castle, has some monuments worthy of notice. Here is a prize monument by Ritchie, erected to the memory of "Margaret Wilson, virgin martyr of the wave." "She was bound to a stake, within flood mark of the Solway tide, and died a martyr's death, on May 11th, 1685." The inscription on the monument, to this true blue Presbyterian maiden, reads thus :—

"Love many waters cannot quench,
   God saves His chaste impearled ones in covenant true.
   O Scotia's Daughters, earnest scan the page,
   And prize this flower of Grace, blood bought for you."
                              "Psalm ix. 9."

Here is a pyramidal monument, to the heroic "Covenanters." On the sides, the "Crown of Life," the "Star of Light," and the open Bible, are beautifully chiseled. How the blood warms, while we walk through this city of the dead, and gaze upon the graves of our ancestors! How fearless of danger; how ready to die in defence of truth, were those heroes of the "Covenant"!

A quaint inscription this, upon the tombstone of A. Meffin, Chief Constable of Stirlingshire :—

> "Our life is but a winter day,
>   Some only breakfast and away,
>   Others to dinner stay, and are well fed,
>   The oldest man but sups and goes to bed,
>   Large is his debt, that lingers out the day,
>   He that goes soonest, has the least to pay."

From Stirling we proceed to Linlithgow, by way of Bannockburn, and visit the palace famous as the residence of the Stuart kings, and the birth-place of the beautiful Queen of Scots.

The ruins of the palace, stand upon the margin of a crescent shaped lake, and command a charming view of the surrounding country. We wander through the deserted halls, now the home of the wild birds; and are startled, as out from the ivy-clad, crumbling walls, sweeps the black-winged, screaming hawk, or flies the affrighted swallow.

Here is the dining-hall, 98 feet long, 33 broad, and 38 high. And this is the room that witnessed the birth of Queen Mary, in 1542; and yonder the apartment sacred to the confessional.

It was from this room, in which we now stand, that James escaped—by an opening in the floor—when the nobles came to assassinate him. Some of the tender-hearted ladies covered the subterranean passage with a spinning wheel, and thus aided their royal master in his untimely flight. Every apartment, in this once royal palace, has a history.

And could these crumbling walls speak, what a tale would they unfold !

From Linlithgow to Edinburgh: the route lies through well-cultivated farms. Sturdy women toil in the fields, hoeing the potatoes. The houses are built of stone, and the roofs are slated, or tiled. These red-roofed houses, shine quite conspicuously through the green trees, by which they are shaded and surrounded.

Edinburgh is, unquestionably, a beautiful city. It is built upon a number of hills; and the relative position of the structures, and the varying style of architecture, present a scene exceedingly picturesque. The city is divided into two parts, the old and the new. The old is separated from the new, by a wide valley, beautified with flower gardens, and spanned by two bridges. A mound, also, 800 feet long, 300 feet wide, and nearly 100 feet high, serves the purpose of a bridge, in uniting the old town and the new. In the " new " section, the streets are wide, and the edifices, many of them, costly and magnificent. In the aristocratic quarter, there are a number of handsome terraces, crescents, and squares, ornamented by stately trees, and sparkling lawns. Over the valley, in the " old " town, the houses, unlike in structure, and unequal in height, stand along the sloping hillsides, or crown the summits, in the most charming irregularity.  Some of these edifices, climb to a height of eight or ten stories!  Here, indeed, we behold " castles in the air."

The scene after dark, is exceedingly brilliant. The inequalities of the surface, render visible the thousands of flickering lights, that in wavy lines span the valleys, climb the acclivities, and encircle the summits.

But a stranger is unequal to the task, of giving a graphic description of this modern Athens.  We will therefore call upon a local writer, to describe one or two interesting localities.  To the clear head of a Scotchman, he adds a thorough knowledge of geology, and a loving appreciation of the beauful and picturesque.  " Arthur's Seat culminates in a point, lifts a truncated, conical summit to an altitude of 822 feet, southeast ; descends rollingly to the east and northeast, projects an abrupt shoulder to the south ; breaks down precipitously to the west ; presents to the south and west an undulating outline, similar to that of the sculptured figure of a lion couchant, and contains indications of successive outbursts of igneous rock."  In the following language, he describes the beauty of Salisbury Crag.

" Salisbury Crag ascends in regular gradient, over 700 yards ; makes a semicircular sweep of three quarters of a mile, with convexity to the west ; breaks perpendicularly down round the face of that sweep, in naked, rugged, greenstone crag, 60 feet ; is girt round the foot of its entire sweep of crag by a broad path ; then descends in a talus partly detrited, but mostly verdant,—and all so smooth, so rapid, so regularly declivitous as to be transversable only by an adventurous and sure-footed pedestrian."

That this is an excellent place to study geology, may readily be inferred, when we are informed " that the locality must have acquired its contour from a stupendous series of shocks, upheavals, and surging denudations : that it contains remarkable masses of igneous and stratified rocks, in varieties, compositions, dips, and mutual relations illustrative of many of the most striking changes which have occurred in the crust of the earth ; it gives charming lessons, in much of the departments of volcanic action, oversurging sea, fossiliferous deposit, and mineral distribution ; and presents in the logical inferences of a geologist, and in the enlightened imagination of any ordinary intelligent thinker, a long diversified bygone blaze of wonders."

Now, to our mind, the character of the place, accounts for the genius of the people. Up to this very moment, we have found it difficult to understand, why the inhabitants of Edinburgh, were, mentally and morally, so superior to their neighbors. But this writer has shed a "blaze" of light upon the subject. How could men, born upon these marvelous crags, and encircled by, and breathing such an atmosphere, fail to be pure in thought, and clear in conception?

There are a number of splendid monuments, erected in different parts of the city. Nelson's crowns Calton Hill; and close beside it, stand monuments to the memory of Dugald Stewart, the mental philosopher, and Professor Playfair, the mathematician. On Prince's Street—the "Broadway" of Edinburgh—Scott's monument is quite conspicuous. The Poet was born in Edinburgh, August, 1771, and died at Abbottsford, September, 1832. This monument was erected in 1844; is two hundred feet high; and cost seventy-five thousand dollars. A bronze statue of Professor Wilson—Christopher North—adorns one of the beautiful West Prince's Street gardens.

On Prince's Street, stands the Antiquarian Museum, an institution well worth visiting. Here, we find stone implements used by the Celts and Picts; swords, daggers and axe-heads in bronze; curiously sculptured urns; and many beautiful ornaments in silver and gold.

And here is a silver tea-spoon, used by Prince Charles Edward, at Holyrood Palace; the sea-chest, and drinking cup, belonging to Alexander

6

Selkirk, when he sojourned on the Island of Juan Fernandez; and a brass collar, on which the following words are engraved: — "Alex$^r$ Steuart found guilty of death for theft at Perth the 5th of December 1701 and gifted by the Justiciars as a perpetual servant to Sir Jo. Araskin of Alva." If all thieves of the present day were thus necklaced, and compelled to work without wages, how quickly the price of brass would rise, and that of labor fall! And this is John Knox's pulpit from St. Giles. And there is the " Maiden," or Scotch guillotine, used in the beheading of the Earl of Argyle, and still stained with blood! Here are the thumbikins, and other instruments of torture used against the Covenanters. And yonder, is Jennie Geddes' stool,—the very one—which that sinewy and orthodox lady hurled at the Dean of St. Giles, on the 23rd of July 1637. This gentleman had just commenced reading the service, when Jennie hurled the stool at his head, accompanied with the indignant outburst, "Villain! dost thou say mass at my lug?"

Above us, is one of the blue banners of the " Covenant." This was borne by the Covenanters, at the battle of Bothwell Bridge. And here too, is the "Solemn League and Covenant," signed by Archbishop Leighton. There are several " Leagues;" and the signatures to some of these "solemn" documents, are written in *blood!* And many of those were penned by Christian women, who were willing to die for the "faith, once delivered unto the Saints."

We will now walk through Canon Gate and High Street, from Holyrood Abbey to the Castle. This palace was once the seat of Scottish royalty; and in the Chapel Royal—a fragment of the ancient Abbey—are buried, many of the kings and queens of Scotland. The rooms occupied by Queen Mary, are the chief attraction, to all tourists. Our guide points out the dressing-rooms, the private supping-room, the audience-room, and the sleeping-room. Here stands, with fragments of the blankets, QUEEN MARY'S BED. The decayed hangings, are of crimson damask, with green silk fringes, and tassels. The Queen's work-box, and the needlework—worked by her own fair hands, and representing Jacob's Dream are upon the table,—just as she left them!

The Picture Room is 150 feet long, 27 feet wide, and 20 feet high. It was used by Prince Charles as a banquetting hall, and is now used for the election of Scottish Peers, and for the annual levees, of the Commissioners to the General Assembly of the Church of Scotland.

Queen Victoria, and the royal family, occupy the royal private apartments in Holyrood Palace, during their visits to Edinburgh.

On our right as we march up the Hill, is the Canongate Church. Here, Adam Smith, author of "The Wealth of Nations," Dugald Stewart, and Ferguson the poet, are buried.

And this is John Knox's house. In this quaint, many-cornered old building, the fearless reformer resided, from 1560, until his death in 1572. The house consists of three rooms,—sitting-room, bed-room, and study. It is by no means attractive, internally or externally; and yet, how many pilgrims coming from afar, wend their way to old High Street, to gaze upon the edifice, once tenanted by this heroic man!

A little further along is the old Parliament House, now occupied by the Supreme Court. It was erected between 1632, and 1640. The great hall is 122 feet long, 49 feet wide, and has a lofty roof of carved oak. The walls are decorated with portraits of Lords Brougham, Cockburn, Mansfield, and other distinguished lawyers. Here, the attorneys and counsellors promenade, when off duty; and here they consult with clients, and banter each other upon the losing or winning of suits.

In the adjoining rooms, are seated the clear-headed "Lords" of Justice, clothed in purple and scarlet, and crowned with curiously woven wigs; while in their august presence, the dark-robed lawyers dissect, analyze, unravel, and make lumi-

St. Giles, Edinburgh.

nous, that which would puzzle even a Philadelphia brother—in the law.  We highly enjoy an hour in the court rooms, listening to the keen logic, and fluent speech, of these Edinburgh advocates.

And here is old St. Giles,—the church of the Patron Saint, and memorable as the place, where October 13th, 1643, the Solemn League was signed.

It is 206 feet in length, and from 76 to 130 feet in breadth.  In the days when Rome was in power, it had forty altars, and was served by seventy priests.  The building is now divided into three parochial places of worship.  Here, Queen Mary worshipped, and John Knox preached; here, Jennie Geddes hurled the stool at the Dean's head, and the Solemn League and Covenant was sworn to; and here also, the Covenanters were imprisoned!  The old female guide has all the historic facts at her finger's end.  She is enthusiastic, eloquent; and many of her statements are quite interesting.  Pointing to a certain corner of the building, she informs us that "In yonder corner the queen did sit; above, at the joining of the arches is a wreath beautifully carved, having four M's.  These four M's represent her four maids of honor, viz.: Mary Beaton, Mary Seaton, Mary Fleming, and Mary Kir Mackle."

Climbing the Hill, we reach the famous old Castle. It is built upon a precipitous rock, 383 feet above the level of the sea. The Castle covers an area of $9\frac{1}{2}$ acres, and the outlook, from the battlements, is magnificent.

Of the numerous apartments, the "Crown" room is the most interesting. Here, the crown jewels are carefully guarded. The "Regalia," consist of a golden crown,—sparkling with gems, and surmounted by a cross; a Sceptre,—a slender silver rod, thirty-nine inches in length, and beautifully ornamented; and the Sword of state,—some five feet long,—the gift of Pope Julius II. to James IV.

The history of these symbols of sovereignty, during the centuries of internal and external strife, preceding the Union with England, is exceedingly romantic. And it is stipulated in the Treaty of Union, that they "shall remain in all coming time" in Scotland.

The University of Edinburgh is visited, by invitation of Professor Calderwood,—successor of Sir Wm. Hamilton in the chair of Metaphysics. The University dates from 1582. The buildings form a hollow parallelogram, extending 255 feet from north to south, and 358 feet from east to west. The library hall is 198 long, and 50 feet wide, and is ornamented with busts of Sir

Wm. Hamilton, Dugald Stewart, Professor Playfair, and other distinguished scholars.   It has
upon its shelves, 250,000 volumes, arranged in
the most convenient, and admirable manner.   In
the class rooms, the benches and the black-boards
are not a whit more intelligent-looking, than those
used in the most unhistoric, and unpretending, of
American Colleges!

A short distance from the University buildings,
we find the old *Greyfriars Church*, surrounded by
an ancient Church-yard.   In this cemetery, some
notable Scotsmen are buried.   Here are the tombs
of George Buchanan, Principal Robertson, Dr.
Hugh Blair, Dr. McCrie, Colin Maclaurin, and
Ramsay, the poet.   A monument of Peter Head
granite, marks the poet's resting-place ; and the
following lines form the epitaph :—

> "Tho' here you're buried worthy Allan
> We'll ne'er forget you canly callan,
> For while your soul lives in the sky,
> Your Gentle Shepherd ne'er can die."

But by far the most interesting monument, is that
erected to the memory of the Covenanters.   The
inscription, both in prose and poetry, is quite instructive, and we copy it.

" From May 27, '61 that the most noble Marquis of Argyle was beheaded, to 17 February '88,
that Mr James Renwick suffered, were one way

and another murdered, and destroyed, for the same cause about 18,000 ; of whom at Edinburgh were executed about 100 noblemen, gentlemen, ministers, and others, noble martyrs for Jesus Christ. The most of them lie here."

> "Halt, passenger, take heed what you do see,
>   This tomb doth shew for what some men would die,
>   Here lies the dust of those who stood,
>   'Gainst perjury resisting unto blood;
>   Adhering to the Covenants and the laws
>   Establishing the same ; which was the cause
>   Their lives were sacrific'd unto the lust
>   Of Prelatists abjured.   Though here their dust
>   Lies mixed with murderers, and other crew
>   Whom justice justly did to death pursue ;
>   But as for them, no cause was to be found
>   Worthy of death ; but only they were found
>   Constant and steadfast. zealous witnessing
>   For the Prerogatives of Christ their King.
>   Which truths were sealed with famous Guthrie's head,
>   And all along to Mr. Renwick's blood,
>   They did endure the wrath of enemies,
>   Reproaches, torments, deaths and injuries,
>   But yet they're those from whom such troubles came,
>   And now triumph in glory with the Lamb."

In this city, we find the finest specimens of the Scotchman. At every turn, on the street, in bank, and store, you meet with the genuine Scot,— pure and unalloyed. In looks, dialect, and dress, the Edinburgh Scotchman exhibits all the national peculiarities. How clearly, shrewdness, forethought, and philosophic reflectiveness, are mirrored in that somewhat rugged countenance! Even the Scotch beggar, is a peculiar individual—His strategy is masterly; and if he fails to capture a sixpence or a shilling, he does not lose his equanimity, but rather reflects upon the best method of improving his tactics.

The city has a population of 200,000, is beautiful for situation; and the people are distinguished for intelligence, refinement, and culture.

Standing upon one of those picturesque elevations, for which the city is so famous, and looking down upon this Scottish Metropolis, what memories of men, and events, crowd upon the mind! Here, Knox, Chalmers, and Guthrie, preached; and Hamilton, Stewart, and Playfair taught; here Jeffrey, and Wilson, wrote; and Scott, and Ramsay, sang. And here, the solemn Covenant was signed; and in these graveyards, the Covenanters sleep! Is it surprising, that the Scotch should love this city on the hills? Is it to be wondered at, that Scott should write of it,—

> "The wandering eye could o'er it go,
>   And mark the distant city glow;
>     With gloomy splendor red;
>   For on the smoke-wreaths huge and slow,
>   That round her sable turrets flow,
>     The morning beams were shed;
>   And tinged them with a lustre proud,

> Like that which streaks a thunder cloud,
> Such dusky grandeur clothed the height,
> Where the huge castle holds its state,
>     And all the steep slope down,
> Whose ridgy back heaves to the sky
> Piled deep and massy, close and high
>     Mine own romantic town !"

Bidding farewell to Edinburgh, we take the train for Melrose Abbey. The distance is 37 miles. This famous Abbey, was founded by David I. early in the twelfth century, and was rebuilt during the reign of Robert the Bruce. In the choir, on the site of the high altar, the heart of King Robert, the Bruce, is interred.

The doorways and arches are richly ornamented.

> " The keystone that locks each ribbed aisle
>     Is a fleur-de-lis or a quatrefeuille ;
>     The corbels are carved grotesque and grim,
>     And the pillars with cluster'd shafts so trim,
>     With base and with capital flourish'd around,
>     Seem bundles of lances which garlands have bound."

There are several beautiful windows. The tracery in stone, is the finest we have yet seen ; and, excels that of any other Scottish ruin, except that of Roslin Chapel.

> " Thou would'st have thought some fairy's hand
>     'Twixt poplars straight the osier wand
>         In many a freaking knot had twined ;
>     Then framed a spell when the work was done,
>     And changed the willow wreaths to stone."

We would love to linger here till moonlight, if

other scenes did not extend a pressing invitation
to visit them.  Sir Walter Scott informs us, in
the "Lay of the Last Minstrel," that the moonlight scene is the loveliest.

> " If thou would'st view fair Melrose aright,
>     Go visit it by the pale moonlight ;
>     For the gay beams of lightsome day
>     Gild, but to flout, the ruins gray.
>     When the broken arches are black in night,
>     And each shafted oriel glimmers white ;
>     When the cold light's uncertain shower
>     Streams on the ruined central tower ;
>     When buttress and buttress alternately,
>     Seem framed of ebon and ivory ;
>     Then go—but go alone the while—
>     Then view St. David's ruined pile ;
>     And, home returning, soothly swear,
>     Was never scene so sad and fair !"

Three miles westward—from Melrose—is Abbottsford,—the home of Sir Walter Scott.  We
hire a carriage, and have a pleasant drive over a
good road, through a charming country, to this
beautiful mansion on the banks of the Tweed.
The entrance is by a porchway, adorned with petrified stags' horns.  The hall is pannelled with
finely carved oak ; the floor paved with black and
white marble ; and the walls covered with ancient
armor.

The library contains 20,000 volumes,—each
volume being selected by Sir Walter.  The arm-

chair he occupied during his literary labors, and the large table, stand in the centre of the room, and from their size and position, immediately attract the visitor's attention.

The furniture in the various apartments, is of the finest material, and most curious workmanship. The numerous gifts bestowed by admiring friends, constitute quite a little museum. Some of these articles are of great historic, and intrinsic value. Here is a little box, once the property of Mary Queen of Scots; and a curiously shaped candle-stick, belonging to The Bruce. Here is the sword of Montrose, Rob Roy's gun, and a brandy flask, once carried by James VI.

The walls of the various apartments, are de-corated with numerous pictures. Among these, one is particularly conspicuous,—representing the head of Queen Mary, in a charger, the day after her execution. Here is a picture of Claverhouse, —the terror of the Covenanters ; and yonder hangs a portrait of Scott's grandfather,—a long-bearded and venerable-looking patriarch.

But the Bard of the North is silent ! The harp that thrilled the Scottish heart, is heard no more on the banks of the Tweed !

> " Harp of the North ! that mouldering long hast hung
>     On the witch-elm that shades Saint Fillan's spring,
>   And down the fitful breeze thy numbers flung,

> Till envious ivy did around thee cling,
> Muffling with verdant ringlet every string—
> Oh minstrel Harp! still must thine accents sleep?
> Mid rustling leaves and fountains murmuring;
> Still must thy sweeter sounds their silence keep,
> Nor bid a warrior smile, nor teach a maid to weep?"

Sir Walter seized this harp, and those trembling strings, responsive to his magic touch, swayed Scottish hearts, and made them "higher throb."

But to the harp, and to the Tweed, he bade a long, and sad, farewell. And on the 21st September, 1832, he might have addressed both, in the tender language of an old Welch Bard :—

> " Then adieu, Silver Trivi! I quit thy lov'd scene,
> To join the dim choir of the bards that have been;
> And thou whose faint warblings my weakness can tell,
> Farewell, my lov'd Harp! my last treasure, farewell!"

He rests quietly, in the beautiful Abbey of Dryburg,—a few miles distant. This abbey was founded in the 12th century, during the reign of David I.

The nave of the church is 190 feet long, and 75 feet broad. The great dining-room of the monks, was 100 feet long, 30 feet broad, and 60 feet high.

The west end gable of this refectory, is triangular, has a beautiful starlike window, and is overgrown with ivy. Near the entrance door, a yew-tree,—said to be 700 years old—generously shades the inquisitive tourist. How many dark-robed mourners, have walked in the shadow of this still stately tree! To how many soft whisperings of love, has it listened, when the moonbeams danced over the silvery surface of the murmuring Tweed! Over how many joyous bridal processions, has it waved, when the old Abbey bell summoned lovers to the altar, there to pledge their mutual, and perpetual love!

St. Mary's Aisle, the most beautiful part of the ruin, contains the tomb of the poet. A very plain monument of Peter-Head granite, marks the resting place of the illustrious dead.

Here, within the old Abbey grounds, is a house, once occupied by Ebenezer, and Ralph Erskine,—the eminent Scottish divines; and yonder, crowning the rocky summit, is a rude statue of the patriot Bruce.

The country surrounding the Abbey is beautiful. The trees are tall; the meadows green; and the air is sweet with the mingled fragrance of many flowers.

But the sighing of the winds, and the sobbing of the waters, give voice to nature's sadness, over the ruin time has wrought.

How quiet to-day along the borders! Not the sound of a bugle can be heard; not the flash of a sabre can be seen! The steel-clad warriors, and the clang of arms, have passed away; and bards shall sing no more,—of border strife. Crossing the Tweed, we bid farewell to Scotland ;—

> "Sweet Teviot! on thy silver tide
>     The glaring bale-fires blaze no more;
> No longer steel-clad warriors ride
>     Along thy wild and willowed shore.
> Where'er thou wind'st by dale or hill,
> All, all is peaceful, all is still,
>     As if thy waves, since Time was born,
> Since first they rolled upon the Tweed,
> Had only heard the shepherd's reed,
>     Nor started at the bugle-horn."

# CHAPTER VII.



TAKING the train, at a station a few miles distant from Dryburgh, we cross the border, and roll over the Cheviot Hills. The scene, along these hills, is desolate. Here and there a shepherd's cot may be seen, surrounded by flocks of sheep, and herds of hornless cattle. Our train thunders past Carlisle, and down through northern England, to Leeds and York.

The city of York, is of great antiquity, and its magnificent Cathedral attracts hither, annually, thousands of tourists. The building of the city, is ascribed to Agricola, in the year 50. Here also the Emperor Severus died, about the year 211. At a short distance from the city, the funeral pile was kindled by the Emperor's sons, while the whole army in solemn procession, marched thrice around the burning body. The ashes of the cremated monarch were deposited in an urn, and sent to Rome.

In York also, Constantius, the father of Constan-

144

tine the Great, died in 306, and some writers contend that the latter,—the first Christian Emperor,—was born in York. In the neighborhood of York, many battles were fought between the Scots and Picts, and the ancient Britons. It was in the vicinity of York, that the Saxons, after expelling the Picts and Scots, first turned their arms against the Britons, who had invited them to the Island.

But to view the Minster, or Cathedral, is the object of our visit. The present building, stands upon the site of an ancient heathen temple. The erection of the south transept was commenced in the year 1220. The edifice as it now appears, was completed about the year 1400. The architecture is gothic, of which there are five different styles exhibited, in various parts of the structure.

This stately edifice is 524 feet long, and 221 feet broad. The Great Tower is 214 feet high. The ornamentation in some parts of the building is very beautiful. The slender pillars, pointed arches, ornamented capitals, and magnificent stained glass windows, arrest the eye at every step. The east window is 75 feet high, and 32 feet broad, and this vast illuminated space is occupied with representations of the leading events in Bible history. The great clock bell cost $10,000 and weighs $12\frac{1}{2}$ tons. There are a number of handsome monuments in the aisles, and in the Lady Chapel. For 200 years, the Minster has been celebrated for its music. The organ is played as we wander through the building, and the crowd of tourists seem startled, as if expecting to see the dead arise, and come forth. Groups of men and women stand in the nave, transepts, aisles, under arches 100 feet high, and listen with the most marked attention, and manifest feelings of wonder and delight. And why should they not? The scene, and the sounds, are they not inspiring? This lofty and magnificent building, with its forest of pillars, its archways 100 feet high, its gorgeously decorated windows, and the "pealing organ" filling the vast edifice with music, melodious and inspiring, does, we are free to admit, affect us strangely.

We have never seen such a building, and we have never heard such music. A desire long cherished is to-day gratified. But this pealing organ, is inviting us to morning service. We enter the choir, and occupy a "stall." The seat is comfortable, and the reflection that it may, on former occasions, have been occupied by some royal duke, or noble earl, adds much to the pleasure of our visit. It is 10 o'clock, and the clergy, in slow and solemn procession, are entering the choir. At these week-day services the attendance is small, and to-day, it is composed chiefly of tourists. The officiating clergymen, are tidily attired, in the customary ecclesiastical garments. The litany is chanted, and the Scriptures read. The Bible, rests upon the expanded wings of a brazen eagle, which serves the purpose of a desk. There are so many objects novel and strange, that the majority of the audience, seem more interested in the carvings and paintings, than in the readings or responses.

But the clergy proceed with as much seriousness, and solemnity, as if thousands were listening and responding. Both the service, and the surroundings, impress us. It is our first "Cathedral service," and we enjoy it.

After purchasing a photographic picture of the "Minster," we resume our journey. The route lies through the centre of old England. Our train whirls along past Sheffield, and Chesterfield. We linger a season in Birmingham. The whole city is enveloped in smoke. There are forests of tall chimney's, emitting smoke of all colors. Furnaces are blazing for miles in every direction. Trains thunder along with the greatest rapidity.

We are informed by an Englishman, that the number of trains arriving at, and departing from, the Birmingham station exceeds that of any other Rail Road station in England. Trains pass the East station at the average rate of one every minute! Three trains are now moving past this busy station ; and the clanging of bells, screaming of whistles, and puffing of engines, fill the air with sounds most discordant. The traffic, through this smoking and blazing city, is enormous. But the work goes on, also, underground. The city is undermined. The ground, for miles, trembles as heavily laden trains go thundering over it. And to avoid possible, and fatal accident, the building of a new rail-road is seriously contemplated.

The whole country from Birmingham to Wolverhampton,—a distance of ten miles,—is covered with smoke and flames. Shafts, leading to deep mines, are sunk in every direction. Blazing furnaces, in brilliant succession, illumine the country, by day and by night. Here, the sons of Vulcan toil, " wrapped in drifts of lurid smoke."

The manufacturing cities of England, have each their specialty :—viz., Leeds manufactures, cheap cloth ; Sheffield, steel ; Birmingham, iron ; Wolverhampton, japanned goods ; Manchester, dry goods ; and London,—everything.

Leaving this noisy bustling city, we visit Rugby. And what cultivated fields, rich pasturage, and charming cottages, lie along the route ! How lovely, is this part of old England !

Rugby, is celebrated for its school. Clean winding streets, lead us, between rows of neat two, and three story brick buildings, along the hillside, to the Parish Church.

Inside the gate, is a beautiful fountain, with an image of the Saviour pointing at the words, "If any man thirst, let him come unto me and drink."

The notices posted at the door of this venerable edifice, are not strictly ecclesiastical. Here, are the names of persons licensed to keep dogs! Now, there are two kinds of dogs: viz., those that go upon four legs, and those that walk upon two. And of those dogs that walk upon two legs, there are several species,—such as the "sly dogs," and, the "lazy dogs." Which of these, the pious people of Rugby are "licensed" to keep, is not specifically stated.

And here also, are the names of all the qualified voters, in the town, or parish of Rugby! This looks very much like the union of church, and state. Whether the elections are held in the church building, and the parson is appointed judge, we are not informed.

Rugby Academy, crowns the eminence upon which the town is built. It is a brick edifice, flanked with towers, that give it the appearance of a castle. Some parts of the building are two, and some three, stories high. The chapel is a very large structure, built of red and white brick. Stately trees shade the walks, that lead through the closely shaven, and sparkling lawns. Here indeed, are "goodliest trees, planted with walks and bowers." But we see no form, we hear no footstep. All is silent, save the rooks. These black-winged noisy birds, are cawing in the trees, and flying over the grounds, as if they were the only, and legitimate, occupants of these lawns and bowers.

Remembering that "Tom Brown" went from Rugby to Oxford, we imitate his example, and arrive in the "University town," early in the afternoon. What fields, and flocks, are there in the vicinity of Oxford! Such sheep and oxen, and such sturdy men and women, we have not seen elsewhere in England.

It is now "vacation," and the University is closed. Several hours are spent in wandering through the "quadrangles," that constitute the various college buildings. What venerable structures, and velvety lawns, and giant oaks! Here is Baliol College, or quadrangle; and this the spot where Thomas Cranmer, the first Protestant archbishop of Canterbury, died at the stake, on the 21st day of March, 1556!

Through the kindness of a polite and gentlemanly old janitor, we are admitted to the grand dining hall, of Christ Church College. It is the largest in the University. The hall is 115 feet long, 40 feet wide, and 50 feet high. Portraits of Queen Elizabeth, and Cardinal Wolsey, decorate

the wall, at the upper end of the room. The intelligent janitor assures us, that those distinguished
personages were "patrons" of the institution.

Wolsey, was educated at Magdalen College,
Oxford,—graduating in 1486, at fifteen years of
age. In the year 1525, he founded "Cardinal
College," Oxford. This College was subsequently
altered by Henry VIII., and called the "College of King Henry VIII." It is now called
"Christ Church College." In addition to the
effigies of those distinguished "patrons," there
are portraits of sixty eminent men, graduates of
this College; and among these we recognize that
of John Locke.

The founding of the University of Oxford, is
traced back to Alfred, in the year 880. What
multitudes of students have walked these streets,
during the past thousand years! In 1231, there
were thirty thousand students in attendance!

There are some eminent scholars connected with
the University at the present time;—and among
them, Max Müller, the linguist, and our old friend
Professor Liddell, whose Greek lexicon, was a con-
stant college companion while perusing the ancient
Classic worthies. And here, the scholarly, and
so-called heretical Pusey, flourishes, in the 74th
year of his age, after having written and published, nearly "sixty separate productions!"

The University of Cambridge, was founded in the year 1229. It is 77 miles distant from Oxford, and while not quite as ancient an institution as its rival, is still worthy of a visit.

The town of Cambridge, is by no means as attractive in appearance, as the town of Oxford. The streets are paved with large cobble-stones. The houses are built of brick, and the surrounding country is flat and uninteresting.

The College buildings are erected in "quadrangles." The "Emmanuel" college buildings, are two stories high; and the beautiful lawn, is tastefully ornamented with fragrant and blooming flowers. Some of the college buildings are ivy-covered, and look quite venerable.

The library, and the Chapel of King's college, are the most conspicuous, and highly ornamented edifices, that we have seen. Some of these quadrangles are built fronting upon a public highway; some stand at a distance from the street; and many of them are widely separated. A considerable portion of the town intervenes, between Emmanuel's college, and King's college. The space covered by these several buildings, with the lawns surrounding, is quite extensive.

As we walk through the streets, and gaze upon these gothic structures, and beautiful quadrangles, we think of the noble and gifted men, who were educated at this University.   Among its graduates we find the names of Milton, Dryden, Wordsworth, Bacon, Barrow, Latimer, Coleridge, Paley, Jeremy Taylor, Tillotson, Trench, and Alford.

But we must leave for the Metropolis.   London is distant from Cambridge just sixty miles.   The country is level; the pasturage and crops excellent.   Some of the houses are built of brick, and some of stone.   Some are thatched, and some are tiled.

Yonder is the Metropolis, with its palaces, temples, and towers!

> " This city now doth, like a garment wear
>     The beauty of the morning silent, fair,
>     Ships, towers, domes, palaces, and temples lie
>     Open unto the fields and to the sky."

The great city is entered, and comfortable " lodgings " secured.   On Cheapside, near St. Paul's, between the Post Office and the Bank, in the very heart of this modern Babel, we are pleasantly located.

London is built, principally, in a valley, surrounded by gently rising hills.   It is situated upon the river Thames, and by it—rolling eastward—divided into two unequal parts.   The distance from the city, to the sea, is about 50 miles. The city covers an area of 78,000 acres,—equal to

7

122 square miles.  The population is estimated at four millions.  The annual increase, is over 40,-000.  The average density of the population, is 40 persons to an acre.  Truly this is

> " A spacious city,
> The seat where England from her ancient reign
> Doth rule the ocean as her own domain."

There are over 500,000 houses within the city limits.  And the rent paid annually for the use or occupancy of these houses, amounts to $100,000,000 !

The houses are built—largely—of brick and have a somewhat dingy appearance.  There are over 10,000 streets, squares, terraces, and lanes.  Many of the streets are wide, and—for a considerable distance—straight, but the larger proportion are narrow, and crooked.  They are well paved, and considering the enormous traffic, quite clean.  These 6,600 miles of streets, are illumined every night by 360,000 gas lights, — burning 13,000,000 cubic feet of gas, every twenty-four hours.

Every day 44,000,000 gallons of water flow into London ; and every day 9,000,000 cubic feet of refuse matter flows out of London.  For the accommodation of its millions, thirteen railroads, over and under ground, enter the city ; scores of steamboats ply upon the Thames, stopping at twenty different landings ; and 8,000 public cabs, and 1,500 omnibusses, roll through the streets. And is it any wonder that the city is occasionally smoky, when 5,000,000 tons of coal are annually consumed ? And what quantities of food, and drink, are annually swallowed by these millions of hungry and thirsty metropolitans !

1,600,000 quarters of wheat ; 1,700,000 sheep ; 4,000,000 head of game ; 3,000,000 salmon ; 300,000 bullocks ; 35,000 pigs ; 28,000 calves, with large quantities of other "fish, flesh, and fowl," are washed down by 65,000 pipes of wine, 2,000,000 gallons of spirits, and 43,000,000 gallons of porter and ale ! The milk of 13,000 cows, is required to keep the "cream jugs" full.

And what a grand army of men and women, is engaged in providing for the bodily comfort, the mental culture, and the religious training of these hosts of Londoners ! Let us marshal them.

Here marches 2,500 bakers, followed by 1,700 butchers. Next comes 2,600 tea-dealers, accompanied by 1,200 coffee-room keepers ; while 1,500 dairy-men tramp close in the rear.

The next brigade, is headed by 3,000 tailors ; then follows 3,000 boot and shoe makers ; 1,500 milliners and dressmakers ; and 1,100 linen-drapers. And to settle disputes, here comes 3,000 attorneys, and 4,000 barristers ; and to keep the physical system in harmony, 2,400 doctors walk in procession. Then follow the teachers in 1,500 private schools, while 2,000 clergymen, representing over 1,000 places of worship, give dignity to this unique, and wonderful parade. But even metropolitans will not live always ; and now, behold a gloomy band of 500 undertakers, whose funereal services are required in the burial of the 75,000 that annually die, within the city limits. This provisioning, clothing, educating and governing a city of four millions, is a wonderful work.

But where shall we go? There are so many objects claiming attention, that we scarcely know where to begin. London is not only the greatest manufacturing city, but also the greatest commercial city, in the world. We will therefore honor the " Docks," by paying them a visit. The chosen route, passes " Billingsgate " market. This market is celebrated for the sale of fine fish, and the use of foul language. What rough specimens of Londoners! What brutal faces, and shameful speech ! And how the " King's English," is mercilessly murdered, even in sight of the Tower ! Of the discussions this morning it may be truthfully said,—

" There, stripped, fair rhetoric languished on the ground,
  And shameful Billingsgate her robes adorn."

Here are St. Katherine Docks, covering a space of 24 acres, and costing over $8,000,000. The warehouses, in connection with these docks, usually contain some 120,000 tons of merchandize,—principally from America, and the Mediterranean.

We now pass to the London Docks. These docks employ a capital of $20,000,000. Here are ships from every quarter of the globe, manned by seamen of all colors, who chatter up and down the decks, in strange and unknown tongues. Along these wharves lie heaps of hides, and oil cake, casks of cocoa, bags of rice, barrels of tallow, with immense quantities of sugar, tea, coffee, drugs, spices, oils, wines, wool and cotton. The Tobacco Dock, has warehouses adjoining, capable of holding 30,000,000 pounds of tobacco, and 9,000,000 gallons of wine and spirits. How closely united do we here find tobacco and whiskey? Smoking, and drinking,—do they not often walk hand in hand through life?

In connection with this Eastern Dock, is a wine and spirit vault, covering an area of seven acres! Admission is free, but we have no *taste* for the beverage.

The docks of London, cover an area of 900 acres. The Port of London, extends four miles; is entered by over 40,000 vessels annually; and the customs collected amount to $55,000,000 a year!

> " Where has commerce such a mart,—
> So rich, so thronged, so drained, and so supplied,
> As London?   Opulent, enlarged, and still
> Increasing London !"

*Lloyd's shipping office*, is next visited.   The scene, in and about the building, is a busy one. Flaming placards on the walls point out the home, colonial, and foreign, departments.   Huge books lie upon the desks, and the names of vessels arriving at, and departing from, the various ports all over the world, are carefully recorded. Merchants eagerly scan the lists, and hurry off with smiling or frowning faces.   A stately Englishman, wearing a scarlet robe, guards the entrance, and none can enter the room, or examine the books, without his permission.

The Thames, is spanned by a number of bridges ; and of some of these, the Londoners are justly proud.   Wandering through streets flanked with massive structures, and crowded with hurrying merchants, and thundering vehicles, we arrive at the London Bridge.   This bridge is 928 feet long, 54 feet wide, and cost $12,000,000.

It is not the longest, nor the widest bridge,— the " Waterloo " being 1380 feet long, and the " Westminster " 85 feet wide,—but the traffic over it is immense.   It is estimated that 1000 vehicles, and 10,000 pedestrians, pass over this bridge every hour!

*The Bank of England*, is famous and worthy of a visit. Passing through Broad and Lombard streets, and looking upon the sitting statue of the philanthropic Peabody, we are face to face with the "old lady in Threadneedle street."

This bank was founded in 1691, by a Scotchman named Patterson. The business is conducted by a governor, deputy governor. and 24 directors.

The capital is over $70,000,000. The par value of the stock is $500, and the market price, $1250. There are 1000 persons employed, and the salaries range from $250 to $6,000 a year. The management of the National Debt, amounting to $4,000,-000,000, is intrusted to this Bank. On this "Debt," dividends are paid to the amount of $125,000,000 a year. And the Bank receives annually, from the Government, as compensation for its services, $1,000,000.

At the entrance door, sits a gorgeously robed Englishman, closely inspecting every visitor. Gentlemen, with shining silk hats, dark green coats, crimson colored vests, and stylish knee breeches, walk hither and thither, keeping order in the establishment. We are conducted through the Bank-note and gold rooms, and the " Consol " department. Here are men shoveling gold, as if it were nothing more than the " dust of the earth." And here are curious machines, capable of weighing 33 sovereigns a minute; and also of instantly detecting, and rejecting, every light weighted coin! And yonder is a clock with 16 dials, so arranged, that a "face" may be seen in 16 different offices. What crowds of people, and yet what order, in this the greatest banking establishment in the world!

The next public building visited is the *Post Office*. Passing along Cheapside and Newgate streets, we arrive at this building, about four in the afternoon. As business in London is transacted between the hours of 10 A. M. and 4 P. M., the scene at the " office," at the latter hour, is exceedingly lively. Letters, carried by all manner of conveyance, are tumbled into the receiving boxes by the thousands. Scores of men and boys, are rushing with full baskets, to the various receptacles. Wagon loads of precious documents, are whirled through the gates, at the utmost speed. Crowds of lazy people, wonderingly— stare at these swift-footed messengers.

But the quickness of movement inside, fully equals the rapidity of motion outside. 1,500 clerks are engaged in assorting, and despatching. And the mail matter handled annually at this office, is said to be 12,000,000 book parcels : 80,000,000 newspapers; and 800,000,000 letters.

*The Tower of London,* is the most celebrated

fortress in Great Britain. It is, or has been, both a citadel, a palace, a prison, an armory, and a treasury. Tradition ascribes its foundation to Cæsar. Shakespeare, in King Richard, speaks thus of this ancient structure :—

> " Prince.   Where shall we sojourn till our coronation?
> " Gloster.   Where it seems best unto your royal self.
>   If I may counsel you, some day or two
>   Your Highness will repose you at the Tower.
> " Prince.   I do not like the Tower, of any place,—
>   Did Julius Cæsar build that place, my lord ?
> " Buck.   He did, my gracious lord, begin that place,
>   Which since succeeding ages have re-edified."

It is situated on the north bank of the Thames, and the area of the Tower, within the walls, is twelve acres. How many famous men were here imprisoned ! John, King of France; the Duke of Orleans; the Duke of Buckingham; the Duke of Marlborough; the Earl of Shaftesbury ; Lord Russell ; and Sir Walter Raleigh, had free lodgings furnished in these gloomy apartments !

And here Sir Thomas More, Lady Jane Grey (1553), Queen Anne Boleyn (1536), and Queen Katherine Howard (1542), fourth wife of Henry VIII., were beheaded. Lord Lovat, was the last gentlemen left headless on Tower Hill. This occurred in 1747.

A sturdy old pensioner, dressed in quaint military cos.ume, conducts visitors through the building. It contains 70,000 stands of arms. It also contains a large collection of ancient armor, and curious weapons used in attack and defense, on the battle-fields of centuries ago. And these are so systematically arranged, in separate apartments, that they not only illustrate the methods of ancient warfare, but also reveal the successive changes effected in the ministry of war, from the earliest ages until the present time. Here are weapons, taken in the Indian campaigns from the Sikhs, Burmese, and Chinese. And here are equestrian figures, clothed in the armor "fashionable" between the years 1272 and 1688. These mail-sheathed steeds, mounted by steel-clad effigies, so bright and burnished, and in such eager attitude, seem ready to rush forth to battle. We instinctively shrink back from that well poised lance, lest haply it should pierce a tourist's panoply,—our linen duster! Here is a suit of damasked armor, worn by Henry VIII. And yonder an effigy of Queen Elizabeth, arrayed in the armor worn by Her Majesty at Tilbury, in 1588, when she made her memorable speech to the soldiers.

The small arms, are so arranged as to "strike the eye," harmlessly and agreeably. They form numerous devices. Here is a balustrade of swords, and a floor made of ram-rods. And along the walls, are representations of stars, and flowers. And above us, suspended from the ceiling, is a shining chandelier, in the construction of which over 3,000 arms have been used, including swords and bayonets!

But we enter the " Bloody Tower," and climb to the " Jewel House."  Here, in a glazed iron cage, in the centre of a well-lighted room, we find the Regalia, and crown jewels of England.  This is Victoria's crown—a cap of purple velvet, enclosed by silver hoops, and studded with diamonds. It weighs $1\frac{3}{4}$ lbs., and is valued at $600,000.  St. Edward's Staff—of beaten gold—is 4 feet 7 inches long.  The Royal Sceptre, is of pure gold, and 2 feet 9 inches in length.  The Rod of Equity,—3 feet 7 inches long—is of gold, and set with diamonds.  In this carefully guarded cage, are also the Royal Spurs, used at the coronation ; the Gold Coronation Spoon, from which oil is poured upon the Sovereign ; and the Baptismal Font—silver gilt —used at the christening of the Royal children.

And shining conspicuously amidst these silver, and golden, and jewelled ornaments, is the famous Koh-i-Noor diamond.  This diamond belonged to Runjeet Singh, and was captured by the army that conquered the city of Lahore, Northern India.  It is of large size, and great brilliancy.  The jewels in this " case," are valued at $15,000,000 !

*The British Museum,* is an object of great interest, not only to the citizens of London, but to visitors at the British Metropolis. Leaving the Tower, and walking through Lombard St., Cheapside, under Temple Bar, and along the Strand and Drury Lane, an afternoon is delightfully and profitably spent, in this treasure-house of Science and Art. The building cost over $5,000,000. The cost of buildings and collections, from the founding of the Museum in 1753, until 1872, amounted to over $17,000,000. The buildings are erected in the form of a quadrangle. The reading-room is circular, surmounted by a dome 140 feet in diameter, and 106 feet in height. In this room 300 readers are accommodated with separate desks. The Library of the Museum, contains over 700,000 volumes.

On the tables, in the George III. library, are some beautiful specimens of printing, illustrating the progress made in that art, since the days of Guttenbergh, and Faust.

There are 30,000 manuscripts in the library ; and some of these date back to the 4th and 5th centuries. The largest collection of Hebrew books in the world, rests on these shelves. The Mazarine Bible, printed by Guttenberg's press at Mainz, in 1455,—and the earliest printed book known,—

is one of the many rare books owned by the Museum.

*The Sculpture Gallery*, is exceedingly interesting. Here, in the Egyptian Saloon, is a colossal head of Rameses II., 9 feet high; and here is also the celebrated Rosetta stone.  It is a piece of black basalt 3 feet long, 2 feet 5 inches broad, and about 12 inches thick.  Its tri-lingual inscription, furnished a key, by which to unlock the mysteries of Egyptian hieroglyphics.  It rests upon a very modest pedestal, in the centre of the room, and yet it has shed more light upon the path of anti-quarian, and historian, than all the giant statues by which it is surrounded.

Among the *Assyrian Antiquities*, stands a monument of Sennacherib, pointing back to 800 B. C.; and a beautiful obelisk, ascribed to an earlier date.

In the Elgin Hall, are some of the finest Greek sculptures.

It is supposed that some of these were executed by Phidias.  Here are statues that once decorated the Parthenon; and this the " Frieze," of that matchless Temple.

How the glory of Greece has departed, when the sculptures that beautified her most splendid edifices, have been removed from her soil, and placed on exhibition in England's metropolis!

*The Kensington Museum*, is of more recent

origin, and to certain classes, much more attractive than the "British." It was founded by Prince Albert in 1852; and the total outlay,—including the cost of the buildings,—from 1852 until 1872, amounted to $8,000,000.

The objects exhibited, consist principally of paintings, sculptures, porcelain, pottery, ornamented furniture, metal-work, tapestries, embroideries, &c. There is also a loan exhibition, in connection with the Museum. What a wealth of material is contained in these beautifully decorated courts! Here, painter, and sculptor, artist and artizan, manufacturer and merchant, may find objects worthy of study.

This is the musical court. What a number, and what a variety of wind and stringed instruments, are here collected!

In looking at these curiously constructed music-making machines, we are inclined to believe that some of them were fashioned by Jubal, and that they travelled to the Museum over Mount Ararat. Here is an old bag-pipe with velvet bags, and ivory keys. And yonder is a finger-organ owned by Luther; while close beside it is the harpischord played by Handel!

In an adjoining room, is the royal robe of *Theodore, King of Abyssinia*. It was captured by General Wolsey, on the 8th of April, 1874, at the taking of Magdala.  It is of damask silk, shining with gold.  How his sable majesty must have shone in the presence of his dusky warriors, when robed with this glittering garment!

If we are correctly informed, love was the cause of this monarch's downfall.  In an unlucky hour, he "proposed" to Victoria; and being cruelly, but most politely rejected, he laid violent hands upon a few wayfaring Englishmen.  General Wolsey, with British battalions, released the prisoners and slew the king.  Poor Theodore!  And yet he was not the first man who lost his head,—by "falling in love."

In the picture gallery, occupying a separate apartment, are the celebrated Cartoons of Raphael.  These were executed in 1514, at the request of Leo X.  They are drawings on cardboard, in chalk, tinted with distemper.  The subjects are scriptural, viz. : Christ's Charge to Peter ; The Death of Ananias ; Peter and John at the beautiful gate ; Healing the Lame Man ; Paul and Barnabas at Lystra ; Elymas the Sorcerer struck Blind ; Paul Preaching at Athens ; The Miraculous Draught of Fishes.  They are owned by the Queen, and loaned by Her Majesty to the Exhibition.  They are regarded by competent critics, as "the grandest productions of Christian art."

There is one painting in the gallery that attracts universal attention. It is "The worship of Bacchus, or the drinking customs of society from the cradle to the grave." The picture is most impressive. In the foreground is a group of bright, innocent, happy children; in the background, the first social gathering around the wine cup; the reeling drunkard; the station house; the house of correction; the hospital; the magdalen house; the work house; and the lunatic asylum!

*The Houses of Parliament*, are on the left bank of the "silver-streaming Thames." The building covers an area of 8 acres, has 100 staircases, 1100 apartments, and more than two miles of corridors. It is heated by 16 miles of steam pipes; and the gas consumed in lighting it costs annually over $17,000.

The River Front, is 900 feet in length; and the " Victoria Tower" 75 feet square, and 340 feet high. At the east end of the building, the " Clock Tower" rises to a height of 320 feet. The " Palace Clock" placed in this Tower, strikes the hours, and chimes the quarters, upon 8 bells; and shows the time upon four dials, each 30 feet in diameter. The entire cost of erecting these magnificent buildings, is estimated at $15,000,000.

But, for profit and enjoyment, let us inspect this

"New Palace" a little more closely. An excellent opportunity is afforded, as the Court sits, and Parliament is in session. Adjoining Westminster Hall, are the crowded court rooms. The judges are robed in "purple and scarlet," and crowned with curly wigs. Yonder, presiding with great dignity, sits the Lord Chief Justice of England,— Judge Cockburn. But how unmasculine does this distinguished lawyer appear, clothed in his judicial garments! That full, florid, beardless face, set in a framework of horse hair, with long curly appendages, might be taken, or mistaken, for the amiable countenance of some good-natured, well-preserved, English grandmother. Pardon us, Judge,—but this is the exact impression.

In the next room Sir John D. Coleridge presides. In a lively discussion between an inquisitive juryman, and a fractious witness, Sir John reveals rare powers of analysis, keen wit, and brilliant repartee.

To reach the House of Commons, we must pass through Westminster Hall. This hall was built in 1399, and is 270 feet long, 74 feet wide, and 90 feet high.

Here Richard II. kept his Christmas, entertaining 10,000 guests each day. It was in this magnificent hall,— fitted up as a court,— that Charles I. was tried, and Warren Hastings impeached.  Passing from Westminster Hall, we enter St. Stephen's Hall, 95 feet long, 34 feet wide, 56 feet high, and beautifully decorated. On either side are statues of eminent statesmen.  Here is the somewhat bulky figure of Fox, and the more slender forms of Pitt, Burke, and Grattan,—each in their characteristic attitudes.   And how expressive are those marble features ; how eloquent those marble gestures !

We now enter the Octagon Hall, a most elaborately ornamented room, 70 feet square, and 80 feet high.  To our left, is the *House of Commons*, 62 feet long, 45 broad, and 45 high.  Having secured a ticket of admission, we take a seat in the visitors' gallery.  The House is quite full this afternoon, and the debate in progress.  These Commoners, sitting with covered heads, look like a company of Quakers.  The only member of this great deliberative body with head uncovered, is the distinguished leader of the Conservatives,— Benjamin Disraeli.  Close beside him on the ministerial bench, sit Messrs. Hunt, and Cross. When a strong speech is made by some liberal opponent, these staff officers consult with the chief, and carry out his orders by immediately " moving on the enemy."  The subject under discussion, relates to the manufacturing interests of different parts of the kingdom.

Irishmen from the north, and the south, Scotchmen, and Englishmen, present the claims of their respective constituencies.  As England and Wales returns 500 members, Ireland 105, and Scotland 53, the Englishmen are in the majority: and when united, can legislate just as they please.

In all the turmoil, the "hear," "hear," and the clapping of hands, the Premier sits unmoved. How quiet and indifferent, and yet how watchful and wily, is this distinguished Jewish statesman!

Retracing our steps, we enter the *House of Lords*.  This chamber is 97 feet long, 45 wide, 45 high, and most richly and elaborately ornamented.  The wood-carving is exquisite.  Yonder is the Throne,—occupied by her Majesty when she visits the House.  In the centre of the chamber, is the Woolsack, on which the Lord Chancellor sits.  At the east end of the room, a committee of the House of Lords is now in session.  Lord Chancellor Cairns is pointed out by an obsequious attendant; and the noble "Lord" really looks like an ordinary mortal.

In passing from the "Lords," we are approached by a policeman, and politely informed that the "Duke" is in an adjoining room.  And without further ceremony, we are ushered into the committee-room, and into the presence of His Royal Highness the Duke of Cambridge, cousin of the Queen, and commander-in-chief of the British army. The royal warrior, is surrounded by a joint committee of the Lords and Commons and is being closely interrogated respecting the condition, and disposition of the British forces in India. His Highness receives the small salary of $17,000 a year, as commander-in-chief. The soldiers of the " line " receive as pay the large sum of $105 annually. From the very simple considerations of safety, and salary, most men would prefer being commander-in-chief.

The London Parks, ornamented with winding flower-bordered pathways, stately oaks, sparkling fountains, miniature lakes, and marble monuments,—are charming places of recreation and amusement.

The Englishman's love for the green sward, is revealed in the number and location of these " city lungs." The Surrey Gardens, covering an area of 16 acres, are in the southern section of the city. Victoria Park, situated in the north-east, contains 290 acres. This may be styled the poor man's park, as the laboring-classes reside in the immediate vicinity. Regent's Park, in the north-west, covers an area of 472 acres, and contains within its limits the beautiful " Royal Botanical Gardens," and the popular and unrivalled " Zoological Gardens." Two thousand animals are here exhibited. The arrangements for bird and beast are most admirable. By the labels on the doors and cages, we are informed that a large number of the " inhabitants " were presented to the management by ship captains, travelers, and various explorers on land and sea.

James' Park, containing 91 acres, Green Park 60 acres, Hyde Park 390 acres, and Kensington Gardens 210 acres, are all in the western part of the city, and quite close to each other. The distance from the east end of James' Park, to the west end of Kensington Gardens, is nearly three miles; and in traveling between the two points, the pedestrian traverses these four parks in succession, and may walk almost continuously over the smooth green turf.

In this pleasant three miles excursion, we pass the Pall Mall, Piccadilly, and Buckingham Palace; and are surrounded on all sides by the costly and magnificent residences of princely merchants, eminent bankers, noble lords, and royal dukes.

# CHAPTER VIII.



WINDSOR CASTLE, about twenty miles distant from London, is the principal residence of the English monarchs. It was founded by William the Conqueror, and is situated upon an eminence commanding a most extensive, and charming view of the surrounding country.

The day is bright and beautiful, and an hour's ride brings us in sight of this royal Palace. The flag floats on the Tower, indicating that the Queen is at home. By climbing 160 steps, and proceeding to the "Terrace," we have the grandest view of English rural scenery thus far enjoyed. What waving woods, lovely parks, and winding silvery streams greet the eye!

From the Castle Terrace, we see

> "Where the silver Thames first rural grows."

The sloping grounds are tastefully ornamented with shrubbery, and flower-beds curiously arranged, while the winding pathways are pleasantly

174

shaded by stately trees.  Along these smooth flower-bordered walks, over and through these emerald velvety lawns, where the atmosphere is sweet with fragrance, and vocal with song, England's Queen rambles daily.

Her Majesty is driving in the Park this afternoon, and paying a visit to the tomb of her beloved Albert.  Victoria and Albert were "lovely and pleasant in their lives," and the manner in which his memory is cherished by the widowed Queen, does honor to her sex, and sheds a brighter lustre on England's Crown.

This great Windsor Park, where the deer run wild, and royal game is in abundance, contains 3800 acres; and the Forest is 56 miles in circumference.

But here comes the Queen, accompanied by Princess Beatrice,—the only unmarried daughter. They are seated in a very plain open carriage.  A splendid pair of gray horses seem proud of their traces, while the driver is as imperious as a Prince. The Queen is robed in dark-colored garments; is quite unassuming in manner; has a serious and thoughtful expression of countenance;—and such a real, true motherly look!

Beatrice is a comely, modest maiden.  She seems quite unconscious of her position, title, and surroundings.  How could she be vain, and trifling, in the presence of such a thoughtful, wise, and godly mother?

John Brown,—Prince Albert's faithful Scotch servant,—accompanies the royal party.  How easily a " lord" might envy him his position,—the Queen's ever-present attendant!

The gate-keeper's daughter, a Scotch lassie, who has a brother in America, is quite talkative, and communicates sundry items of information respecting the royal household.  This young woman converses daily with the Queen, who seems to be strongly attached to the Scotch.  A Highland piper, we are informed, plays every afternoon under the palace window, for the amusement and pleasure of Her Majesty.

When the Queen is " in residence," visitors are not permitted to inspect the royal apartments. But to view these grand old Gothic structures, lofty towers, and palace courts ; to see England's Queen and Windsor Castle, is quite sufficient for one afternoon.

Buckingham Palace, the city residence of the Sovereign, is this evening brilliantly illuminated.

Taking tea, in the neighborhood of the Palace, and being attracted by whirling equipages, and prancing steeds, we inquire the cause of this commotion among the aristocracy.  A policeman on the " Mall " informs us that the Queen has ordered a " State reception," and requested the Prince of Wales to represent Her Majesty.  As this is one of the very few royal receptions given since the death of the Prince Consort, it awakens quite an interest among the fashionables of the West End. And as Parliament is in session, and the noblemen of Britain are all at the metropolis, the attendance is large, and the display most brilliant.  Just picture the audience, with the following individuals in "full dress," viz.: 6 Princes, and 3 Princesses; 116 members of the diplomatic corps, representing 24 different nations; 19 Dukes, and 19 Duchesses; 21 Marquises, and 23 Marchionesses; 76 Earls, and 53 Countesses; 43 Counts, and 23 Viscountesses; 103 Lords, and 800 Ladies; 40 Right Honourables, 80 Honourables, and 140 Honourable Mesdames; 75 Sirs, 160 Messieurs, and 125 Mesdames; 33 Admirals, 22 Captains, 10 Commanders, 50 Generals, and 57 Colonels !

The Scots Fusilier Guards, mounted in the Palace Court, act as a guard of honor.  The Royal Body Guard of the Yeomen, are on duty in the interior of the palace.

In company with a large number of un-titled individuals, we attend this royal reception,—outside the Palace gate.

But even at this distance, there are " streaming
8

glorics," quite sufficient to dazzle our republican eyes. Hundreds of carriages come whirling to the palace gate:—from the two-wheeled Hansom cab, drawn by a spirited pony, to the royal chariot thundering at the heels of six richly caparisoned horses. These numerous vehicles, with their lamps all trimmed and burning, sweeping through the upper gate, winding around the stately palace, and rolling homeward through the southern entrance, form lines and circles of wavy light, that are beautiful to behold. The appearance is that of a hurried torchlight procession, marching in single file.

But there is quite an excitement. Policemen are running to and fro. There is lively cheering along the streets. The "clatter of street pacing steeds" are heard in the distance ; and a stentorian loyal Britisher thrills the expectant crowd by shouting "here comes the Prince!" Along the wide "Mall" from Marlborough House, the royal chariot, drawn by six richly caparisoned galloping horses, comes thundering towards the gate. There are two mounted "coachmen," and four gorgeously appareled "footmen." A detachment of the royal Horse Guards, in full military uniform, and brandishing glittering swords, surround His Royal Highness. The spectacle is brilliant. Loud cheers ring out from the enthusiastic spectators. And

when this royal procession is lost to view behind
the stately palace, we wander homeward, wishing
that we were the Prince of Wales,—or, indeed,
any other member of the Royal Family.

But we imagine that some of our lady readers,
are exceedingly anxious to know how these Princesses were adorned.  " What did the Princess of
Wales wear ? "  " What kind of head-dress
crowned the Princess Christian ? "  " Please do
tell us."  Having the slightest possible knowledge
of the millinery business, and yet wishing to gratify
the desires of our inquisitive readers, we consult
the critic of the London *Times*.  This gentleman
is regarded as " authority," among the " higher "
circles of Metropolitan society.  He solemnly
assures us that " Her Royal Highness, the Princess
of Wales, wore a dress of brown poult-de-soie with
plaitings of brown tulle and Honiton lace, ornamented with garlands of the rose-de-thé and veiled
with silver spotted tulle.  Head-dress and ornaments of pearls and diamonds.  Orders, Victoria
and Albert, and the Danish Family Order."  The
same reliable authority informs us that " Her
Royal Highness, the Princess Christian, wore a
dress of white moire antique and satin trimmed
with Brussels lace, white orchids, and tulle.  Head-
dress, tiara of torquoises and diamonds with
bunches of orchids.  Ornaments, torquoise, and

diamonds. Orders, Victoria and Albert, and the Prussian, Portuguese, and Russian Orders." Any further explanation seems quite unnecessary.

*The Crystal Palace*, crowning the heights of Sydenham, is one of the most attractive, and instructive places of popular resort in all Europe. To reach it, in the distant suburbs, we take the " Rail Road of the Rats." This is the name given by the " Cockneys" to the underground passage. A ticket is purchased for the Thames Tunnel, in order that we may travel, neither above, nor on, but *under* the river. Descending several flights of stairs, we stand in an underground station, awaiting the arrival of the train. This Tunnel consists of two arched passages 1200 feet long, 14 feet wide, $16\frac{1}{2}$ feet high, separated by a brick wall 4 feet thick. The crown of the arch is 16 feet below the bed of the river.

The total cost was over $2,225,000. Strange how a little insect, suggested to Brunel the plan by which this marvel of engineering could be accomplished. In studying the form of this little creature, and the manner in which it cuts its way through the hardest wood, the great engineer was enabled to pierce beneath the bed of the Thames. How wise is the great Architect; and how His wisdom shines even in the structure of the tiniest insect. Well might the Psalmist exclaim, " O

Lord how manifold are thy works! in wisdom hast thou made them all!"

The passage through the Tunnel is made without any real discomfort, only we emerge upon the other side with a better appreciation of sunlight, and the beauties of the "upper world."

The Palace grounds are reached and explored. These grounds, including the Garden, and Park, contain over 200 acres.  The undulating and sloping surface, is intersected by winding pathways, and ornamented with terraces, temples, fountains, cascades, close-cut lawns, shrubbery, and flowers, most artistically and beautifully arranged.  The shining "Crystal" edifice crowns the eminence, and commands the most extensive view within 20 miles of London.  The building cost $7,250,000. The whole scene is a perfect surprise.

But let us walk up the hillside noting a few of the most interesting objects.  Here in the valley, is the largest educational model we have ever seen on exhibition.  It covers several acres; and combines land and water.  It is a most successful effort to illustrate the structure of the earth, by presenting the various strata, in the same relative position disclosed by geology.

Here is a little mountain artificially constructed. It contains several thousand tons of various kind of rocks.  These rocks are arranged according to the teachings of geology. Beneath is the old red sandstone, concerning which Hugh Miller wrote so eloquently. Then follows mountain limestone, millstone grit, bands of ironstone, beds of coal, and the new red sandstone.

But standing along these artificial mounds, are the forms of animals inhabiting the lakes and the forests, in those far-distant and uncertain ages. Here is the Magalosaurus, and Mososaurus, and Plesiosaurus, and Hylæosaurus. What strange and frightful-looking creatures!

As we ascend the sloping hillside, the fountains begin to "play." The basin of this fountain is 784 feet long, with a diameter of 468 feet. The central jet leaps 250 feet into the air! When all the fountains are sporting themselves, 11,788 jets sparkle in the sunlight! And 120,000 gallons of water are forced through the pipes in a minute. In a single complete display, 2,000,000 gallons of water are sent bounding towards the sky in fifteen minutes!

Passing the cascades and climbing the stairway, we enter the building. The interior is most beautifully arranged. Along the nave on either side, are a number of "courts," designed to illustrate the style of architecture peculiar to the different nations, or prevalent in certain centuries. This is a most interesting department. Here are the

Egyptian, Grecian, Roman, Byzantine, Italian, and French Courts, each ornamented with such decorations as were most admired, by the artists of these several countries.

The entertainments this afternoon are varied. In one of the concert-rooms, the "Mountaineers of the Apennines" are amusing an immense audience, by playing upon their novel instruments. At $3\frac{1}{2}$ o'clock the "orchestral band," makes the air musical; at $5\frac{1}{2}$ the "Mexican athlete" performs on the "High Bars," while Mr. Coward, the great organist, delights the music-loving visitors, with selections from the compositions of Rossini, Handel, and Mozart.

The annual expense of the "Palace" amounts to $300,000. The price of admission is 25 cents each day except Saturday, when the charge is 60 cents. None of the London Art Galleries or Exhibition Palaces are open on the Sabbath.

By climbing, spirally, 400 steps, we stand upon the Palace Tower. The elevation is 200 feet higher than the cross on St. Paul's and 550 feet above the surface of the Thames. Yonder is London lying along the banks of the river, a veritable "smoky hollow." The panorama of woods, and meadows, shining cottages and blooming gardens, is quite picturesque.

*St. Paul's Cathedral*, is considered by the crities "the noblest building in Great Britain in the Classic style." It is built in the form of a Latin cross; is 550 feet east and west; 250 feet north and south; and the distance from the pavement to the cross is 370 feet. The cross is 30 feet in height and weighs 3360 lbs. The great bell weighs 11.000 lbs. The building was 35 years in course of erection: was completed in 1710; and cost $3.750.000.

This enormous sum was raised by a "small" tax on coal. The circumference of the building is 2292 feet. It is located in the very midst of the business section of the city, being surrounded by two streets, called the "Bow" and "the String." Land in the vicinity of St. Paul's is valued at $5.000.000 an acre!

The Cathedral contains several beautiful monuments; and many illustrious men,—poets, philosophers, soldiers, and sailors, have found in St. Paul's their last resting-place. Here are the tombs of the Duke of Wellington, Lord Nelson, Sir Joshua Reynolds, and Benjamin West.

On Sabbath evening, an immense audience is seated under the dome, and in the nave, and transepts. The Lord Bishop of Manchester is the preacher. The celebration of the anniversary of the "Society for the Prevention of Cruelty to Animals" is the occasion. The audience is es-

timated at 10,000.  The hymns are printed upon
"slips," that all may unite in the service of song.
Some of these hymns are very familiar :—

> " Jesus lover of my soul
>     Let me to thy bosom fly,"

and

> " Hark! hark, my soul; Angelic songs are swelling
>     O'er earth's green fields, and ocean's wave-beat shore:
> How sweet the truth those blessed strains are telling
>     Of that new life when sin shall be no more."

The distinguished preacher is enabled, with the
assistance of a sounding board, to scatter his well-
rounded periods among the audience, making himself quite intelligible to the thousands of listeners.
The music and the singing is grand! That magnificent organ handled by a celebrated " performer ;"
the trained cathedral choir ; and the 10,000 worshipers,—all in unison—is most impressive, and
inspiring.  Never did we enjoy such a service of
song.  And we can never forget this beautiful
Sabbath evening, spent in St. Paul's.

*Westminster Abbey*, is the most venerable-looking, and the most interesting Church edifice we
have ever visited.  It is 416 feet long, and 203
broad ; the height of the roof from the pavement
is 101 feet ; and the height of the Towers 225
feet.  It is built in the form of a Latin Cross ; in

the pointed style of architecture ; and the erection of some parts of the edifice, is ascribed to Edward the Confessor, who ruled 800 years ago.

The beautiful stained glass windows, are ornamented with representations of Old and New Testament worthies :—Moses, Aaron, the Patriarchs, Christ, and the Apostles. The aisles, transepts and chapels, contain numerous and costly monuments, erected to the memory of the illustrious dead. The Choir is wainscoted, and elegantly fitted up with stalls and seats.

This is Monday afternoon, and the entire building is open to visitors free of charge. Beginning at the " *Poet's Corner*," in the south transept, we will slowly ramble through this venerable Abbey Minster. In this " corner " we find monuments erected to Shakspeare, Chaucer, Spenser, Dryden, Addison, Goldsmith, Campbell, Gray, and to several other distinguished literary men. Here also Thackeray, Dickens, Grote, and David Livingstone are buried.

In the south transept we find a gravestone marking the resting place of " Old Parr," who lived in the reigns of three princes, and who died in 1635, aged 152 years !

In the north transept, there is a noble monument to Lord Chatham. It was erected by the King and Parliament, and cost $30,000.

> " Bacon there
> Gives more than female beauty to a stone,
> And Chatham's eloquence to marble lips."

Here also is a standing statue of Sir Robert Peel ; and these are the smooth stones covering the graves of Pitt and Fox.

> "The mighty chiefs sleep side by side ;
> Drop upon Fox's grave the tear,
> 'Twill trickle to his rival's bier."

In the nave, are monuments to Sir William Temple, Sir Isaac Newton, Sir James Mackintosh, William Pitt, C. J. Fox, and Major Andre ! Andre was executed by the Americans as a spy in 1780; and the monument to his memory was erected at the expense of George III.

*Henry VII.'S Chapel* contains the tombs and effigies of Henry VII. and Queen: the work was executed by an Italian artist, and was regarded by Lord Bacon, as "one of the stateliest and daintiest tombs in Europe."  In the south aisle of the chapel is a tomb, with a recumbent effigy of Mary Queen of Scots.  This was erected by her son, James I. The marble face is beautiful ; and around it gather crowds of visitors,—men and women,—who frequently exclaim,—what a lovely face !  The north aisle contains the tomb and effigy of Queen Elizabeth.  Her sister, Queen Mary, is buried in the same grave. In this chapel the " Westminster Assembly " held a number of meetings.

*The " Chapel of Edward the Confessor "* is perhaps the most interesting of these royal cemeteries. The shrine of this somewhat superstitious monarch, is erected in the centre of the chapel, and surrounded by the graves and monuments of Kings and Queens. Here is a bronze effigy of Henry III.; and the altar tombs of Edward I., Edward III., and Henry V. Twenty Kings and Queens of England are buried in these chapels.

*The " Coronation chairs "* are kept in the " Confessor's " Chapel. In this modest old chair, the Kings and Queens of England have been crowned during the past 600 years! A very strange-looking stone is attached to the bottom of the chair, by cramps of iron. How came this piece of reddish gray sandstone, 26 inches long, 16 inches wide, and 11 inches thick into such a position? Why has this been strapped to England's coronation chair? The explanation is very simple.

On this stone the Kings of Scotland, in the " guid auld " days were crowned. Edward I. captured it, and carried it to England as evidence of England's supremacy. And thus England and Scotland became united, in the " Chapel of Edward the Confessor,"—by bands of iron.

But the sun is sinking in the west; and the

aisles and monuments are faintly illumined by "the dim religious light" streaming through the stained glass windows.  Standing in the choir, where for centuries the monarchs have been crowned, and looking upon those statues designed to perpetuate their memory, we reflect upon the scenes this venerable building has witnessed, and the generations that have worshiped within its walls.  How many brilliant coronation processions have marched, during the past 600 years, through yonder gateway!  How many sad and sorrowing assemblages have crowded this stately temple, when the Abbey bell summoned a weeping nation, to behold the open grave of a sovereign beloved!  To how many stormy debates, and to what thrilling eloquence, has the old Chapter-house listened, during the 300 years it was the "home" of the Commons of England!  And to what learned discussions, and profound theological disquisitions did these walls listen, during the 1163 sessions of the memorable Assembly, that presented to the world our grand old "Confession of Faith!"

How many of England's greatest warriors, statesmen, poets, were borne along these aisles to solemn burial.  By how many strange voices has the mass been chanted, and the service-book read beneath this vaulted roof.  And what numbers of

God's elect,—saintly men and women,—have here
knelt in prayer, or united in the glad responses!

And what changes political and ecclesiastical;
what struggles for supremacy on the part of diverse
races and hostile clans: what battle fields red with
the blood of Saxon, Norman, and English; what
establishing and overthrowing of dynasties; and
what improvement in the moral and physical condition of the people of England, have the watch-
men on the walls of this Zion beheld, from the
days of Henry III. to those of Victoria I!

But now the twilight fadeth into darkness, and
we must depart. A solemn silence reigns over all.
In passing along the nave, these erect statues, in
striking attitudes and flowing marble robes, seem
to beckon us with their uplifted hands. We experience strange emotions in presence of such a
scene; and stepping over the threshold, cease com-
muning with the dead, and again look upon and
mingle with the living.

The Sabbath afternoon services at Westminster
Abbey, are well attended. The choir and transepts are crowded. Tourists from all quarters,
come to hear the eloquent Dean Stanley. And
during the "season," the audience is exceedingly
aristocratic. What "noble" men, and "honor-
able" women this afternoon occupy these cathedral stalls! Here, during the sessions of Parlia-

ment, the "lords" of earth worship the Lord of Heaven.

The scene indeed is strange and striking. All around are the tombs of the departed. Close beside us are the statues of the immortal dead. From the stained glass windows, Moses, Aaron, and the Patriarchs, look benignantly down upon the worshipping assembly. A charming life-size portrait of the Queen, smiles upon us from the chancel. Clergymen robed " in spotless white," read from the desk, while the distant aisles, and lofty arches, resound with the responses of organ and choir· The Dean is not present to-day ; but a " Canon" discourses on Christian benevolence. The sermon is simple, earnest, evangelical. Whether he be a broad-churchman or not, there is certainly a broad charity inculcated. Would that all the sacred citadels of England were defended by just such "Canon"!

*Mr. Spurgeon's Tabernacle*, is on the south side of the Thames. Externally it has very little to excite admiration. Strangers would never regard it as a church edifice. It is 145 feet long, 81 broad, 62 high, and cost $150,000. We arrive in time to inspect the Sabbath-school, and attend the morning prayer-meeting. The superintendent is a pleasant, genial Englishman. The majority of the teachers are young, and seem thoroughly in earnest. In the infant department we find just fifty small men and little women. The teacher seems well-adapted for the work of "juvenile" instruction; and by suitable questions enables the "little ones" to give the stranger some information respecting the Sabbath school lesson.

The walls of the school-rooms are decorated with beautiful and appropriate Scripture mottoes. The entire service is conducted in a quiet, yet earnest manner. There is no attempt at "display." There are no "striking" portraits grinning on the black-board; no representations of human hearts in red, white, and blue chalk. And the hymn-books are not "just issued!" They are well-thumbed; contain many of those Christian songs sung for generations; and are remarkably free from jingling nonsense. The tunes are also appropriate. The children in singing, are worshiping and not waltzing. In all parts of the service, there is a simplicity, a sincerity, an earnestness, that is both beautiful and impressive. A morning prayer-meeting is held, just before the preaching service. It is conducted by a very plain-looking individual, who enjoins the brethren to be "prompt and brief." The number present, —of both sexes,— is quite large, the singing spirited, and the prayers tender and beseeching. What prayers are offered for a blessing upon the Pastor,—just about to enter the pulpit! We have never listened to such pleadings for a blessing upon the labors of any preacher. And may not this be the secret of Spurgeon's marvelous success?

The church is well-filled when the service begins. And yet many come late. Some people are always lagging behind, but are especially slow in attending the church. But the preacher is prompt, and the service is conducted in the following order:—Invocation; hymn beginning, "God in His Church is known;" Scripture reading, and exposition; hymn "I'm not ashamed to own my Lord;" prayer occupying about 12 minutes; church notices; sermon; hymn:—

> "Leave thee—never!
> Where for safety could I go?"

benediction.

The Tabernacle is elliptical in form, and two deep galleries run round the interior of the building. The preacher stands upon a raised platform, nearly on a plane with the lower gallery. He thus commands the audience, and the audience commands him. The congregation bow in prayer, and stand in singing. Upon the reading of a hymn, the tune to which it is sung, is announced. If the singing is slow or spiritless, the preacher urges the people to "sing more quickly and joyously brethren!" And the response, from the

5,000, or 6,000, is hearty and inspiring. The great majority of the people are shop-keepers, mechanics, laboring men; and the galleries are crowded with the young of both sexes. In the pews, immediately in front of the preacher, there are a number of plump, sleek, well-dressed men and women, who might be numbered among the wealthy. And when the service is concluded a few of the worshipers are carried homeward in stylish conveyances.

Mr. Spurgeon is a short thick-set man. There is nothing in his appearance to indicate his power. He looks as unlike the stereotyped ecclesiastic, as the exterior of the Tabernacle looks unlike a modern church edifice. He has the manner of a business man; is quick in his movements; mirthful and mirth-provoking: and really appears like a big, well-fed, overgrown boy. But what a voice; what fluency of speech and lofty eloquence; what familiarity with Scripture and profound knowledge of human nature; what convincing argument and thrilling appeal; what consuming earnestness, and complete self-forgetfulness! No pulpit or table intervenes between him and his audience. He stands behind the low railing that surrounds the platform, and addresses the immense assemblage with the most perfect abandon. The morning theme was " The Christian Afflicted ;" the evening sermon discussed "Retribution." In the morning, the audience laughed and wept; in the evening, there were many that trembled.

The Tabernacle, it is said, holds 6,000, and is always full. Good seats are in great demand. The pew-holders have always the preference until the service begins. A somewhat worldly-wise policy is adopted by the "Deacons" on the Sabbath evenings. They stand at the outer gates and distribute small envelopes to those who are eager to gain admittance. These envelopes are a polite invitation to subscribe a "little," for the support of the benevolent work of the church. Those who thus subscribe are admitted to the interior of the building, and have the choice of the unoccupied seats when the service commences. And yet some will not subscribe! Not even a choice seat in the great Metropolitan Tabernacle, with the eloquent Spurgeon on the platform, will induce some of these mean, miserly church-goers to contribute a single sixpence.

They will take all, and give nothing. Others must pay for lighting, heating, cleaning, and repairing the building; others must pay the pastor's salary, and contribute to objects of benevolence, but *they* will pay *nothing*. Common sense, conscience, would suggest that if they share in the enjoyments, they should share in the expenses. Why should they be so lacking in self-respect; why should they be so stingy and miserly, as to allow others to pay their church expenses? And yet here they linger around the gate, waiting until they can march in, and take a "free seat." Shame on such delinquents, when they are *able to pay!*

Doctor Parker, represented "The Modern Pulpit" at the meeting of the Evangelical Alliance in New York City. His new "Temple Church" has just been completed, and the Doctor's reputation attracts a large and brilliant audience. A front pew has been sacredly set apart in this new church for the use of Americans. A gentlemanly usher conducts us to the "front," where we find pleasantly seated a few Yankee pilgrims, who have come in this morning "from going to, and fro in the earth."

The congregation at the "Temple" differs much from that assembling at the "Tabernacle." It is not as large, but is much more "select." The preachers are also quite unlike. Dr. Parker is undoubtedly a most eloquent preacher. He has one of the finest pulpit voices to which we have ever listened. His sermons are thoroughly elaborated. He is enthusiastic; and occasionally there are sudden outbursts of passionate eloquence, that thrill the entire audience. But he is shielded by a desk; reads pretty closely; appears self-conscious ; is somewhat affected in manner : and in his arguments and illustrations, is quaint and conceited. He is ecclesiastically, a "congregationalist ;" but we would infer that in theology, and in everything else, he is pretty "independent." To this brilliant metropolitan, we might address the words of Shakespeare :—

> "You were glad to be employed
> To show how *quaint* an orator you are."

The population of London is exceedingly "mixed."  Along these crowded thoroughfares walk representatives of every nation on the globe, and of every isle of the sea.  And here meet the paupers and the princes.  Wealth and poverty stand face to face.  In the eastern districts, the houses are crowded, the streets are filthy, and the condition of the people, pitiable.  But the poor are not forgotten.  $20,000,000 are expended annually, in aiding the distrest. Some of the wealthy Londoners, following in the footsteps of Peabody, are erecting "improved dwellings."  Others are employing the missionary, the tract distributor, and providing places of worship.  And yet in this city of millions, " the harvest truly is great, but the laborers are few."

Around Hyde Park, and along " Rotten Row," the scene at 3 or 4 o'clock in the afternoon is exceedingly brilliant.  The magnificent and costly equipages ; the prancing steeds gaily caparisoned ; the princes, dukes, and lords, arrayed in richest garb ; the liveried coachmen, with silver-clasped shoes, silken stockings, velvet breeches, scarlet vests, gorgeously glittering coats, and silken hats ornamented with flashing cockades : what a spectacle to look upon, on a lovely afternoon in the month of June !

Rotten Row, is set apart for the equestrians. Here, the finest saddle-horses in the world, mounted by the most graceful riders of both sexes, canter and gallop, watched by hundreds and thousands of admiring spectators. The coaches move along 5 and 6 abreast ; and the saddle-horses come pacing down the " Row " 8 and 10 in a line, whipped and spurred by the " beautiful contestants."

The signs over the doors of the "shops" are somewhat amusing, and instructive. The proprietors, with an eye to business, inform the vulgar public of their royal or noble patrons. This man is "confectioner to the Queen," or " stationer to the Prince of Wales," or " draper to His Royal Highness the Duke of Cambridge ; " and this woman is " patronized by the Royal Family." They appreciate good customers.

The English people treat us very kindly ; and although occasionally boastful, are nevertheless very agreeable companions. In dress, they differ

in some respects from Americans.  They prefer
comfort, to fashion.  Their garments are somewhat
loose, and lacking in "style."  Boots and shoes
are large and strong.  Paper soles, and high heels,
are not the most popular.  The ladies never waste
time in pushing a large foot into a Chinese boot.
They walk on their feet, and not on their toes,
even at the risk of being large-footed.

The English,—like the Irish and Scotch,—have
their national beverage.  They drink porter and
ale.  And the amount of these liquids swallowed
daily by an average-sized drayman, is surprising.
At an outdoor festival, where the laboring classes
meet to spend a "holiday," the drinking scenes
are novel and amusing.  A dozen men sit around
a table; a stone jug holding nearly a gallon is
placed before them filled with the frothy fluid; and
this is seized with both hands by each of the party
in succession, until its contents is poured down
the thirsty throats of these boozy Britons.  Tumb-
lers and goblets they despise.  And the spectacle
of a bulky little Englishman with puffy cheeks
and scarlet nose, hoisting this foaming gallon measure to his giddy head, would be ludicrous if it
were not sad.  Porter and ale are not so intensely
stimulating as Irish and Scotch whisky; but these
English topers are as round as the barrels they
have emptied, and smell very much like them.

Before bidding good-bye to London, and leaving for the Continent, we may state that the charges,—in hotels and boarding-houses, or on railroads, are by no means excessive. The railroad coaches are similar, in pattern and style, to those already described. There are three classes of cars,—first, second, and third. By act of Parliament the charges are as follows:—1st class cars per mile 6 cents; 2nd class, 4½ cents; 3rd class 3 cents. Only the very wealthy travel in the 1st class. There are also what are termed the " Parliamentary trains." By act of Parliament, railroad companies are obliged to run two daily trains over their respective roads, at a charge of 2 cents a mile. We have traveled over the country on these trains at a high rate of speed, rejoicing in the reduced fare, and thanking Providence that there were some legislatures that could not be bought, by conscienceless corporations.

"High life" in London, has been enjoyed at a moderate expense. We have a nicely furnished room, the privilege of a beautiful parlor, the London daily papers, and the society of a most refined company of guests. We rejoice every day over the choicest cutlets, the juiciest steaks, and the most delicious soups. After rushing through tunnels, climbing towers, exploring docks, traversing parks, inspecting museums, wandering through libraries, listening to wrangling lawyers and debating "Commoners," and walking a dozen miles through winding streets,—how the "ebbing" life of the tourist is changed into a "full-tide" of physical vitality, by a dish of nutritious English mutton broth! This we have tested and found to be an unfailing stimulant.

But what are the charges per week for these rare privileges? Why just ten dollars a week! But this is the result of close study and careful planning.

The Sabbath day in London is remarkably quiet. God, by the Sabbath day, lays His hand upon the throbbing heart of the great metropolis, —and behold how still! The libraries, art galleries, museums, and places of business, are all closed.

How grand is London,—with her docks crowded with shipping; her merchant princes controlling the world's commerce; her bankers shaping the financial policy of kings; her Parliament debating questions affecting the interests of hundreds of millions on distant continents! But how beautiful is London, when in obedience to the voice of God, business ceases, quiet reigns, the church bells invite to worship, and from temples dedicated to the Most High, prayer and praise ascend to Heaven! Love for law human and divine,—this is England's glory. May Britannia never cease to rule the waves!

9

# CHAPTER IX.



LEAVING London in the afternoon, we go direct to Antwerp. The train carries us to Harwich; and from Harwich the steamer conveys us over the German Ocean, and up the Scheldt, to this Belgic city. Dutch galleys, with red and white sails, and yellow painted rudders, are floating on the river, while from the distant banks, the revolving vanes of towering windmills seem to beckon us ashore. A number of ships are resting in the harbor, and great activity prevails along the wharves. But here comes that cruel "custom-house officer." Our innocent valise is turned inside out, and every article carefully examined. We protest in vigorous English, but without the slightest effect. This faithful official replies to all our protests and inquiries, in a language that, in our ears, sounds like a mixture of French and Dutch. In all our linguistic studies; in all our rambles through the German and French " quarters" in London, we never heard or read anything that could compare with this gentleman's language. If all the Belgians talk in this manner, our progress through this most populous little kingdom must indeed be slow.

In Antwerp, the houses are built of stone and brick, and the streets are paved with Belgic blocks. In the wide avenues are pretty booths, where jewelry and various " notions," are sold at very tempting prices. The people dress somewhat picturesquely. Clog shoes rattle along the pavement. Old men wear woolen hose of three different colors,—blue, red, and striped. The women pace the streets proud of their purple petticoats. A new mode of conveyance greets the eye,—the dog wagon. Yonder is a sturdy dog pulling a lazy woman! The sight is ludicrous. The husband leads the dog, and the wife sits in the wagon !

The cathedral steeple is 416 feet high, and by climbing 616 steps we reach the summit. The view is magnificent. The city, the river, the dykes, and the country for scores of miles, are clearly seen. This Cathedral has a chime of 40 bells. And while in the steeple we have the pleasure of listening to the " chiming of the bells." They chime every quarter of an hour. The smallest bell weighs 40 lb. ; the largest 12,000 lb. It requires 16 men to ring the latter. In this city Rubens was born, and in the Cathedral may be seen one of his masterpieces;—"The Descent from the Cross." It is a wonderful painting. The grouping, posturing and coloring, give such an appearance of reality, that we, almost, expect to see the figures move. How the figure of "the dead Christ," contrasts with the forms of those who stand around the cross! In some of these churches, the altar and pulpit decorations, are costly and beautiful. The polished black, white and red marbles, shine like mirrors. And the organs are embellished with representations of cherubs and angels, holding violins, trumpets, and harps. These carvings in walnut, are of exquisite workmanship.

From *Antwerp* to *Brussels*, is a pleasant ride through a charming country. There are no hedges, or fences. Long rows of elms and poplars, mark the boundaries of fields, or farms. Men and women are toiling in the meadows. Some swing the scythe; others rake the hay, and pile it on the waiting wagons. The crops look beautiful.

*Brussels* is the pride of the Belgians. It has magnificent promenades; charming parks, ornamented with statues and fountains; and some large and imposing edifices. This being Saturday evening the streets are crowded, and the shops brilliantly illuminated.  The Belgians appear to be fond of beer,—and the drinking is done in public.  The open paved squares are transformed into bar rooms and beer gardens.  Long lines of small marble-topped tables are surrounded by men and women, who sit chatting and drinking with the most absolute freedom.  Here are hundreds of husbands and wives, emptying their wine and beer glasses with wonderful rapidity.  Clouds of segar smoke hang heavily over these increasingly talkative, and occasionally belligerent tipplers.  And here sit women apart by themselves, holding a high debate over the sparkling wine glass, or foaming beer mug!  And all this along a public highway!  We have seen women enter public houses in England, Ireland, and Scotland; but never have we seen the most degraded touch the beverage in an open square, in full view of the public.  And these Belgic women are well dressed, haughty in manner, and really seem proud of their evening occupation.

The Sabbath day in Brussels is not a holyday.  It is simply a holiday.  The shops, stores, and taverns are open.  The market places are thronged.  Bands of music, followed by crowds of men and women, parade through the streets.  And the dog market is well attended!  In attempting to reach the English Church, we are shocked by these scenes of Sabbath desecration. The dog market is to us, quite a new institution. And yet in winding through a crooked street, we are suddenly confronted by this Continental method of keeping holy the Sabbath day. Here scores of dogs, of all sizes, colors, and breeds, are being sold and bought. They are held by cords tied round the neck,—and the larger number are exhibited by women! How they leap, yelp, bark and bite! And here are pups in baskets, carried by children who rock to sleep the troublesome curs, by swinging the baskets! This is the kind of Sunday-school these little boys and girls are trained to attend. Is not the spectacle a sad one?

In returning from the Episcopal Church, the route leads us past several of the Roman Catholic places of worship. The attendance is not large. In some of the churches the priests are giving instruction to the children. Here and there in different parts of the building, groups of boys and girls surround the monk or priest, and are being carefully catechised. But how cold and formal do these instructions appear! And the children act and answer as if they were under an unpleasant restraint. They may occasionally move an elbow, or indulge in a smile; but by a sudden shake of that closely shaven head, or a frown of that beardless face, order is quickly restored.

The Palace of King Leopold is carefully guarded by Belgic soldiers. They are sturdy men ; and as they pace the Palace Court dressed in scarlet breeches, and dark-green coats with yellow facings, attract considerable attention.

The "Brussels carpet," and "lace," are not manufactured within the city limits. These celebrated fabrics, are spun and woven in the neighboring towns. A young merchant informs us that the laces are manufactured principally in the nunneries, or in schools controlled and managed by the nuns. The young women receive as compensation, tuition and board.

In the month of June, 1815,

"There was a sound of revelry by night ;
  And Belgium's capital had gathered then
Her beauty, and her chivalry ; and bright
  The lamps shone o'er fair women and brave men ;
And all went merry as a marriage-bell.—
  But hush ! hark ! a deep sound strikes like a rising knell !
And nearer, clearer, deadlier than before !
  Arm ! arm ! it is—it is the cannon's opening roar !

And there was mounting in hot haste ; the steed,
  The mustering squadron, and the clattering car,
Went pouring forward with impetuous speed,
  And swiftly forming in the ranks of war ;
And the deep thunder peal on peal afar :
  And near the beat of the alarming drum
Roused up the soldier ere the morning star ;
  While thronged the citizens with terror dumb."

Waterloo, is not far distant from " Belgium's capital," and an early morning train conveys us to this scene of mortal strife. The "Hotel du Musee," stands on the battle-field ; and while enjoying an excellent breakfast we chat pleasantly with the proprietor, who imparts considerable information respecting Wellington and Napoleon. In the Museum—posted on the wall,—is Napoleon's address to his "soldiers!" Here also the silver spurs, and the cross of the "Legion of Honor," worn by the Emperor on the battle-field, are exhibited.

A mound or monument, erected by the Belgians and the Dutch, affords a fine view of this scene of strife. This monument is 500 yards round the base, and 200 feet high. It is composed of earthy matter, mingled with the remains of the soldiers who fell on either side, during that memorable engagement. In its erection 200 men were employed for a space of three years ; and the cost was nearly $1,000,000.

226 steps lead to the summit, which is crowned by a " Belgic lion." We are quite fortunate in our guide. He is nearly 80 years of age ; was born on the soil ; and was present at the battle. And from this elevated position, standing upon the accumulated remains of slaughtered heroes, we view these valleys and plains over and through

which, 60 years ago, sabres flashed, and cannon thundered.

Our guide points out the position occupied by Napoleon, and the "Iron Duke;" the order of battle array; the extent of the opposing "lines;" the valley lying between the embattled hosts; and the distant village through which Blucher marched in attacking the French.  And here, close by the monument, the "Imperial Guard" was shattered and victory won, by the uprising "Grenadiers."

But to-day, no flag floats; no bugle sounds; and no sword glitters over the peaceful plain. The grass waves, the crops grow, and the flowers bloom, as if "Waterloo" had never been fought!

# CHAPTER X.



Aix la Chapelle is the first German city
visited. The route from Brussels leads through
Louvain, Liege, Verviers, and the distance is about
100 miles. Aix is situated in a valley, surrounded
by gently sloping hills, has a population of 73,000,
and is famous as the birth-place, and the burial-
place of the Emperor Charlemagne. He died in
this city in 814. And here also 37 of the kings
of Germany were crowned, from 814 to 1531.

Wooden representations of the crucifixion are
erected at the street corners; and in the evenings
these crooked streets are crowded with jostling
Germans. Along the winding thoroughfares, rival
merchants present their wares, with violent gestures
and deafening shouts. Yonder, an auctioneer
thunders in the ears of a gaping crowd of lion-
headed men. On the opposite side stands a tall
muscular feminine praising her tin merchandize,
and dazzling the eyes of her customers, by turning

210

the blazing jets on the shining tin. And here are groups of men and boys surrounding the "wheel of fortune," and risking a kreutzer on a chance for a big brown cake. After dark the whole town seems to be in motion. We are surprised and delighted. The spectacle is amusing, and we enjoy it exceedingly.

In the early morning the market place is visited. Here are milk-wagons holding 5 or 6 prettily-painted cans, drawn by dogs. And yonder trembling in the traces, is a fine mastiff,—with shapely limbs, noble bearing, and head like a German professor,—while behind him stands a wagon containing about a hundred heads of cabbage; all, —we presume—to be converted into the most delicious saur-krout. The cows are also harnessed, and come toiling up the hill wheeling heavy burdens. Upon a pedestal in the market-place, looking calmly down upon the bustling crowd, is a bronze statue of Charlemagne. A sceptre is held in the right hand, while the left holds a globe and a cross.

Aix la Chapelle, since the days of the Romans, has been famous for its "Springs." In a lovely garden intersected by winding flower-bordered paths, shaded by stately trees, we find aristocratic Teutons taking their morning "bitters." They walk and drink, and drink and walk to the charm-

ing music discoursed by a well-trained band.
These mineral waters are warm, and are sipped as
they come steaming from the bubbling fountain.

The Münster, or " Dome," is an interesting
edifice. We enter during the morning service.
Some 300 or 400 children are in attendance. The
priests are chanting in the choir, and the children
are uniting in the responses. Taking a seat in
one of the " stalls " and opening a " Psalm-book,"
we read, " Ad te, Domine, levavi animam meam :"
—Unto thee, O Lord, do I lift up my soul. The
words are from the 25th Psalm as translated in the
Latin Vulgate. And how musically do these
Psalms in Latin sound, when chanted by these
German ecclesiastics!

This Münster is said to be the oldest church in
Germany. It was built, in part, by Charlemagne,
more than 1,000 years ago, and the great monarch
was buried under the dome. A large stone with
the inscription "Carolo Magno," marks the place
where he was buried, over which and suspended
from the dome, swings a bronze chandelier, the
gift of the Emperor Frederick Barbarossa. Frederick was called the " Xerxes of the Middle
Ages." He reigned as King and Emperor of
Germany from 1152 till 1190. And this chandelier has illumined the old church for 700
years!

But the sacred "*Relics*" in this church constitute its chief attraction. Here are exhibited a lock of the virgin's hair; a piece of the true cross; Christ's leathern girdle; the cord that bound the rod that smote Christ; a nail of the cross; the sponge that was filled with vinegar; some of the blood and bones of St Stephen; some manna from the wilderness; a few bits of Aaron's rod. These are presented as all genuine. And upon these sacred relics the Emperors of Germany swore at their coronation!

The "*Grand Relics*," are exhibited to vulgar eyes only once in seven years. They consist of the robe worn by the virgin at the nativity,—of cotton and five feet long; the swaddling clothes in which Jesus was wrapped,—coarse yellow cloth; the cloth in which the head of John the Baptist was laid; the scarf worn by our Saviour at the crucifixion,—marked with blood.

These sacred relics were presented by the Patriarch of Jerusalem to Charlemagne, over 1000 years ago. And from the 10th to the 24th of July, 1874, more than 500,000 pilgrims and relic-worshippers, thronged this ancient edifice and paid their respects to these "Grand Relics."

We express no opinion regarding the objects thus exhibited. They are certainly very valuable,—to the priests. Their salaries will be promptly paid while these "relics" remain on exhibition. The admission fee is quite respectable. And what immense sums are collected every seventh year from these multitudes of pilgrims!

In Aix la Chapelle German is universally spoken. In wandering through the winding streets,— with our eyes dazzled by the brilliant reflection of the sparkling jets,—we go astray. The crooked streets tempted us, and we followed on. But our position is critical,—alone, in a foreign land, in a crooked city, in the dead of night, and everybody talking Dutch! We pay our politest respects to a policeman, informing him of our "lost" condition, and hinting that his services as guide to the "Hotel du Dragon," would be keenly appreciated. This communication is made in the very best German at command, expressed with due emphasis, proper inflexion, and in such a "sweet guttural accent." In fact when struggling for college honors, we never recited Schiller, Göethe, or Bürger, so forcibly or impressively, as we recite the tale of our misfortunes in the ear of this preserver of the peace. But there is no response, save an ugly shrug of that Dutch shoulder. We again repeat, and resorting to the tactics of the street merchants, suit the action to the word,—but still no response! At length, excited beyond measure, we "lay hands" tenderly upon what we regard as the "stupidest man in creation," and urge a compliance with our request:—when lo! he speaks, and from the very depths of the lowest diaphragm comes the saddening response in language like this, "Menchen, Ich-weiss nicht, was du sagest":—which being freely translated means, "My dear tourist, I do not understand Pennsylvania Dutch"!

*Cologne,* on the banks of the Rhine, has a population of 150,000.  The streets and side-walks, are narrow and rough, and do not always smell of "cologne."  Some of the public buildings are stately structures, and many of the private residences are quite handsome.

The Church of St. Ursula, is a strange build-ing, both in the manner of its erection, and the "relics" it contains.  It is built, largely, of "human bones."  The walls, partions, and decorations are composed, in part, of this strange material.  A sad looking monk, devoutly leads us through this sepulchral church edifice, point-ing out the objects worthy of pious regard.  Here are scores of skulls, tastily arranged, grinning at us from scores of shelves.  And there are the toes, finger-nails. and teeth of departed saints, who died long, long ago.  Nails of the "true" cross, and sundry sacred relics too valuable to be purchased, are pointed out to us by this simple-minded and tender-hearted ecclesiastic. On a centre-table, is a precious casket made from "selected portions" of the sainted dead. This is of exquisite workmanship, sparkles with gems. and is, by all visitors, curiously and carefully inspected.

But how came these bones, and skulls, these teeth, and toe nails to dwell in St. Ursula? The explanation is very simple,—if the reader is simple enough to believe it. St. Ursula, a princess of Britain, marshaling a force of 11,000 virgins, migrated to this region just 1600 years ago. This virgin band came to unite in happy wedlock, with the brave British soldiers keeping watch on the Rhine. They were seized and cruelly murdered by the barbarous Huns. And to perpetuate the memory of their love and their suffering, these relics have been preserved! An eminent anatomist has discovered among these "remains" the bones of animals; and this fact leads us to suspect, that some little deception may have been practised by certain ecclesiastical architects, during the "dark ages." But may not the story of the virgins be true?

The Cathedral of Cologne is a most magnificent structure. The foundation stone was laid in 1248, and the edifice is not yet quite completed. Scores of men are, this afternoon, hammering on the roof. This cathedral is regarded by critics as the

"finest specimen of gothic architecture in Europe."
It is 511 feet long, and 231 feet broad.  It has
9 aisles, 116 cloisters, 128 windows, 576 statues,
and 5000 turrets.  The south entrance has recently been completed at a cost of $500,000.  On
the walls hang ten large and costly paintings, five
of which were presented by the King of Bavaria.
The symmetry of this majestic edifice, is not marred
by any of those projections or graceless ornamentations, that so frequently disfigure similar structures.  The harmony is complete.

At three o'clock in the afternoon we enter the
building.  The organ is being played by some
master-hand.  And the music,—how sweet, solemn, sublime!  On a sultry afternoon, wearied by
excessive walking, how restful to the body, and
inspiring to the soul, to sit in this temple and
listen to this music!

But are there no "relics" on exhibition?  Yes,
quite a variety.  No building could survive for
600 years along the banks of the Rhine, if it were
not guarded by the sacred dust of some departed
saints.  The sacristan informs the traveler, that in
the rear of the high altar, the "Wise men from the
east" lie sleeping!  By what strange star their
wandering footsteps were guided hither, we are not
informed.  Certainly they showed "wisdom" in the
selection of their last resting-place.  And as it re-

quires the jingling of several German coins to awaken these sleeping ones, we will not disturb their repose.  May they rest in peace!

By the payment of an admission fee, we are permitted to climb to the roof, look upon the statues and turrets, and gaze upon the gently-flowing Rhine.  The prospect is delightful; and from these airy summits we return refreshed.

Before departing for Bonn, we visit Joh. Mar. Farina, No. 10 Wallrafsplatz.  This gentleman claims to be the "original manufacturer" of Cologne water.  His store is a model of neatness; and upon entering,

> "Meseemed I smelt a garden of sweet flowers,
>    That dainty *odors* from them threw around."

Two or three flasks of the "original article" are pushed into our valise; and we leave the city, smelling sweeter than the violet or the rose.

*Bonn* is beautifully situated on the left bank of the Rhine.  The streets are narrow, paved with rough stone,—and many of them have no side-walks.  Some of the houses are very neat; and a few wide streets furnish the "aristocrats" ample room for promenading.  The University is visited. The buildings form a "quadrangle;" and as the hour for recitation arrives, the students march to their respective class-rooms.  They are a lively set of " fellows ;" wear hats of various colors, but are not gowned.  Following in the footsteps of an agreeable young German, we find ourselves seated in the class-room, and listening to Professor Schultz. The topic of the morning lecture is the " German Rebellion."  His manner is earnest; style lucid; and by the frequent flashings of his piercing eyes, a stranger would infer that sometimes even the students at Bonn might be " rebellious."  The library building is 504 feet long, and for the privilege of inspecting it we pay five silbergroshen,— equal to 12 cents.  The room is ornamented with busts of Luther, Melancthon, and other famous men.  On the tables lie 200 periodicals, printed in different languages.  Some of these are specially devoted to the discussion of particular subjects,— History, Philosophy, Geography, Philology.  In counting and examining these 200 current publications,—coming from all parts of the world, and representing every school of science, philosophy, and religion,— how many do we find representing America?  Only one! "The Journal of Science." Is this the esteem in which the great " Republic of America " is held, by this German University? Where is the " North American," the " Bibliotheca Sacra," or our own orthodox " Princeton ?"

Prince Albert was a student at Bonn ; and some of the musical compositions of Mendelssohn

in manuscript, are pointed out by the librarian.
Several of the present Professors are well known
in America.  Lange, the distinguished Commen-
tator gives instruction in Theology; and Christ-
lieb, whose brilliant essay on "Modern Doubt,"
so thrilled the Evangelical Alliance in New York
city, is also a Professor.  We should like to linger
and form their acquaintance, but the shrill whistle
of the steamboat, summons us to the wharf to take
passage up the Rhine.

*The Rhine*, is famous in history, legend, and
song.  It is the pride of the Germans.  And those
who have listened to the " Watch on the Rhine,"
know what enthusiasm that song excites, among
those who love the dear old " Vaterland."  The
Rhine has its rise in the Alps, and rolls onward to
the sea.  The waters from 370 glaciers, and 2700
larger and smaller streams, unite in forming this
majestic river.  It is not uniform in width or
depth.  At Mentz, it is over 1500 yards wide,
while at Basle the width is only 500.  In depth
it varies from 10, to 200 feet.  In its march it
sweeps past Basle, Mentz, Bingen, Coblentz, Bonn,
and Cologne.  Along its banks the vine is cultivated.  And the sloping hillsides are, for scores of
miles, covered with smiling vineyards, while the
shining summits are crowned with hoary ruins,—
where in ages past dwelt the " robbers of the

Rhine." The frequent and sudden bends in the course of the river,—revealing at each curve new scenes of beauty,—form a succession of delightful surprises, and keep the admiring tourist continually on the alert.

Here indeed, looking from the ample deck of our stately steamer, we behold

> "A blending of all beauties, streams and dells,
> Fruit, foliage, crag, wood, corn-field, mountain, vine,
> And chiefless castles breathing stern farewells
> From gray but leafy walls, where ruin greenly dwells."

These monuments of the past, those castle-ruins, appear so lonely, and yet so proud !

> "And there they stand, as stands a lofty mind,
> Worn, but unstooping to the baser crowd,
> All tenantless, save to the crannying wind,
> Or holding dark communion with the cloud.
> There was a day when they were young and proud,
> Banners on high, and battles pass'd below,
> But they who fought are in a bloody shroud,
> And those who waved are shredless dust ere now,
> And the black battlements shall bear no future blow.
> Beneath these battlements, within those walls,'
> Power dwelt amidst her passions; in proud state
> Each robber chief upheld his armed halls,
> Doing his evil will, nor less elate
> Than mighty heroes of a longer date."

What fierce contests by rival Barons were witnessed in the distant ages, along these vine-clad hills ! How steel-clad knights flashed over bloody fields, and shining spears were waved in triumph over the prostrate forms of fallen foes!

> "In their baronial feuds and single fields,
>   What deeds of prowess unrecorded died!
> And love, which lent a blazon to their shields,
>   With emblems well devised by amorous pride,
> Through all the mail of iron hearts would glide;
> And many a tower for some fair mischief won,
> Saw the discolor'd Rhine beneath its ruin run."

Yonder is the Castle of Drachenfels, crowning the highest summit of the "seven mountains." It was rebuilt by the Archbishop of Cologne in the 12th century.

> "The castled crag of Drachenfels
>     Frowns o'er the wide and winding Rhine,
>   Whose breast of waters broadly swells
>     Between the banks which bear the vine,
> And hills all rich with blossom'd trees,
>     And fields which promise corn and wine,
> And scattered cities crowning these,
>     Whose far white walls along them shine."

And here, at the confluence of the *Mosel*—" The Pearl of German rivers"—and the Rhine, stands the old historic city of Coblentz. The city is blazing with banners; and the valley of the Rhine echoes this afternoon with the thundering of cannon. King William is paying a visit to the city. The Kaiser has come from Ems, a few miles distant, and the town is as joyously excited as if France had been conquered the second time. This

city is strongly fortified; and the country surrounding it is beautiful and picturesque.

> "Here Ehrenbreitstein, with her shatter'd wall,
>   Black with the miner's blast, upon her height
>   Yet shows of what she was, when shell and ball
>   Rebounding idly on her strength did light;
>   A tower of victory! from whence the flight
>   Of baffled foes was watched along the plain
>   And on which the iron shower for years had pour'd in vain."

We are now at Bingen.  This town is situated
on the left bank of the river, at the influx of the
Nahe into the Rhine, and at the foot of the Rochus
Mountain.  Here we rest during the night; and
from the piazza of the " Hôtel Victoria," listen to
the murmuring waters, and gaze upon the ruins of
Castle Klopp.  In this Castle Henry IV. was imprisoned in 1105.

How beautiful the scene this lovely evening of
the 2nd July!  And how expressive of the feelings of a lonely maiden, is this simple Rhine-land
song :—

> "The moon looks down upon the wave,
>     And calmly flows the Rhine,
>   The fisherman now spreads his nets,
>     Beneath the pale moonshine;
>   I sit within my silent room,
>     And list the waves' low tone,
>   I cannot mind my spinning wheel,
>     For I am all alone."

Perhaps her lover was on the distant battle field.

Was it of this maiden of Bingen, the dying soldier spake?   Was it to her he sent that tender message, ere he breathed his life away?

> "There's another,—not a sister; in the happy days gone by
>   You'd have known her by the merriment that sparkled in
>       her eye;
>   Too innocent for coquetry,—too fond for idle scorning,—
>   O friend! I fear the lightest heart makes sometimes heavi-
>       est mourning!
>   I saw the blue Rhine sweep along; I heard, or seemed to
>       hear,
>   The German songs we used to sing, in chorus sweet and
>       clear;
>   And her glad blue eyes were on me, as we passed, with
>       friendly talk,
>   Down many a path beloved of yore, and well-remembered
>       walk!
>   And her little hand lay lightly, confidingly in mine.—
>   But we'll meet no more at Bingen,—loved Bingen on the
>       Rhine."

*Mentz*, was founded by Drusus, step-son of Augustus, in the year 14 B. C.   It has a population of some 50,000, and is strongly fortified.

The Cathedral is a stately building.  It contains some interesting monuments, which are pointed out and explained to us by the "sexton's" daughter. This maiden speaks three different languages!— and appears delighted when complimented for her excellent English.   Here is the tomb of the "Sweet Singer."  The sculptured marble represents a shrouded coffin, borne upon the shoulders

of weeping women, and followed by a mournful
procession of the " gentler sex."  This poet was so
beloved for his sweet and tender melodies, that the
women whose hearts he won by his purity and
pathos, carried him to the tomb, and erected the
monument to perpetuate his memory !

In this town Guttenberg lived ; and on one of
the prominent streets we find a monument descriptive of his labors, and crowned by a statue of
this,—the first,—printer.

But we must bid the Rhine farewell.  Its winding current, and picturesque scenery, have been
both a surprise and delight.  From Bonn to
Mentz,

> " The river nobly foams and flows,
>     The charm of this enchanted ground,
> And all its thousand turns disclose
>     Some fresher beauty varying round :
> And peasant girls with deep-blue eyes,
>     And hands which offer early flowers
> Walk smiling o'er this paradise;
>     Above, the frequent feudal towers
> Through green leaves lift their walls of gray,
>     And many a rock which steeply lours,
> And noble arch in proud decay,
>     Look on this vale of vintage-bowers."

But the country invites us, and we must bid
this winding stream, and those shining towers a
sad farewell.

10

> " Adieu to thee, fair Rhine ! How long delighted
>    The stranger would fain linger on his way !
> Thine is a scene alike where souls united
>    Or lonely contemplation thus might stray :
> Adieu to thee again ! a vain adieu !
>    There can be no farewell to scene like thine;
> The mind is color'd by thy every hue ;
>    And if reluctantly the eyes resign
> Their cherish'd gaze upon thee, lovely Rhine !
>    'Tis with the thankful glance of parting praise ;
> More mighty spots may rise—more glaring shine,
>    But none unite in one attaching maze
> The brilliant, fair, and soft,—the glories of old days."

*Weisbaden,* is a delightful summer resort. The houses are large, and the streets wide and clean. There are a number of beautiful arcades, containing the choicest and costliest fabrics, and the most brilliant ornaments. Crowds of aristocratic Germans are marching along shaded avenues to the mineral springs. These healing waters are warm, and quite palatable ; but they are neither as pungent as the Saratoga " Hathorn," nor as sparkling as the " Geyser."

*Frankfort,* is an old German town, remarkable for narrow, crooked streets, and houses of strangest structure. What antiquated-looking windows hang over these winding stony pavements ! There are a few large and well-stocked bookstores. And yonder is the " Bourse," where Rothschild rules as king. Around its doors, the " long " and "short" gentlemen are already gathering. They do not appear in the least excited; but look as calm and bright as this peaceful summer morning. Stocks, we presume, are "steady;" and the next quarterly dividends are "assured." There has been no "overissue" by the Darmstadt-Aschaffenburg railroad; and no "embezzlement" by the Treasurer of the Cottbus-Gorlitz. He simply went "over the line" to visit a sick stepmother, and intends returning from Stuttgart, at a "convenient" season. The traffic on the Deutz-Barmen-Hagen-Soest has been much increased by the "Centennial" at Alten Hundern. The "immense" number of heavy Germans who were carried by weight, has relieved it from "temporary embarrassment," and placed it in a "sound financial condition." The "equipment" of the Eydtknahnen-Konigsberg-Bromberg is in "first-class order;" and the "discrepancy" in the cash account was due to a "slight mistake" in charging a certain amount to "construction," instead of to "current expenses." There may be some little anxiety respecting the "actual condition" of the Frauzensfeste-Villach-Marburg road, but by the skilful management of a few "leading directors," the stockholders will not "eventually" suffer loss. The well-known ability of these gentlemen to "borrow" on large interest, assures the owners that the "next quarterly" will be forthcoming.

The large amount of real estate owned by the Regensburg-Schwan'dof-Eger, although " unproductive " at present, will in the course of twenty years be a most " profitable investment."  This valuable property consisting of mountains and mines, which cannot be easily stolen, and can only be sold at a great " sacrifice," is considered by competent judges a good " permanent " investment.  Surely, with such a happy and " prosperous " state of affairs reported in the editorial columns of the " Blatherskite," and other " trustworthy " journals who have just received their information from " headquarters," the " investing public " should neither be " alarmed," nor " scared " by the deep growling of German " bears."  And hence the calmness, and serenity, of these phlegmatic financiers.

A few of the streets in Frankfort are straight and wide ; there are some very pleasant promenades, and many stately buildings.  Here Goethe was born in 1749 ; and a beautiful monument to his memory stands quite conspicuous on a leading thoroughfare.

*Darmstadt*, is visited in journeying to Worms. The Ducal Palace, surrounded by groves and gardens, and guarded by watchful soldiers, is the charming residence of a local prince.  Ludwig's monument challenges inspection.  The streets are, —many of them,—wide and treeless.

*Worms*, is associated with the name of Luther. In this town was held the celebrated "Diet," before which this reformer appeared. This Diet was, in accordance with the " Golden Bull " of Pope Leo, convoked to meet at Worms on the 6th of January 1521. This "solemn" assemblage was composed of "electors, dukes, archbishops, landgraves, margraves, counts, bishops, barons ; " and the "ambassadors" of the kings of Christendom. Some of these distinguished men came to Worms, as warriors march to a scene of strife. Philip of Hesse, enters the town surrounded by 600 horsemen ! Charles V. by the " grace of God Emperor elect of the Romans, always august, King of Spain, of the Two Sicilies, of Jerusalem, of Hungary, of Dalmatia and of Croatia, Archduke of Austria, Duke of Burgundy, Count of Hapsburg, of Flanders, and of the Tyrol," presided over the deliberations of the Diet. And before this august body Luther was commanded to appear. What would be his fate none but the Omniscient knew. His friends remonstrated ; they urged him to remain away lest his life should be forfeited. But this brave man responded to the tender appeals of the people of Eisenach in the following language :—" Though they should kindle a fire all the way from Worms to Wittemberg, the flames of which reached to heaven, I would walk through it in the name of the Lord ; I would appear before them ; I would enter the jaws of this behemoth, and break his teeth, confessing the Lord Jesus Christ." To the entreaties of dear friends at Frankfort, he replies, " but Christ lives, and I shall enter Worms in despite of all the gates of hell." Before he arrived at Worms, a special messenger sent by the chaplain, urges him not to enter ; but Luther sends back the answer :—" Go and tell your master, that even should there be as many devils in Worms as tiles on the housetops, still I would enter it !"

What sublime courage had this humble monk, who was regarded by his friends as marching to martyrdom ! And with what interest we look upon the ruins of the old building, in which Luther made his defence in presence of that august assemblage. And here are the old tiled houses, that have watched the flight of centuries, and sheltered the "delegates to this German General Assembly."

Luther's Monument, is well conceived, and admirably executed. The substructure is of granite, 42 feet on each side. Three sides are inclosed by battlemented walls, of polished syenite, three and five feet high. At the four corners, on pedestals eight feet high, are the statues of Melancthon, Reuchlin, Frederick the Wise, and Philip the Magnanimous. On the inner faces of the battlements, are the arms of the 24 cities which fought for the Reformation. In the centre of this enclosure are four pillars, on which are the statues of Wicliffe, Huss, Waldus, and Savonarola; while on a pedestal 28 feet high, in the centre of this inner group, stands the bronze statue of Luther,—nearly twelve feet in height. In front we read the words: "Here I stand. I cannot retract. God help me, Amen!" There are a number of finely executed bas-reliefs illustrating memorable scenes in the life of the Reformer. The inhabitants of Worms look with pride upon this noble monument; and the "guardian" of the premises, points out the various ornamentations with a sparkling eye.

*Heidelberg,*—between the hills,—is a charming town. Such beautiful avenues, shaded by stately trees! What a place for meditation,—or the quiet perusal of the classic page! If we had not already "completed our education," the beauties of the place would tempt us to matriculate. But to make it still "more complete," we will this morning "go through" a German university. The buildings are old and venerable; the recitation rooms somewhat dingy; but the "boys"—42 of whom are Americans,—seem bright and cheerful. We listen to some lectures; learn something respecting the methods of instruction; and are vigorously "stamped," because we slip away before the recitation closes.

In the wide paved market-place the goods for "sale," are arranged in parallel lines ; and the anxious purchasers march up and down between these lines, picking from the pavement the articles required, and paying if possible the "lowest prices." And these articles vary in size, from a fresh egg, to a newly skinned ox. The old Castle of Heidelberg overlooks the town, and by its position and architecture, constitutes one of the special attractions.

*Baden-Baden*,—a fashionable summer resort,— is in some respects the most attractive, and alluring little city we have thus far visited. It is situated in "one of those fair vales by nature formed to please," through which, a swift shallow stream flowing, "makes sweet music with the enameled stones."

Here is the great gambling palace, where in former days, kingdoms were lost and won. Gambling is now prohibited by law, but the palace is open, and may be quietly inspected. A *tageskarte* is purchased for 18 kreutzers, which admits to the Conversationhause, the Trinkhalle, the Spielzimmer, and affords the privilege of a Promenade-stüle, after we are tired marching through the Gebünde. Lest in our ignorance we might make a

mistake, this *card* informs us that "Zum Besuch der Reunions—Bälle, Küntstler-Concerte, Sonstiger besonderer Veranstaltungen und Festlichkeiten, aussergewohnlicher Reunions und Bals pares berechtigt diese Karte nicht."

Thus instructed, we enter the grand hall. In this room, kings and princes formerly gambled. The floors are of oak, and smooth as polished marble. Large mirrors in gilt and elaborately carved frames, reach from the ceiling to the floor. Magnificent paintings decorate the walls. The ceiling is frescoed in the most sumptuous style. Luxurious couches, and gilded chairs, are artistically arranged in shining groups. Reclining on one of those royal couches, and gazing upon this spacious hall, thus brilliantly ornamented,

> "We dare not trust these eyes:
>   They dance in mists, and dazzle with surprise."

The most delightful music is discoursed daily, in presence of aristocratic audiences, by famous German bands. Many wealthy Americans mingle in these scenes, and spend restful days in these shady and fragrant bowers. In leaving for Strassburg, we meet a prominent New York banker, with family and servants,—passengers on the Abyssinia,—speeding to this delightful place of rest.

*Strassburg*, is famous for its Cathedral, and its

clock.   The houses five stories high, have an ancient aspect, and by their crooked ranks, point back to the distant ages.   How crooked people must have been in the "middle ages" to build such streets!   It suffered terribly during the Franco-Prussian war; and is now occupied by the German forces.   New fortifications girdle the conquered city; and Krupp cannon thunder along the left bank of the Rhine.   Large numbers of the French, have left the city and the surrounding country, since the close of the war; but equal, or larger numbers of Germans have entered the conquered territory during the same period.   The population is therefore "mixed."   But there is no sympathy or fellowship, between the victors and the vanquished.   In business, society, amusements, they stand as far apart as possible.   The Cathedral is a stately edifice.   Hundreds of statues ornament the grand Gothic entrance; and a steeple and spire over 460 feet high, crowns the noble structure.   The Cathedral was struck several times during the bombardment of the city by the Germans, but not seriously damaged.   The pious sacristan points out the sacred pictures, that were so singularly preserved, when the walls surrounding were riddled with shot and shell.

The clock,—placed in one of the corners of the Cathedral,—is a marvelous piece of mechanism.

The position and motion of the heavenly bodies; the day of the week, month and year; and other "signs" among the "heavenly host" are most beautifully and strikingly presented. The quarters of the hour are struck by figures representing Infancy, Youth, Manhood, and Old Age. The hour is struck by the figure of an old man. At noon each day the scene is novel, and exciting. The figure of an old man steps forward and strikes the hour. The effigy of the Saviour appears and around it march the figures of the twelve apostles. Each apostolic effigy bows when passing the Saviour, as if in adoration, and the Saviour's hand is extended, as if in the act of blessing. But when the old man ceases striking the hour, and as the last apostle has bowed and been blest, a cock appears, flaps his wings vigorously and crows lustily three times!

The Sabbath-day in Strassburg is not religiously observed. In the morning, the places of business are all open; in the afternoon, bands of music parade the streets, and the lager beer gardens are crowded: while in the evening, the open squares are covered with noisy bibbers of wine and beer.

The peasant costume is quite picturesque. Both men and women delight in brilliant colors. And how pretty they look when marching gracefully in pairs! Yonder, sweetly smiling, walks a "fair couple," linked apparently "in happy nuptial league." The man wears leggins tightly buttoned, tightly-fitting and fancy knee-breeches, scarlet-colored vest, swallow-tailed coat, and low-crowned hat. The woman wears neatly embroidered slippers, garments of red, green and blue, and her head is crowned with a rainbow-tinted material of indescribable shape. And with all this "finery," there is a simplicity of manners, an absence of pride, that fairly captivates.

The scenery along the railroad between Strassburg and Basle is beautiful. Westward are the Vosges mountains; to the east is the peacefully flowing Rhine; while through the fertile fields Alsacian peasantry, gaily dressed, toss the hay or gather the corn.

Before leaving Germany and visiting Switzerland, some information may be given respecting the railroad and hotel charges, and the manners and customs of the people. The railroads in Germany, are most admirably managed. The stations are guarded by military officers. In the depots are pleasant rooms for the 1st, 2nd and 3rd class passengers. Before the arrival of trains, persons who have purchased tickets, are locked in these rooms, and are not permitted to approach the train until all the passengers stopping at that station have left the cars. Then the doors are opened, and the various " classes " walk to the open cars for which tickets have been purchased. All rushing,—with the consequent disorder, and frequent accidents,— is thus prevented. The order is complete.

The Germans smoke so universally, that every car may be called a " smoking-car." And being " smoked out " of the " upper class " cars, we ride in the " lower class," where the smoke is not so dense, by reason of " better circulation." In the 3rd class cars, the partitions separating the compartments, are only three or four feet high. Passengers in the several compartments freely converse, and occasionally pass from one compartment to another. The benches are hard, but more agreeable on a hot day, than padded crimson cushions. Then we are under no restraint. We can study character; take notes; breathe a purer air; and,—well,—save a little money. One hundred miles for $1.20 is not expensive traveling.

The hotel charges vary according to time, and place. At Bonn, for the privilege of sleeping in the largest hotel in town, one dollar is paid; while at Bingen, for supper, bed and breakfast, the charge is $1.50. In Frankfort we sleep snugly between two feather beds on the night of the 2nd of July! For breakfast, we have bread, butter, coffee or tea, and a little honey,—for which 30 cents is paid. But not being particularly lack-

ing in sweetness, we exchange the honey for a
beefsteak. Hot water is placed upon the table
to *weaken* the tea or coffee. What mirth would
be excited, if some American boarding-house man-
ager would imitate the example! The butter is
frequently saltless; and rarely is soap found in
the bed-chamber. A bougie, or candle, costs 12
cents, and occasionally two of these costly candles
are placed upon our table,—tempting us to an
"illumination." There are no carpets; but the
oaken floors are smooth and shining. The hotels
in all their arrangements, are models of neatness,
and order. The greatest inconvenience arises from
the numerous and curious coins that are current
in the Empire. Just think of the florins, thalers,
marks, kreutzers, silbergrochens, and pfennings
that jingle in our pockets, and pity us!

# CHAPTER XI.

### SWITZERLAND. BASEL. ZÜRICH.

BASEL is pleasantly situated on the left bank of the Rhine, and is of great antiquity. It is the first republican city visited since leaving America. It has a population of some 44,000; a University founded in 1459; an interesting museum and picture gallery; and a magnificent Protestant Münster. It was in this church edifice that the celebrated "Council of Basel" was held in 1431. During the sessions of this Council, pope Eugene was deposed; and the 500 ecclesiastics then assembled, solemnly declared that "a general Council is superior to the pope." Here also the "Helvetic Confession" was composed, in 1530. The city, in its position, political and ecclesiastical history, and Protestant character, is a pleasing introduction to the land of the hardy Swiss.

In Switzerland there are 22 Cantons united in a Confederacy. The population in 1870 was 2,670-000; of this number 1,566,000 were Protestant, and 1,084,665 Roman Catholic. There are four languages,—the German, French, Italian and Romansch,—spoken within the limits of the Confederacy. "Of every 1000 souls, 585 are Protestant and 411 Roman Catholic. Of every 1000, 702 speak German, 226 French, 55 Italian, and 17 Romansch. Of the 566,000 households of Switzerland, 465,000 possess landed property. Of 100 square leagues of land, 20 are pasture, 17 forest, 11 arable, 20 meadow, 1 vineyards, and 31 uncultivated, or occupied by roads, lakes or dwellings."

The scenery between Basel and Zürich is charming and inspiring. The train thunders along the lovely valley of the Aare, and onward past Brugg, where the Reuss, Limmat, and Aare,—three of the principal rivers of Switzerland,—unite their streams, and rush northward to mingle with the Rhine.

The joyous groups of quaintly costumed peasants; the neat Swiss cottages surrounded by blooming gardens, and smiling vineyards; the newly mown meadows and fields of ripening grain; and the distant hills crowned with waving woods,—how beautiful!

*Zurich*, is situated on the banks of the green and swiftly flowing Limmat, and by it divided into two parts. It is one of the most flourishing manufacturing towns in Switzerland. It has a number of schools; a college; a botanic garden containing 800 Alpine plants; and is regarded as the "literary centre of German Switzerland." Here, Zwingle, the great Swiss Reformer, lived and preached. His Greek Bible, with Hebrew annotations in his own handwriting, is preserved in the Town Library.

In the Museum, we find models—and some of the materials used in the construction—of the Swiss houses, found imbedded in the peat at Robenhausen. Arriving in the evening, and selecting the " Hotel et Pension Bellevue du Lac" as a temporary abode, we catch the first glimpse of a Swiss lake. How beautiful in the moonlight is the Lake of Zurich!  And how the young Swiss of both sexes, enjoy floating upon its smooth and shining surface.  From our chamber window, we count forty-four little row-boats moving hither and thither over these silvery waters!  And here we sit alone, far from home, looking down upon this scene of love and beauty.

But morning comes and behold the distant Alps!  Yonder is the Pfannstock; the snow-clad Bifertenstock; and on either side are the lofty glistening peaks of those " everlasting hills."  How gloriously they shine when illumined by the rising sun !

> " Above me are the Alps,
> The palaces of nature, whose vast walls
> Have pinnacled clouds their snowy scalps,
> And throned eternity in icy halls
> Of cold sublimity, where forms and falls
> The avalanche—the thunderbolt of snow !
> All that expands the spirit, yet appals,
> Gather around these summits, as to show
> How earth may pierce to heaven, yet leave man below."

But in order to enjoy a better view of those snow-clad summits, we must journey towards the south.

*Lucerne,* is a pretty little town, charmingly situated on the banks of the green and rapid Reuss, and on the margin of the lake to which it gives its name. The Lake of Lucerne, is regarded as the " Queen of Swiss Lakes."   It is cruciform in shape, and is bounded by four of the Swiss cantons :—Uri, Schwyz, Unterwalden, and Lucerne.   The length of the lake from Lucerne to Fluelen is 25 miles; the distance between the extremities of the two arms 15 miles; the width from one to four miles; and the greatest depth 510 feet.   It is surrounded by scenery the most magnificent.   The lakes of Killarney and Scotland, vanish in the presence of Lucerne.

In order to enjoy the beauty of this lake, and better appreciate the grandeur of the scenery, we purchase a ticket, secure a pleasant position on

board a lively little Swiss steamer, and sail over
the shining waters, with prow pointed towards
Fluelen.  The ticket for the round trip,—50
miles,—costs 66 cents.

Just look at those mountain sentinels that guard
this enchanted land !  To the right, is the cloud-
capped Pilatus over 6,000 feet high,—and promising a bright and happy day.

> " If Pilatus wears his cap, serene will be the day ;
> If his collar he puts on, you may venture on the way ;
> But if his sword he wields, at home you'd better stay. "

To the left rises the Rigi,—5,000 feet. In front
the Buochser, the Stanzerhorn, and the Burgen-
stock proudly lift their heads. Here, are bald and
barren peaks ; yonder, are mountain sides clothed
with verdure.  On the right are frowning forest-
clad hills ; on the left, are shining cottages, blooming gardens, and fruit trees, bearing chestnuts,
almonds, figs !  How beautiful, wild and grand !
The village of Gersau, with its broad-roofed
cottages, is now in sight.  Here once existed the
smallest independent State in Europe.  The small
territory of 8 square miles, and 1,000 inhabitants,
—guarded by the Hochfluh and the Vitznauer-
stock,—was, during 400 years, an independent
State !  Every mountain peak, bubbling spring
and sparkling meadow, speaks of the heroic deeds

of patriotic Swiss. Tell's Chapel, shaded by over-
hanging trees, and standing on the margin of the
lake is now in sight; and not far distant is Altorf,
where the Swiss liberator aimed at the apple placed
upon his son's head, at the command of the tyrant
Gessler. The Gitchen (8,000 feet), the Bristen-
stock (10,000 feet), the Windgelle (10,400 feet),
tower majestically above us. These "crags and
peaks" witnessed both the skill and patriotism, of
this mountain chieftain; and to them, as the
"guards of liberty," he might with propriety hold
out his hands, to show they still were free.

> "Ye crags, and peaks, I'm with you once again;
> I hold to you the hands you first beheld,
> To show they still are free.
> Again! O sacred forms, how proud you look!
> How high you lift your heads into the sky!
> How huge, you are! how mighty, and how free!
>                         Ye guards of liberty
> I'm with you once again!—I call to you
> With all my voice!—I hold my hands to you
> To show they still are free—I rush to you
> As though I could embrace you!"

But the ascent of the Rigi must be made, in order
to view the Alps at sunrise. The mountain is
5,000 feet high, and the ascent is made by railroad.
This mountain road is, in construction and method
of operation, similar to the road climbing Mt.
Washington. It is 7,755 yards long; the fare to

the summit is $1.40; and up and down these slanting heights 50,000 passengers are carried annually.  The hotel on the mountain is a well-kept establishment, and furnishes an excellent supper and good bed for $1.40.  For less comfortable quarters on Mt. Washington we paid $3.00.  By special arrangement, the tourists are to be aroused from sleep by the "Alpine Horn."  And faithfully and honestly does this Swiss bugler fulfil the terms of the contract.  For long ere Aurora with "rosy finger opens the portals of the East," —long before "the moon began to nod, her eyes becoming dim,"—did the Alpine horn begin to "blow."  And what a "blower!"  It would seem that all the wind sporting around the lofty heights of the Rigi was marching through that horn! There is, of course, great excitement.  The sleepers are quickly aroused.  Garments are hastily snatched, and shivering tourists quickly clad.  A rush is made to the highest point; guide books are opened;  opera glasses properly adjusted,—and then, the babble begins.  Rigi this morning is a very tower of Babel.  Men and women, representing all the world,—and some of them "the rest of mankind,"—are either scolding the "bugler," or censuring the absent sun for tardiness in rising, or chattering with their teeth.  But the sun appears: and the scene is inspiring.

We have climbed the Alleghenies and the Berkshire hills; stood upon the summits of the Green and White mountains; but never witnessed such beauty, grandeur and sublimity combined, as the rising sun now reveals. The eye sweeps a circuit of 300 miles! Thirteen Swiss lakes sparkle in the sunlight! What cities, rivers, woods, meadows, valleys, plains, forests, emerge from the darkness, and greet the coming day! But look eastward. What beacon lights are being kindled along the snow-clad Alps! From North to South,—along the East,—a range of mountains 120 miles in length stands revealed. And along this mountain path 132 peaks, from 5,000 to 13,000 feet in height, are clearly visible. 132 peaks shining along a snowy pathway of 120 miles!

The beacon lights kindled to herald the fall of the Trojan city, never flashed so quickly from Troy to Argos, as those Alpine heights announce the coming of the king of day.

Mont Sentis, in the far East, tells it to the Glärnish; and the Glärnish repeats it to the Todi; and the Todi flashes it to the Jungfrau; and the radiant snowy Jungfrau,—13,000 feet high,—beams upon the distant West, and heralds the rising sun! Many are the exclamations of surprise and delight, as peak after peak glows and glitters, and lake after lake sparkles and shines. But like Peter,

James, and John, we must descend from this mount of transfiguration.  And in order that we may better study the manners and habits of the Swiss, we walk from the summit to the base of the Rigi.

Among the Swiss mountains the cattle are led up the hillsides in the early spring, and do not return until late in the Fall.  Every cow has a bell attached; and the ringing and jingling of these scores of bells, makes the mountain air musical.  This bright, beautiful morning we listen

"To the tintinnabulation that so musically wells,
From the bells, bells, bells, bells,
From the jingling and the tinkling of the bells."

Here and there, like birds' nests in the clefts of the rocks, are the chalets of the herdsmen.  Along those steep declivities, the Swiss peasant, assisted by an iron-pointed Alpenstock and spiked shoes, is climbing.  On his back he carries a long, shallow basket, in which are placed the milk-pails.  He moves from height to height until the cows are milked, and then slowly descends to his mountain home.  Here are maidens moving with heavy burdens where goats might fear to climb.  They are singing strange melodies, and their happy voices are sweetly ringing through these wild ravines.  Alpine horns sound from peak to peak along  this mountain range,—herdsman answering herdsman.   We enter a Swiss cottage, and ask for some milk.   The floor is ˙paved with stone,—perhaps to prevent it from sliding down the hill.  The woman talks pleasantly ;  is very polite ; and  presents the thirsty tourist with  such an excellent article.   This milk has never tasted of the mountain stream, although  that stream dances  merrily past the door-way.   Thus refreshed we press down the hill to Vitznau.   The scenes along this morning's pathway, recall some beautiful passages of descriptive poetry.

> " When hums the mountain bee in May's glad ear,
>     And emerald isles to spot the heights appear,
>     When shouts and lowing herds the valley fill,
>     And louder torrents stem the noon-tide hill,
>     When fragrant scents beneath the enchanted tread
>     Spring up, his choicest wealth around him spread,
>     The pastoral Swiss begins the cliff to scale,
>     To silence leaving the deserted vale,
>     Mounts where the verdure leads, from stage to stage,
>     And pastures on, as in the patriarchs' age ;
>     O'er loftier heights serene and still they go,
>     And hear the rattling thunder far below—
>     I see him up the midway cliff, he creeps
>     To where a scanty knot of verdure peeps ;
>     Thence down the steep a pile of grass he throws,
>     The fodder of his herds in winter snows.
>     An idle voice the Sabbath region fills,
>     Of deep that calls to deep across the hills ;

> Broke only by the melancholy sound
> Of drowsy bells forever tinkling round."

After glancing at the "Lion of Lucerne,"—sculptured by Thorvaldsen out of the sandstone rock, and dedicated to the memory of the Swiss soldiers who were slain in Paris in 1792,—we charter a Swiss "Diligence," and proceed to Briens, over the Brünig Pass. The distance is 17 miles, and the fare $2.20. Our coach is drawn by a lively pair of horses; the roads are broad, hard and smooth; and the scenery,—mountains, lakes, Swiss cottages, foaming cataracts and flashing cascades,—is beautiful.

In the village of Sachseln on the east bank of Lake Sarnen, we visit St. Nikolaus, or St. Klaus. In 1487 this venerable man died; and for his piety and good works he was quickly canonized. His skeleton is carefully preserved in the village church, and exhibited to all those who pay a small admission fee. Here also may be seen the home-spun garments worn by this sainted Swiss. It is said that during the 20 years of his hermit life, he subsisted upon the sacred elements, of which he partook monthly. And in this old church the skeleton and the garments, have been sacredly kept the past 400 years! As we look upon these fleshless bones, glittering with cheap ornaments, we sympathize with all those pious Swiss who may yet be " canonized."

Brienz, is a village of wooden houses, situated at the foot of the Brienzer Grat,—over 7,000 feet high,—and on the margin of lake Briens. This town is famous for its wood carving. Some 600 of the inhabitants are carvers in wood. A visit is paid to a dozen of these private manufactories. By purchasing some trifling articles, we are permitted to sit and watch the men and women at work. These wild mountain artists are very gentle, and exceedingly kind, when the slightest interest is manifested in their handiwork.

And what beautiful toys are made in these humble Swiss homes : what exquisite workmanship comes from the hands of these poor rustic Swiss peasants ! One old artist quickly responds to our expressions of kindly feeling, by carving our name on a rule we purchase, as a memorial of our visit.

Part of the 9th day of July is spent in rowing and fishing upon lake Brienz. A boat is chartered; rod, line, hook, and bait provided; and we "launch into the deep." But after the most tempting, offers of a " crooked hook baited with a vile earth worm," these foolish Swiss fish will not bite. And " having toiled " until twilight, we return to the " Hotel and Pension de l'Ours," having " taken nothing,"—worthy of being recorded.

The *Giesbach Falls*, is formed of seven cascades that leap and foam several hundred feet along the mountain side.  In the summer evenings these falls are brilliantly illuminated.  Upon a signal being given, either by the ringing of a bell, or the flight of a rocket, scores of blazing red white and green lights flash along the cascades, coloring the foaming falling waters, and exciting the greatest enthusiasm among the admiring tourists.

*Interlaken*, situated between the lakes,—lake Brienz and lake Thun,—is a popular summer resort.  Here we find the prettiest Swiss cottages in Switzerland.  Such is the fineness of material, elegance of finish and beauty of decoration, that they look more like large toys than human habitations.  From Interlaken to Bern, we are carried by railroad and steamboat.  While sailing over lake Thun, a storm rages amid the lofty Alps, and the scene from the deck of our steamer is magnificent.  The "Bernese Oberland," numbering 70 Alpine peaks, rises grandly beyond the lake. Thirty of these snow-clad mountains range from 10,000 to 13,000 feet in height.  And how the loud thunder rolls, and shining showers march along those Alpine heights!  The lightning, nimble-footed, leaps from the Wetterhörner to the Finsteraarh, from the Finsteraarh to the Blümlisalp, and encircles the snowy summits of the Mönch

and Jungfrau, with bands of flashing fire!  The
scene is sublime.  We have never witnessed such
a war of the elements, upon a battle-field so grand.
What revelations of the power of the Almighty
are before us!  "He bowed the heavens also, and
came down, and darkness was under his feet.  He
did fly upon the wings of the wind: the Lord
also thundered in the heavens, and the Highest
gave his voice: yea he sent out his arrows and
scattered them: and he shot out lightnings, and
discomfited them."

> "Far along,
> From peak to peak, the rattling crags among
> Leaps the live thunder! Not from one lone cloud,
> But every mountain now hath found a tongue,
> And Jura answers, through her misty shroud,
> Back to the joyous Alps, who call to her aloud!"

*Bern*, is beautifully located on the banks of the
Aare and in view of the Bernese Oberland.  The
houses are very quaint-looking structures;  and
the streets rejoice in the most classic names.  The
principal street is one mile in length, and is labeled
the Spitalgasse, Marktgasse, Kramgasse, and Ge-
richtigkeitsgasse!  Now if all the streets in Bern
are as "gasse" as this one, then indeed the
Bernese Swiss must be very talkative people.

There are some costly edifices in the Swiss
capital.  The Federal Council Hall, in which the

sessions of the two great national Councils are
held, is quite conspicuous.  The debates are conducted in the German, French, and Italian languages; and all the rulings and resolutions, must
be announced in French and German.  The
Cathedral is a beautiful building,—elaborately
and tastefully ornamented.  In the Library,
" Prescott's Histories " in English, and " Paley "
in German, stand side by side.  The university
is attended by about 200 students.  The Museum
contains some objects of interest.  Here, the St.
Bernard dog " Barry " is exhibited.  This dog
during his earthly career along the snowy summits
of St. Bernard, saved the lives " of 15 persons."
And like the canonized St. Nikolaus, Barry is
" preserved " for his " good works."  Here also
is a magnificent specimen of crystal from the
Tiefengletschar, weighing 270 lbs.

The Bears are highly favored by the Bernese.
On the right bank of the Aare, in the Bärengraben,
Bruin is kept at the public expense.  And the
antics of these " privileged characters," are as
amusing on the banks of the Aare, as on the
banks of the Schuylkill.  The specimens we laugh
at this afternoon are large, and in excellent humor.
The Clock Tower, standing on the Kramgasse, is
an object of interest to all visitors.  At the striking
of the hours, two wooden bears march round ; a

wooden cock crows; a wooden man turns an hour glass; and a stone figure strikes the hour on the bell. The scene is amusing, and is witnessed by scores of curiously-costumed Swiss.

On our journey to Lausanne, we visit Frieburg. In the Church of St. Nicholas may be heard one of the finest organs in Europe. It boasts of 67 stops and 7,800 pipes. For the small sum of 20 cents we are permitted to enter the Cathedral, and listen to a "performance." Although the edifice is well filled, the silence is profound,—for who could move the lip or tongue when this organ speaks? Alpine storms thunder along the aisles, and shake the building; and melodies, tender and pathetic, moisten the eye with tears. Could that "vox humana" be any other than a human voice?

*Lausanne* surprises us. The site on the terraced slopes of Mount Jorat is so commanding, and the view so magnificent. On the right,—in the distance,—are the Jura Mountains, separating Switzerland and France; on the left, are the Savoy Hills and Valley of the Rhone; in front, gleaming for more than 30 miles,

> "Lake Leman woos me with its crystal face,
> The mirror where the stars and mountains view
> The stillness of their aspect, in each trace
> Its clear depth yields of their fair height and hue."

At Ouchy, we embark for Geneva. Yonder

along the shining eastern shore is the "Castle of
Chillon :"

> " Lake Leman lies by Chillon's walls;
>     A thousand feet in depth below
>     Its massy waters meet and flow;
>     Thus much the fathom line was sent
>     From Chillon's snow-white battlement,
>     Which round about the wave enthrals."

Here Bonnivard was imprisoned in 1530, by the
Duke of Savoy.

> "Chillon! thy prison is a holy place,
>       And thy sad floor an altar,—for 'twas trod,
>     Until his very steps have left a trace
>       Worn, as if thy cold pavement were a sod,
>     By Bonnivard!—May none those marks efface!
>       For they appeal from tyranny to God."

Lake Leman, or Geneva, is shaped like a half-
moon.  It is 55 miles in length along the north
bank; 48 miles along the south bank; and is
from 1½ to 9 miles wide.  As it differs from lakes
Zurich and Lucerne in form, and the character of
the scenery by which it is surrounded, so it differs
from these lakes in color.  Zurich and Lucerne
are of a pale green color, Geneva is of a deep blue.
The banks are fringed with the walnut, magnolia,
cedar of Lebanon, and vine.  And here and there
over the shining waters, float Swiss craft with
lateen or "goose-wings" sail.  The air this afternoon is balmy; the sky is bright; and the excur-

sion from Ouchy to Geneva, is delightful and refreshing.

*Geneva*, is situated on the banks of the river Rhone,—by which it is divided into two parts,—and on the margin of lake Leman.  Six bridges span the swiftly flowing Rhone, and reunite the divided city.  The population is nearly 50,000.  Along the quays there are handsome houses, magnificent hotels, and charming little lawns furnished with seats, and "shaded with branching trees." The view from the Quai du Montblanc is grand. Yonder, lifting his snowy head 16,000 feet high, stands the monarch of the Alps,—the glorious Mont Blanc!    Just 50 miles to this shining mountain ; and yet how near it seems to be !

> " Mont Blanc is the monarch of mountains ;
>     They crowned him long ago
> On a throne of rocks, in a robe of clouds,
>     With a diadem of snow.
> Around his waist are forests braced
>     The avalanche in his hand ;
> But ere it fall, that thundering ball
>     Must pause for my command."

Geneva, from its situation, and surroundings, is a popular resort.  The English and Americans love to linger here.  Hundreds of aristocratic tourists are either strolling through the streets, lounging in the Jardin Anglais, or visiting the brilliant shops that adorn the leading thoroughfares.

The principal industry is watchmaking.  100,000 watches are made and sold every year.  We are conducted through one of the largest manufacturing establishments by a member of the firm, who exhibits all the parts, and explains all the processes necessary in the construction of a watch. And the stores and windows so tastefully ornamented with " warranted timekeepers " of all sizes, materials, and prices, tempt us to exchange our ugly German coins for pretty Swiss watches.

Geneva was the home of Calvin.  Here he lived, and here he died in 1564.  Climbing the hill, we visit the Cathedral in which he so eloquently preached; and seated in a chair once used by the great Reformer, reflect upon his character, labors, and system of theology.  What an amount of work was accomplished by this austere man :— preaching daily, lecturing two or three times a week, founding and superintending schools of learning, legislating for Geneva, corresponding with eminent men on subjects of gravest interest that required the closest study, and writing those learned commentaries that have made his name immortal! In labors and in trials, how much like the great apostle, of whose divinely inspired system of theology he is the admired expounder !

He died at the age of 56, was buried in Geneva, but his resting place is not known,—and no monument seeks to perpetuate his memory. He requested that no monument should be erected. In the Public Library are exhibited the autographs of Calvin, Rousseau, and other Genevese celebrities. Here also we find portraits of Calvin, Turretin, Coligny, Beza, Erasmus and Grotius.

The Sabbath-day is much more religiously observed in Geneva, than in the German towns through which we have passed. And the services in some of the churches are exceedingly interesting and instructive. This afternoon at the close of the service, a child is baptized. In the front pews are seated father, mother, and all the family. When the child is presented to the minister, the members of the family stand; the mother pours from a vial the baptismal water into the minister's open hand; and as the baptismal name is being pronounced, the entire congregation rise, as if to welcome "the little stranger" to the " communion of saints." This is the most expressive, and beautiful baptismal service we have ever witnessed.

From Geneva to Mont Blanc, and the Valley of Chamouny, is 50 miles. Selecting from our valise a few "changes" of raiment, and bracing them in a neat Genevese strap, we purchase a ticket, take a seat with the driver and roll on to Chamouny. The road is broad and smooth; the scenery picturesque; and the atmosphere exhilarating. Through the valley of the Arva; around the mountains of Savoy; in sight of castle ruins and flashing cascades; and over lovely meadows breathing perfume, our chariot rolls. How these horses love to gallop; and how grandly the Diligence sways and thunders behind their flying feet! Here is the Breson 6,000 feet high; and yonder the Aiguilles de Varens, 9,000 feet above the level of the sea. Down along these mountains cascades leap 1000 feet; and swerved by passing winds, they look like shining serpents scaling the lofty heights.

At St. Martin's the shining peaks of Mont Blanc suddenly appear. The mountain is 12 miles distant, but really seems to overshadow us. How lofty, grand, and dazzling, are those snow-clad summits! We are now in the lovely valley of Chamouny; and for this enjoyable ride of 50 miles pay $4.20.

The *Valley of Chamouny*, is 15 miles long, and nearly one mile wide. It is a verdant vale. Alpine flowers bloom, and corn grows along the line of perpetual snow. Streams of purest ice water rush from melting glaciers, and swell the foaming Arva. A dozen snow-clad peaks, ranging from 10,000 to 16,000 feet high, glitter in the sunlight.

From the village of Chamouny, tourists make the ascent of Mont Blanc. It was ascended for the first time in 1786. In fine weather, and under the leadership of experienced guides, it may be climbed in safety ; but if the weather be cloudy or stormy, serious and sometimes fatal accidents befall the explorers. During 1870 eleven persons perished in a storm ! Guides charge $20 to make this mountain excursion.

The " *Mer de Glace*," is, after Mont Blanc, the principal attraction. To view this " Sea of Ice," we must climb on mule-back to the Montanvert,—6000 feet high. We hire a guide and mule for the entire day,—paying $6.50 for the services of both,—and at 5 o'clock on the morning of July 16th, lift our eyes up to those shining hills. The path crosses the track of avalanches ;—and how grand the scene when the summit is reached! Three glaciers, that fill the highest gorges in the Mont Blanc chain of mountains, unite in the form of a surging stream of ice, 12 miles long and a quarter of a mile wide. And there are the frozen billows ! Miles above us are two mountain peaks, each over 10,000 feet high ; and between them,—as through a shining gateway,—this stream of swelling, motionless, icy waves, majestically rolls!

The scene is sublime, awful ; it cannot be described.

"Hast thou a charm to stay the morning star
  In his steep course? So long he seems to pause

On thy bald, awful head, O sovran Blanc!
The Arvé and Arveiron at thy base
Rave ceaselessly ; but thou, most awful Form !
Risest from forth thy silent sea of pines
How silently !
Who filled thy countenance with rosy light ?
Who made thee parent of perpetual streams ?
And you, ye five wild torrents, fiercely glad !
Who gave you your invulnerable life,
Your strength, your speed, your fury, and your joy,
Unceasing thunder and eternal foam ?
And who commanded (and the silence came),
Here let the billows stiffen and have rest ?
    Ye ice-falls! ye that from the mountain's brow
Adown enormous ravines slope amain,—
Torrents, methinks, that heard a mighty voice,
And stopt at once amid their maddest plunge !
Motionless torrents! silent cataracts !
Who made you glorious as the gates of Heaven ?
God ! let the torrents, like a shout of nations,
Answer! and let the ice-plains echo, God !
God! sing, ye meadow-streams, with gladsome voice !
Ye pine-groves, with your soft and soul-like sounds !
And they too have a voice, yon piles of snow,
And in their perilous fall shall thunder, God !
    Ye living flowers that skirt the eternal frost !
Ye wild goats sporting round the eagle's nest !
Ye eagles, playmates of the mountain storm !
Ye signs and wonders of the elements,
Utter forth God, and fill the hills with praise !
    Thou, too, hoar Mount !  Rise, O, ever rise,
Rise like a cloud of incense from the Earth !"


Yonder is the Chapeau, but how shall we reach

it?  By crossing this sea of ice!  Our guide, a sure-footed Alpine climber, leads the way.  Occasionally our slipping feet discourage us, and we "balance" as gracefully as possible on the edge of an iceberg.  Here, is a crevasse gaping wide to the depth of 200 feet; and we listen to the murmurings of a chilly stream that,—far below,—courses along its icy path.  In the midst of our perplexities, and bewilderments, even when we are compelled to wait until the axe cuts a resting place for the foot, our cheerful guide shouts in French, " it is very easy, Sir!"—and sliding forward we reach the other shore.  But we would not recross those icy billows, for one hundred francs!

*Martigny,* lies in the Rhone Valley, beyond the Tête Noire, some 25 miles from Chamouny.  The people along the route are stunted in growth, of sallow complexion, and numbers of them afflicted with the goitre.  The children are very polite. Boys and girls have great respect for strangers ; and bowing most gracefully, greet us in French with the pleasing salutation,—" Good day, Sir!" Might not some of these Alpine lads be imported to teach our city youngsters " manners?"  And the humble priests are " affectioned one to another with brotherly love;" for when they meet along the wayside, they bow, and kiss each other on both cheeks!  Just think of rival preachers, or pulpit

" stars," whose orbits of pastoral duties circle through " neighboring folds," greeting each other in their pious incursions " with a holy kiss "! The little churches are surrounded by stout stone walls, to protect them from the thundering avalanche.

Our four-footed conveyance possesses all the characteristic traits, and excellent qualities of a thorough-bred mule. That gentleness and docility; that yielding and submissive disposition ; that readiness to walk or gallop, which so distinguishes this pliant species of quadruped, find a beautiful illustration in our fiery steed. With the English language he is not familiar ; and his education in French has been " sadly neglected." All spurring with the heel ; all sturdy strokes of the umbrella ; all the appeals for swifter motion, are utterly disregarded. Then in form and movement, this animal is a novelty among quadrupeds,—pos·sessing such a low neck, such a high back, and delighting in such a stylish swing ! In descending mountains, graceful horsemanship is, under the circumstances, quite difficult.  And lest the yielding of crupper, or breaking of stirrups, should precipitate us 1000 feet, and suddenly end our " wanderings," we occasionally dismount.  Then, it is so pleasant to see the owner of the animal ride at our expense !

Accidents along these mountain roads are of

frequent occurrence. Two heavily laden wagons have just been upset in rounding a narrow curve. One of the wagons is completely shattered; the barrels are sent rolling along the hillside; and the mule,—obedient to the laws of gravitation,—after numerous hurried revolutions, reclines on his back, and with "burnished hooves" beckons to the sun. This animal is so accustomed to "back up," that no influence except that of gravitation can compel him to "back down." How many mules there are walking through life,—on two legs!

Martigny, is the starting point for an excursion over the "*Great St. Bernard.*" The ascent is fraught with danger, but we are determined to visit the monks and dogs, or "die in the attempt." Our motto is "Excelsior!" The road climbs zigzag along the mountain, and our Diligence moves slowly. The hillside is terraced, and the poor peasantry are toiling hard to secure a scanty supply of food for man and beast. Here, we behold a new system of irrigation. Swollen torrents rush down from the snow-clad summits. At certain points, artificial streams branching from these torrent-stems, flash through and over those terraced heights, making them bloom "and blossom as the rose." The houses are built of stone; have stony stairways; small doors and small windows. The roofs are covered with large stone slabs, to protect them from the whirling winds.

At Bourg St. Pierre, the Diligence route ends; and up to the Hospice,—four miles distant,—we travel "on foot." The St. Bernard Pass, was climbed by Napoleon in May, 1800. The mountain was then covered with snow. The guns were placed on sledges, and dragged by soldiers over the Pass. And for each cannon pulled through ice and snow, Napoleon paid his warriors $240. As we climb the scenery becomes wild. The road has now dwindled to a crooked pathway, and the last human habitation is passed. On a former and memorable occasion, another young man proceeded along this same bleak and barren mountain, in the afternoon.

> "The shades of night were falling fast,
>     As through an Alpine village passed
>     A youth, who bore, 'mid snow and ice,
>     A banner with the strange device,
>                     'Excelsior!'"

This village has just been passed; but we have no banner, except a faded umbrella; and this is not ornamented with a solitary " device."

> "'Try not the pass!' the old man said;
>     'Dark lowers the tempest overhead,
>     The roaring torrent is deep and wide!'
>     And loud the clarion voice replied,
>                     'Excelsior!'"

But the old man of sallow complexion and baggy

trousers, saluted at the " Bourg," gave no such intimation of the coming storm.

> "' O stay,' the maiden said, 'and rest
> Thy weary head upon this breast!'
> A tear stood in his bright blue eye,
> But still he answered with a sigh,
>             ' Excelsior!'"

The venerable maiden passed on the wayside, was too busily engaged in attempting to shear a big black sheep, to bestow the slightest attention upon the lonely traveler. Her strength was taxed to the utmost, in preserving this kicking quadruped in an inverted position. And in our " blue eye" no " tear stood," while we smiled at the amusing spectacle.

But the storm is coming; and the gathering clouds, pushing the daylight down the valley, suddenly shroud the shining peaks in gloom and darkness. The rain now falls in floods; and the swollen streams rush madly through the glen. Boots and umbrella, have lost their water-proof qualities, and we walk ankle-deep in water, along the steep ascent. The " *Valley of Death*" opens before us. Just here, the accidents are most frequent and disastrous. Seven persons were killed on this spot. Close to the path stands the old " Morgue." And there, lie the bleaching bones of unfortunate travelers, who perished in the blinding snow storm, or were crushed to death beneath the thundering avalanche!  The surrounding scene is wild and dark : and we shudder at the sight of these unburied remains, and tremble lest a similar fate should reward our ambitious efforts. The words of the poet are well remembered :—

> " At break of day, as heavenward
> The pious monks of Saint Bernard
> Uttered the oft-repeated prayer,
> A voice cried through the startled air,
>      ' Excelsior ! '
>
> A traveller, by the faithful hound,
> Half-buried in the snow was found ;
> There in the twilight cold and gray,
> Lifeless, but beautiful, he lay !"

Chilled by the biting blasts, yet inspired by the hope of reaching the summit in safety, we press forward over ice and snow, and upward through the gloomy gorge and " valley of death," until the " Hospice " is reached.

The monks and the dogs receive us kindly,—the former by a kind shake of the hand, the latter by a joyous wagging of bushy tails: we are immediately conducted to a comfortable room, and prompt attention paid to our numerous wants.  Having made a hasty " toilet," placed our weary feet in a pair of monk's soft slippers, and partaken of a refreshing meal, we sit before a blazing fire and take a few " notes."

*The Hospice of St. Bernard,* is the highest winter habitation in the Alps. The latitude is 45° north, and the altitude is over 8000 feet. It was founded in the year 962, by the pious monk whose name it bears, as a refuge for the numerous travelers crossing the Alps. The "brotherhood" consists of 10 to 15 Augustinian monks, and 7 attendants. There are two large buildings: one of these contains the cells of the monks, and rooms with 80 beds for the accommodation of the better class of travelers; the other is used as a granary, and lodging for the poorer classes who are continually passing between France, Switzerland, and Italy. The expenses of the establishment amount to about $8,000 a year; and are paid from subsidies granted by the French and Italian governments, collections made in Switzerland, and the gifts of travelers. About 20,000 persons are annually accommodated; no charge is made for food or lodging; but a box in the chapel marked "Pour Pauvre," invites the kindly disposed to remember "the poor."

The mean temperature at the Hospice is 30°; the large rooms are heated throughout the whole year; and 20 horses are employed during July, August, and September, in transporting fuel from a valley 12 miles distant.

The reception room is neatly furnished: on the

walls hang pictures representing Napoleon crossing the Alps; Jesus teaching; the Apostles separating; Timothy; and St. Agnes. The Library
is large, admirably arranged, and contains a number of valuable works on Natural and Moral
Philosophy and Theology, in the French and German languages. It has also a picture of Washington presented by an American tourist. In the
Museum are a number of photographs representing the "Bernard dogs" seeking for the dead, or
releasing the living from their chilly abode, in the
" beautiful" yet terrible snow. The little church
is a perfect gem; the organ is sweet-toned; and
the early morning services are conducted with
great pomp and ceremony by these pious ecclesiastics. The services this morning are attended
by all the poor wayfarers, who have been furnished with lodging for the night. And most
reverentially do they bow before the altar, which,
to their simple and superstitious minds, presents a
symbol of the presence of that merciful Saviour
who said, " blessed be ye poor, for yours is the
kingdom of God."

*The Morgue*, situated near the Hospice, is a de-
pository for the bodies of persons who have perished
in the snow; and the extreme cold so retards de-
composition, that the features of the dead are recog-
nizable years after death. The dogs accompany

us in a ramble around the buildings, and show a
perfect willingness to climb the snowy heights,
now made so resplendent by the rising sun.

In conversing with guests the monks speak
only French; but they are exceedingly polite, and
quite communicative. After a service of 15 years
in this cold climate, subject to the labors and
excitements incident to their perilous position,
they are compelled to go down the valley, and
spend the remaining years in Martigny. After
dropping our contribution in the box, and taking
leave of these kind friends whose appearance and
manners we admire, and whose self-denying and
heroic labors are warmly appreciated, we march
forth "solitary and alone" to the conquest of
Italy.

# CHAPTER XII.

### ITALY.—HOSPICE TO ROME.

THE route, leads us down the hillside, by a zig-zag path, for several miles; then conducts us, along a good mountain road, to Aosta. With "strap" and map in one hand, umbrella and guide book in the other, we press down the mountain, merry as a lark. On the roadside are numerous shrines, in which are placed images of the "virgin and child," garlanded with flowers.

> "By cells whose image, trembling as he prays,
> Awe-struck, the kneeling peasant scarce surveys."

Little churches are erected in all the villages; the peasants are gathering the harvest; men and women bearing burdens beneath which an ox might bend, are passing along the dizzy heights; maidens in brilliant costume, and crowned with wide-brimmed hats, are gathering the short grass in snow-white sheets, and carrying it down the hillsides for winter fodder; sturdy men with large lustrous eyes, black bushy beard, and "raven locks," are journeying along the winding roads;

mountain streams, fresh from icy fountains, leap joyously from rock to rock, brightly flashing in their downward flight; while soft breezes laden with delicious perfumes, and delightful music chanted by cheerful birds, assure us that we now walk beneath an Italian sky.

> " On as we move, a softer prospect opes—
>   Calm huts, and lawns between, and sylvan slopes:
>   White mists, suspended on th' expiring gale,
>   Moveless o'erhang the deep secluded vale;
>   While pastoral pipes and streams the landscape lull,
>   And bells of passing mules that tinkle dull."

In $4\frac{1}{2}$ hours, we have descended over 6,000 feet; passed from chilling winds and snowy Alps to a valley rich in corn, wine, and oil; from the home of the Swiss, to that of the Italian; and walked twenty miles surrounded by scenery the most varied,—a very pleasant morning walk.

At Aosta, a town founded by the Emperor Augustus to guard the mountain Pass, we dine; and thus refreshed and strengthened, take the Diligence for Ivrea,—distant forty miles. While this our first Italian dinner is being prepared, a walk through the town reveals some strange customs. On the walls of the public square, are notices of " engagements " between some young Italians of Aosta! Just think of the publicity given to that, which, is so often kept a profound secret.

Whenever a young, or old couple, by mutual
courtesies and kindly attentions, attain to that
happy condition of imagining, that they should
be "no more twain, but one flesh," the town or
county official, is immediately informed of the fact.
This delighted Italian hastens to inform the
public, by a printed notice, posted in the most
conspicuous place.  The items, composing this
bill of fare for vulgar eyes, are as follows:—the
man's name, age, residence, trade: his father's
name, residence and profession: the woman's name,
age, (!) residence, and her father's name, residence,
and profession.  With some slight alterations, this
notice would read in English, as follows:—John
Smith,—aged 65, living at 33 Layasse St., son
of Peter Smith of 55 Castellane Alley, proprietor of a cafe,—has just entered into an engagement for life, and for "better or for worse,"
with Miss Delinda Jones, aged 63, (?) residing
at 44 Beldire Row, daughter of Jeremiah Jones,
of 44 Beldire Row, keeper of a refreshment
saloon.  How would lovers in America, of such
tender years, blush at seeing the promised nuptials thus placed on public exhibition !  But these
Italians are reasonable people; and the reason
given for this public announcement is satisfactory
—to wit:—" that persons may have an opportunity of making objections," to the consummation
12

of the union. A splendid opportunity this for rejected lovers;—for all those heart-broken youths of 70, to whom this blooming maiden may have impulsively given that uncomfortable covering for a loving hand,—"the mitten." Would not such a custom of public announcement in America be a healthy restraint upon the loving enthusiasm of beardless boys, and romantic maidens? In Chantillon, the grade, weight, and price of merchandize are printed and posted in the public places; and venders of meats and bread, must state the grade, exhibit the weight, and only charge the "lawful price," upon pain of forfeiture.

Would it work public injury, if laws like those of the Chantillon "Conseil Communal," should be enacted for the government of some American markets?

At Ivrea, some of the women walk into church bare-footed; and every one of these Italian ladies, have both head and shoulders covered with beautiful white handkerchiefs, or shawls. The contrast is striking, and we have not witnessed such a spectacle in any other place of worship.

Since leaving Lausanne, we have traveled by steamboat, diligence, mule, and on foot, just 200 miles. At Ivrea, we are "out of the woods," and the shining "rail" is seen with joy; while the announcement in Italian, placarded at the "station," promising a swift (a grande velocita) flight over the sunny land of Italy, is read with delight.

The morning is simply lovely, and the train sweeps speedily past Chivasso, Vercelli, Novara, the birth-place of Peter Lombard,—" Magister Sententiarum,"—and onward to the beautiful city of Milan. Along the route the corn waves and glistens, and trees bend beneath precious burdens of promising fruit. Men and women, bare-footed, are swinging the flail, and threshing in the open air. Farmers are turning the furrows with shining ploughs, drawn by cream-colored cows. The flowers, blooming around these red-roofed stony cottages, are of the most brilliant hue; while men and maidens, adorned with crimson and orange-colored fabrics, add by their variegated appearance, to the novelty and picturesqueness of the scene.

*Milan*, has a population of over 200,000; is the capital of Lombardy; and one of the most prosperous towns in Italy.

The railroad depot is adorned with frescoes, that feed the eye with scenes of beauty, while the body is being refreshed with a most enjoyable noontide meal. There are several wide and well-shaded promenades, some splendid private residences, and a succession,—for several blocks,—of the most elegantly furnished shops.

The *Galleria Vittorio Emanuele*, is "the most attractive structure of the kind in Europe." It is cruciform in shape, 320 yards long, 16 yards wide, and 94 feet high, and has an octagon in the centre crowned by a cupola 180 feet in height. It is adorned by 24 statues of celebrated Italians, and illuminated in the evening by 2000 sparkling gas-jets. This unique edifice,—where are centered the most attractive and brilliant silk and jewelry establishments,—cost $1,600,000.

Adjoining this gallery, is the *Piazza della Scala*, embellished with the magnificent monument of Leonardo da Vinci. *The Biblioteca Ambrosiana*, containing 60,000 volumes and 15,000 rare manuscripts, is visited. On these shelves, the "fathers" are quietly resting in volumes of immense size, and preserved in wormed wooden binding.

In the Picture Gallery of the Brera, we find the far-famed Sposalizio, or the Nuptials of the Virgin, by Raphael. How the visitors linger to look upon that beautiful face! In a building once used as a monastery, may be seen the faded and celebrated painting of "The Last Supper," by Leonardo da Vinci.

The Cathedral of Milan, is both the pride of the Milanese, and the chief attraction to tourists. Of the 80 churches which adorn the city, this is the largest ; and, excepting St. Peter's at Rome, and the church of Seville, is the largest church edifice in Europe. It is situated in the very heart of the city; and by its gleaming marble turrets, illumines the streets that circle around it. It is 477 feet long, and 183 feet wide; the nave is 465 feet long and 51 wide; the dome is 220 feet in height; and the tower lifts its head 360 feet above the pavement. The edifice is supported by 52 pillars, each 36 feet in circumference; and the broad pavement is of marble mosaic. The roof is adorned with 98 Gothic turrets; and over 2000 marble statues,—like bright guardian angels,—stand as sentinels along the shining battlements of this,—almost,—celestial mansion.

The altar pieces are beautiful, and were painted by some of the most distinguished Italian artists; the vast choir windows are gorgeously decorated with 350 representations of scriptural subjects; while bronze chandeliers of the most curious form, exquisite workmanship, and flashing with gems, swing from the lofty roof. In the Treasury, are life-size statues of St. Ambrose and St. Borromeo, in silver!

This Cathedral differs from the Cathedrals previously described—York, St. Paul's, Westminster Abbey, Cologne, and Strasbourg,—in many respects,—chiefly in being built of marble. The estimated cost of this "miracle in marble," is $100,000,000.

From the Tower, a splendid view of the Alps is obtained; and conspicuous among the shining snow-clad peaks, are those of the lofty Monta Rosa, 15,217 feet high. And the Italian architect, looking upon this pinnacled snowy edifice, erected in imitation of the same, the marble-turreted Cathedral of Milan! What are the grandest works of man, but feeble imitations of the divine handiwork!

The Milanese are dignified in movement, refined in manner, elegant in dress, and quite handsome. We have seen no paintings in the art galleries, more beautiful than are some of those "stylish," "fashionable," and "aristocratic" Milanese, that promenade along the brilliant Galleria Vittorio Emmanuele. In the evening, the Piazza is crowded with men sipping wines, and listening to the most charming music, vocal and instrumental. "Oft in the stilly night" the voice of song may be heard, when the moon shines brightly in the blue Italian sky.

*Venice*, is distant from Milan 200 miles. At four o'clock on a lovely morning, the train,—sent off with the blast of a bugle,—the Italian style of dismissing trains from stations,—goes thundering over the rich and fertile plains of Lombardy. Onward we speed past the cities of Bergamo, Brescia, Verona, Vicenza, and Padova. How beautifully situated are these towns, crowning the heights and commanding magnificent views of the surrounding country ! And how fruitful are these fields ; how sweet with fragrance and merry with song!

The language of the poet is appropriate in presence of such a scene :—

> " Thou art the garden of the world, the home
>   Of all Art yields, and Nature can decree;
>   Even in thy desert, what is like to thee?
>   Thy very weeds are beautiful, thy waste
>   More rich than other climates' fertility,
>   Thy wreck a glory, and thy ruin graced
>   With an immaculate charm which cannot be defaced."

Orchards, vineyards, mulberry plantations, follow in quick succession. Peasants robed in brilliant colored garments are toiling in the fields. The fruit trees, festooned with vines, clasp hands for miles along the track. How beautifully Virgil, the farmer and poet,—who was born in Mantua, a few miles distant,—pictures this peasant life :—

> " Oh peasants, far too blest! if only this
>   Were theirs, the simple knowledge of their bliss !
>   Far from the din of arms, earth's foodful soil
>   With easy nutriment repays their toil.
>   Yet, rich in various wealth, the peasant knows
>   A life ingenuous, and a safe repose.
>   Calm fields, fresh dells, grots, limpid lakes, the breeze,
>   Echoing with herds, and slumbers bowered with trees."

And the Latin poet, Avienus, in a little poem

on "Country Life," refers to the vines hanging from the trees, just as we see them swing this morning :—

> "Safe-roofed my cottage ; swelling rich with wine,
>     Hangs from the twisted elm my clustered vine "

The train halts on the banks of the beautiful Lago di Garda.  This lake is 35 miles long and 7 miles broad.  The surrounding scenery is quite picturesque, and groves of orange trees wave along the western bank.  At Padua we have a fine view of the Tyrolese Alps ; and Venezia with its towers, churches, and palaces, gradually rises from the sea.  The train, with slackened speed, now rolls over the longest bridge in the world,—that which crosses the Laguna.  This bridge is $2\frac{1}{3}$ miles long and 28 feet broad ; has 222 arches; and unites the land to the famous city on the sea.

*Venice.*  Upon the fall of the Western Roman Empire, the inhabitants of those cities bordering on the northern coast of the Adriatic sea, were pushed out upon the small islands of the Lagune, by the hordes of barbarian invaders, by whom the country was overrun.  These islands became subsequently united, and formed the famous island city of Venice.  The present population of Venice is 130,000, and one fourth of these are said to be paupers.  There are in the city 15,000 houses and palaces; and these are erected upon "8 large and 114 small islands, formed by 147 canals, and connected by 378 bridges." The city is 7 miles in circumference, and surrounded by a shallow bay, 25 miles in length and 9 miles in width. It is protected from the sea by long sand hills, which are converted into bulwarks by means of solid masonry 30 feet high, and 50 feet broad.

The houses are built either along the canals, or are separated from them by narrow streets. These streets are paved with broad slabs or brick, and wind in every possible direction. The houses rest upon piles, which, by the action of the salt water become stronger and more durable as they increase in years. Older and stronger is their motto.

*The Grand Canal*, two miles long and 33-66 yards wide—in shape like an inverted S—divides the city into two unequal parts. It is spanned by two bridges, the Ponte Serra Della Canita, and the historic Ponte di Rialto; and is the "aristocratic quarter,"—the 5th Avenue of Venice. Its banks are adorned with magnificent palaces, and handsome houses occupied by the Venetian aristocracy. But how may we travel along this broad avenue, and view these fading glories of ancient Venice,— by steamboat, street car, omnibus, on horseback or on foot? No,—but by gondola. This is,—to us,—a new style of conveyance, and a trifle more poetic than either an Irish jaunting car, or even a Swiss mule. And how we have longed to sit in one of these "romantic" pleasure boats, and be rowed through the streets of Venice!

The afternoon is warm, the gondola chartered, and we are gliding smoothly along the Grand Canal. The "Gondolier," with broad-brimmed straw hat tied with blue ribbon, orange colored necktie, and waist girt with a blue or red scarf, presents quite a picturesque appearance.

Our boat,—painted black, with a low black cabin, furnished with a black leather seat,—is more suggestive of an undertaker's establishment going on a burial excursion, than of a pleasure party composed of merry tourists. But black has been for 300 years the "fashionable" color, and we are delighted at the thought of being in "the fashion." A heavy iron prow counterbalances the weight of the gondolier, who, from the "poppa," rows the boat with a single oar. No other waterman can compare with this tall, graceful, and handsome oarsman. How lithe and agile! And with what ease and skill, he propels his obedient boat through the wandering fleet that float on the Grande Canal!

But the palaces,—faded beauties,—attract the eye. Here is the Giustinian,—the property of the Duchess of Parma; the Manin,—owned by the last Doge of Venice; the Corner della Regina, erected on the site of the house in which Catherine Cornaro, Queen of Cyprus, was born:—and the palace Vendramin Calergi, one of the most magnificent edifices on the canal, owned by the Count de Chambord.

The historic Ponte Rialto, which now shades us, is a very substantial structure, 300 years old, and until 1854 was the only connecting link between the east and west quarters of Venice. The bridge,—158 feet long and 46 feet wide,—consists of a single marble arch of 74 feet span, and 32 feet in height, resting on 12,000 piers. The fish, fruit, and vegetable markets on the right and left banks near this bridge, present a scene both lively and amusing. Here, we look with delight upon the "Merchant of Venice" commending his wares to the purchasing public, and making the air musical with his smoothly flowing Italian. Some of these traders appear to be descendants of Abraham, and perhaps "distant relatives" of the well-known "Shylock."

And was it not at this very bridge, that bargains were made, and monies loaned, in the olden times,— if Shakespeare is to be credited?

"What news on the Rialto?
Antonio:—Well, Shylock, shall we be beholden to you?

Shylock :—Signor Antonio, many a time and oft,
          In the Rialto you have rated me
          About my monies, and my usances;
          Still have I borne it with a patient shrug
          For sufferance is the badge of all our tribe;
          You call me-misbeliever, cut-throat dog,
          And spit upon my Jewish gaberdine,
          And all for use of that which is mine own."

Bidding farewell to our gay gondolier, and threading the labyrinth of narrow streets, we reach St. Mark's Church. This edifice—in the form of a Greek cross,—was erected in the 10th century. The style of architecture is the Romanesque-Byzantine, and the edifice is adorned with no less than 500 marble columns. Marble mosaic pavements cover an area of 45,790 square feet. In the interior, the walls shine with polished oriental marbles; marble statues of the Apostles, and bronze statues of the four Evangelists look serenely down upon us from lofty pedestals; two pulpits in colored marbles, each resting upon seven columns, guard the high altar; the altar-piece, made of plates of gold and silver, is ornamented with flashing gems. In the rear of the high altar are four spiral columns of alabaster,—two of which are said to have adorned the temple of Solomon :— and beneath the high altar repose the remains of St. Mark,—brought hither from Alexandria, in the year 828 !

St. Mark's and Ducal Palace

Four horses in gilded bronze, each 5 feet in height, stand above the principal portal. These bronze steeds once stood upon Nero's triumphal arch in Rome, were conveyed to Constantinople by Constantine, to Paris by Napoleon, and to Venice by the Emperor Francis.

> "Before St. Mark still glow his steeds of brass,
> Their gilded collars glittering in the sun."

*The Palace of the Doges*, erected in 1350, adjoins the church of St. Mark. The council room, where the Nobili once assembled, is 165 feet long, 78 feet broad, and 47 feet high. On the east wall hangs the largest oil painting in the world,— Tintoretto's "Paradise." Portraits of the 76 doges, or chief magistrates of Venice, and 21 large paintings representing famous historic scenes, by such "masters" of the brush as Tintoretto, and Paolo Veronese, decorate the walls. In the upper room, we find the crossing of the "Red Sea,"—a most brilliant picture,—by Titian. The brilliancy of coloring, so characteristic of the "Venetian School" of painting, is admirably illustrated in the life-like and beautiful pictures that adorn these palace halls.

Our guide conducts us to the "Pazzi," or dungeons, where the state prisoners were kept in close confinement; and down to the cell in which they were

strangled.    Here, in these lower depths, where no
ray of sunlight ever comes, and respiration is difficult, the doomed men spent the gloomy days in
perpetual darkness. Upon this wooden pallet now
before us,—the only article of furniture in the cell,
—how many a sorrowing convict, may have slept
the unhappy hours away, while awaiting release
by death!    A bridge spans the canal, and unites
the Ducal palace with the prisons on the opposite
side; and over this bridge,—which we have just
crossed,—the prisoners were led to be executed.
This is the Ponte dei Sospiri, or the " Bridge of
Sighs."

> " I stood in Venice, on the Bridge of Sighs ;
>     A palace and a prison on each hand :
>     I saw from out the waves her structures rise
>     As from the stroke of the enchanter's wand.
>     A thousand years their cloudy wings expand
>     Around me, and a dying glory smiles
>     O'er the far times when many a subject land
>     Look'd to the winged Lion's marble piles,
> Where Venice sat in state, throned on her hundred isles."

*The Piazza of St. Mark*, 192 yards in length
and 60 to 90 yards in breadth, paved with marble
blocks, and enclosed on three sides by imposing
marble edifices, is the centre of attraction at Venice.
Here, we find the shops, where Venetian pearls,
bracelets, necklaces, ornaments in  mosaic, glass

and shells, tempt us to spend a few francs; and here also are the luxurious Cafés, where the wines of Cyprus and Valiaressa are sipped, and delicious "ices," and "creams," are daily enjoyed by aristo-cratic Venetians.  At two o'clock each day, a large flock of pigeons are fed in this square at the public expense.  This custom has prevailed during the past 500 years;  the pigeon being highly revered since the days of the famous Admiral Dandolo, when, by messages borne over the sea by this bird, to and from the Venetian commander, splendid victories were won.

In the evening, the Piazza presents a brilliant spectacle.  A band plays in the centre of the square.  Around scores of little tables are seated hundreds of men and women, robed in the most variegated costume,—Venetians, Austrians, Ori-entals, Greeks and Turks;  while up and down the wide marble pavement, in brilliant procession, march joyous crowds conversing in the liveliest manner, and exchanging pleasant salutations and happy smiles.

After climbing the lofty Campanile, erected in St. Mark's square, and paying a moonlight visit to the Liddo, we leave for Florence.

The distance is 180 miles, and the route lies through Padua, the home of Petrarch,—and where just at present, June, 1874,—the 500th anniversary of his death is being celebrated; and Ferrara, where Ariosto sleeps, and over the fertile plains of Northern Italy to Bologna. *Bologna*,—an ancient Etruscan city,—has a population of 100,000, 130 churches, 20 monasteries, and a celebrated University, founded in 1119. In 1218 there were 10,000 students attending the lectures in this famous school. Anatomy was first taught here in the 14th century: in this university, galvanism was discovered by Jos. Galvani in 1789: and a few talented women have been conspicuous among its distinguished professors. Mme. Manzolina, gave instruction in anatomy; Mme. Bassi, taught mathematics and physical science; and in the 14th century the beautiful Novella d' Andrea,—concealed by a curtain,—lectured the young students of the university! Is this the origin of that delightful literary entertainment known by the name of " curtain lectures?" If it be so, then how indebted is the "sterner sex" for the pleasing instruction thus received,—when the moon looks down from the midnight sky,—to the lovely Novella of Bologna! But must the ladies receive an *appointment* before they can exercise their talents in this direction? This, indeed, may have been the custom in the 14th century, but how changed are the times, and what liberty is enjoyed in the matter of "curtain lectures," in this the 19th century!

The *Library* of Bologna contains 100,000 volumes: and the celebrated linguist, Cardinal Mezzofanti, who was born in Bologna in 1776, and who could speak 42 languages, once occupied the position of librarian. The city is situated in a fertile plain, at the base of the Apennines; and the neighborhood produces excellent fruit, and the most delicious grapes. And how the juice of these grapes, carefully bottled, lie in wait for the weary and thirsty traveler. On the refreshment table, at which we sit sipping excellent tea, there are just 126 bottles of this tempting liquid! And how the corks fly; and the pressed *Ura Paradisa* flows and flows!

Our train, sent off with the blast of a bugle, rolls along the banks of the Reno; through romantic ravines, where cascades flash, and castles shine; over bridges that span the rushing river; through more than twenty tunnels that pierce the Tuscan mountains; and climbing the lofty Apennines, thunders along these sunny slopes, in sight of the lovely Tuscan plains,—the "garden of Italy;"—and halts at the home of Italian Art, the birth-place of Dante, and Michael Angelo.

*Florence.* Florence, formerly the capital of the Grand Duchy of Tuscany, is situated in a beautiful valley, at the foot of the Apennines, and on the banks of the Arno. The population is 170,

000. The streets are,—generally,—narrow, paved
with smooth flags, and flanked with high houses,
ornamented with green blinds. Some of the
promenades are wide; and several of the " Piaz-
zas" are surrounded by magnificent buildings.
The *Piazza Vittorio Emmanuele*, on the right bank
of the Arno, introduces us to the " Cascine," or,
park of Florence. This park,—about two miles
long,—is bounded by the Arno, and Mugnone,
and is the principal rendezvous for aristocratic
Florentines. An afternoon drive, in a "stylish"
cab, along this fashionable thoroughfare, is most
delightful and refreshing. The charges being so
low, and the charioteer so polite, we present him
with a few centessimi as an expression of our
kindly appreciation; and what a graceful bow,
and inimitable swing of the hat, do we receive
from this bushy bearded Florentine! How graceful in movement, are these olive-complexioned
Italians! Men, standing upon the street corners,
look like groups of statuary fresh from the chisel
of Praxiteles, or Michael Angelo. And many of
these poor, unlettered donkey drivers, might be
taken as models for statues of Jupiter or Apollo,
without offending the majesty of those celebrated
divinities.

We follow some of these living statues, in the
track of quick-footed and heavily burdened

donkeys, to the market place. A lively and ludicrous scene is before us. Here, are apples, apricots, pears, plums, cherries, and lemons, in the greatest abundance. And yonder, are street merchants selling hosiery, jewelry, cutlery, and dry goods; each salesman, and saleswoman, shouting the peculiar quality, and the exceeding cheapness of their respective wares, and gesticulating in the most passionate, yet winning manner. Some of these enthusiastic, and ambitious traders, well-nigh embrace reluctant purchasers, and by every imaginable facial, and vocal expression, seek to make quick sales. This is something new. It beats both Jews and Germans. These impetuous Italians, outrun all the " runners " that chase the Jerseymen along Market and 2d Sts., in Philadelphia. The din is terrible, and would be intolerable, in any other language than the musical Italian. When the " bipeds " rest to " take breath," then the quadrupeds wake the echoes in the " Signoria," by their sonorous brayings.

But Florence is distinguished for something better, than braying donkeys, and blatant street merchants. What Rome was in ancient times, Florence has been in modern times,—to Italy. Since the " Middle Ages,"—Florence has been the centre of intellectual life; the home of Italian art. The Italian language, and literature, were born in this city; and here, the fine arts attained the zenith of their glory.

Giovanni Cimabue, the founder of the Italian school of painting, born in 1240; Dante Allighieri, the founder of the modern Italian language, and the author of the "Divine Comedy," born in 1265; Leonardo da Vinci, born in 1452; Michael Angelo Buonarroti, born in 1474; and Galileo, born in 1564, were all natives of Florence. And the treasures of art, contained in these galleries,—both of statuary, engravings, drawings, and paintings are priceless.

Passing through the Piazza della Signoria, once the forum of the republic, and the place where Savonarola the Italian reformer, was burnt at the stake on the 23d May, 1498, we climb a stairway of 126 steps, to the Gallerio degli Uffizi. The east corridor is 534 feet long, and adorned with paintings and statuary, and 534 portraits of princes and eminent men. The Tribuna, an octagonal-shaped hall, built at an expense of $100.000, contains some celebrated statues, and paintings. Here, is the Venus de Medici, found in the 16th century near Tivoli,—a master-piece of ancient sculpture; here also, is "The Youthful John," by Raphael; the "Holy Family," by Michael Angelo; the "Holy Family," by Paolo Veronese,—quite a different conception from the preceding; and the "Flight to Egypt," by Correggio.

There are rooms in which the several schools of painting,—Tuscan, Venetian, Dutch, Flemish, German, and French, exhibit the master-pieces of their most celebrated artists. And here we find young artists, busily engaged in studying and copying the "old masters." In some of these "copies," there is reproduced a striking likeness; but in others, the resemblence to the "original," is exceedingly faint.

*The Cabinet of the Gems*, supported by four columns of oriental alabaster, and four of verde antico, and containing 400 gems, and precious stones,—once the property of the Medici,—is conspicuous and attractive. Here, glitter and sparkle, vessels of lapis lazuli, and onyx; vases of jasper; bas-reliefs in gold, and statuettes in gold, adorned with diamonds.

This Uffizi gallery, stands on the right bank of the Arno, and originated with the Medici collection. On the left bank,—conspiciously situated,—is the *Palazzo Pitti*, built by order of Lucca Pitti, a powerful opponent of the Medici. This palace is now united to the Uffizi gallery, by the Ponte Vecchio; and the ten minutes walk, from the "Uffizi" to the "Pitti," over the flowing Arno, is the most interesting and delightful "artistic" excursion, thus far enjoyed. The stairways and corridor, along which we pass, are ornamented with woodcuts, engravings, drawings, and paintings, by the tens of thousands! In a single collection, there are 30,000 "drawings."! The Pitti Palace, has been the residence of the reigning sovereign since the 16th century. The central structure is 350 feet broad, and 121 feet high. Through these splendid saloons, adorned with 500 pictures —"works of the old masters,"—we wonderingly wander. And reclining on velvet covered seats, we gaze with delight upon tables made of malachite, alabaster, marble, and mosaic,—some of which are valued at $150.000; upon the "Holy Family," by Murillo, and Madonnas, by Raphael.

> "I shall not soon forget that sight;
>   The glow of autumn's westering day,
> A hazy warmth, a dreamy light,
>   On Raphael's picture lay.
>
> "It was a simple print I saw,
>   The fair face of a musing boy;
> Yet, while I gazed, a sense of awe
>   Seemed blending with my joy.
>
> "There drooped thy more than mortal face,
>   O Mother, beautiful and mild!
> Enfolding in one dear embrace
>   Thy Saviour and thy child!"

The famous "Boboli Garden," surrounds the Pitti palace; and with its winding walks, terraced heights, sparkling fountains, beautiful statues, and charming views of Florence and the surrounding country, is a delightful place to spend the afternoon.

The national library contains 200,000 volumes, and 800 manuscripts. Through the kindness of the gentlemanly librarian, we are permitted to look upon the " first printed Homer, and Dante." These volumes are not exposed to vulgar sight, but are carefully guarded by lock and key, in a remote apartment. We scarcely recognize our old Grecian friend of college days, in his typographical dress of 1488.

Florence has 87 churches. A few of these are worthy of mention. Here is the church of St. John the Baptist, octagonal in form, 94 feet in diameter, crowned with a dome, and famous for its three bronze doors. The oldest of these doors, —adorned with representations from the life of St. John,—was completed by Pisano, in 1330. This artist spent 22 years in decorating this door! The second door,—ornamented with ten scenes from Scripture history,—Michael Angelo regarded as worthy of forming an entrance to Paradise. The Cathedral,—556 feet long, and 342 feet across the transepts,—is crowned by a dome, 352 feet in height. The interior decorations, are not so brilliant as some of the cathedrals already described.

The church of St. Lorenzo, is one of the most ancient in Italy. It was consecrated by St.

Ambrose in 393. In the new sacristy, are the monuments of the Medici, executed by Michael Angelo. *The Chapel of the Princes,*—the burial chamber of the grand-dukes—is perhaps the most elaborately ornamented, and the costliest edifice of the kind, in Europe. Here, are granite sarcophagi of the princes, guarded by gilded bronze statues; and the armorial bearings of sixteen Tuscan towns, in the most brilliant marble mosaics. Nearly five millions of dollars were expended by the Medici family, in the construction and ornamentation of this edifice.

The Church of *S. Croce,* is the Pantheon of modern Italy. In this church, are buried some of the most illustrious men of the churches. In the north and south aisles, we find the monuments of Machiavelli, Alfieri, Galileo, and Michael Angelo.

> " In Santa Croce's holy precincts lie
> Ashes which make it holier, dust which is
> Even in itself an immortality,—
>                     Here repose
> Angelo's, Alfieri's bones, and his,
> The starry Galileo, with his woes;
> Here Machiavelli's earth returned to whence it rose."

In the south aisle, there is a beautiful honorary monument to the memory of Dante. The poet was not buried in S. Croce. When the Guelphs were victorious over the Ghibellines, in 1302, Dante was banished from Florence. He died at Ravenna, in September, 1321; and his tomb is in the church of S. Francesca, in that city.

> "Ungrateful Florence! Dante sleeps afar,
> Like Scipio, buried by the upbraiding shore;
> Thy factions, in their worse than civic war,
> Proscribed the bard, whose name for evermore
> Their children's children would in vain adore."

In the *Piazzi S. Croce*, is erected the magnificent public monument to Dante. On a lofty pedestal stands a colossal statue of the poet, 19 feet high. It was inaugurated on the 14th May, 1865; —the 600th anniversary of the birth of the poet.

What a sad-looking face, is that of the author of the "Divine Comedy"! Never have we looked upon such a downcast, dejected, gloomy, marble effigy, as this one, now before us. Why so sad? Was it his early—but unrequited—love for Bearice, that so changed the countenance of this gifted Florentine? Of her death, he tenderly speaks:—

> "Why mourn ye not, as through these gates of woe
> Ye wend along our city's midmost street,
> Even like those who nothing seem to weet
> What chance hath fall'n, why she is grieving so?
> If ye to listen but awhile would stay,
> Well knows this heart, which only sigheth sore,
> That ye would then pass, weeping on your way.
> Oh hear; her Beatrice is no more!"

Her smiles were joy to his soul: her very look, thrilled the Italian poet:—

13

> " I spake: and on me straight
> Beatrice look'd, with eyes that shot forth sparks
> Of love celestial:——Yet blank awe,
> Which lords it o'er me, even at the sound
> Of Beatrice's name, did bow me down
> As one in slumber held.  Not long that mood
> Beatrice suffer'd; she, with such a smile,
> As might have made one blest amid the flames,
> Beaming upon me, thus her words began."

If not sorrow for Beatrice, then was it grief occasioned by the fiery temper of his wife "Gemma," that so troubled the unhappy poet?  To both he makes allusion.   In the Inferno R. speaks thus:—

> " And myself,——
> Who in this torment do partake with them,
> Am R——ci, whom, past doubt, my wife,
> Of savage temper, more than aught beside
> Hath to this evil brought."

His wife's temper pushed him down to Purgatory.

Dante,—rejected by the beautiful Beatrice, and afterwards accepted by the fretful, and ferocious Gemma,—could be none other, than a sorrowful man.  And how many "long" faces there are—not in marble—revealing an inner sadness, inspired by similar causes!  Many mourn the loss of a Beatrice; while others are joyless, because a Gemma has been found.  If,

> " 'Tis better to have loved and lost,
> Than never to have loved at all,"

Then, how much *better,* when the "lost" one,

is "of savage temper," and who, to the home, only "evil" brings?

The distance from *Florence* to *Rome*, is 230 miles.  On Saturday, July 25th, at 5-40 A.M., our train—dismissed as usual, by both steam whistle, bell and bugle,—rolls out of the depot. A thunderstorm, has just swept over the Peninsula; and the rain drops, smitten by the morning sunbeams, sparkle upon tree and flower.  The valley of the Arno, refreshed by genial showers, is sweet with fragrance.  The swollen stream, dashes swiftly along its winding pathway, rejoicing in its newly acquired strength.  On our left, is the mountain chain of Pratomagno, and the monastery of Vallombrosa. The monastery, which was founded by S. Giovanni Gualberto, about the year 1050, has been suppressed; and the buildings are now occupied by a royal school of forestry. The dense forests, that girdle the Apennines in the vicinity of the old monastery buildings, shower autumnal leaves upon the murmuring brooks, and furnish the poets with beautiful imagery.

> " He scarce had ceased, when the superior fiend
> Was moving toward the shore ; . . . . and call'd
> His legions, angel forms, who lay entranc'd
> Thick as autumnal leaves that strow the brooks
> In Vallombrosa, where th' Etrurian shades
> High overarch'd imbow'r :—"

Here is Arezzo, one of the ancient, and once

powerful cities of Etruria. In this city, Mæcenas, the friend of Augustus, and the patron of Virgil and Horace, was born. How frequently college students, who have never seen that "patron" of the poets, *scan* Mæcenas when reading the Odes of Horace! The luxuriant valley of the *Chiana*, now lies before us. And yonder sparkles Lago Trasimeno, surrounded by olive-clad slopes. The train rolls swiftly over the Sanguinetto, or "stream of blood." This was the scene of a bloody battle, fought June 23d, 217 B. C. *Hannibal*, having crossed the Apennines, pressed on towards Rome, leaving the Roman Army at Arezzo. The Consul, *C. Flaminius*, pursued the bold African invader; but the crafty Hannibal, so arranged his forces, that Flaminius was surrounded, and 15,000 Romans killed,—including the Consul. During the battle, the streams flowing into the lake were red with blood! Livy,—lib. xxii.—in one of his peculiar sentences, presents a vivid picture of this terrific struggle. And to-day, in the footsteps of Hannibal, 2,100 years after the battle,

"I roam

By Thrasimene's lake, in the defiles
  Fatal to Roman rashness, more at home;
For there the Carthaginian's warlike wiles
Come back before me, as his skill beguiles
The host between the mountains and the shore,
  Where carnage falls in her despairing files,
And torrents, swollen to rivers with their gore,
Reek through the sultry plain, with legions scattered o'er."

But neither Roman, nor Carthaginian, disturbs
the tourist in his happy wanderings along the
shining shores of this lovely lake.  How peaceful, and how beautiful the scene !

> "Far other scene is Thrasimene now ;
>   Her lake a sheet of silver, and her plain
> Rent by no ravage save the gentle plough ;
>   Her aged trees rise thick as once the slain
> Lay where their roots are ;"—

Yonder, crowning an eminence, and commanding
an extensive view of the valley of the Tiber, is
Perugia,—the capital of the Province of Umbria.
In this city, Pietro Perugino, the founder of a new
school of painting, and master of Raphael, lived.
And in the chapel of S. Severo, Raphael's first
fresco may still be seen.  Our train now rolls
over the Tiber.  On the left is Assisi, the birth-
place of Francis, the founder—in 1208—of the mo-
nastic order of the Franciscans.  He died in 1226 ;
and in 1228, was canonized by Gregory IX.  Dante,
in the " Paradise," eulogizes this pious monk :—

> "The lovers' titles—Poverty and Francis,
>   Their concord and glad looks, wonder and love,
>   And sweet regard gave birth to holy thoughts,
> So much, that venerable Bernard first
> Did bare his feet, and, in pursuit of peace
> So heavenly, ran, yet deem'd his footing slow."

We are now sweeping through the lovely and
luxuriant valley of the Clitumnus.  How beauti-

ful the scene; and how well deserving of the
praise of the poets from Virgil to Byron!

> "But thou Clitumnus! in thy sweetest wave,
> Of the most living crystal that was e'er
> The haunt of river nymph; . . . . thou dost rear
> Thy grassy banks whereon the milk-white steer
> Grazes; the purest god of gentle waters!
> And most serene of aspect, and most clear;
> Surely that stream was unprofaned by slaughters,
> A mirror and a bath for beauty's youngest daughters!"

A striking and attractive feature of this Italian
landscape, is the olive-yards, that give their peculiar olive-green coloring to these sunny and sloping heights. These olive groves wave for miles
along the iron track, and climb the hills, the summits of which are crowned either by historic cities,
ancient castles, or venerable church edifices. The
houses in these cities, are erected terrace-like, and
the highest ground is always occupied by a church.
Is not the church of Rome in America, planting
her standards upon the hill tops; and does she
not point with pride to the conspicuous positions
occupied by her schools, seminaries, and churches?
Are not the most valuable lots, on the most beautiful and commanding sites, in scores of our
western cities, owned by this organization? Italy's
example is being successfully imitated by the
American Roman Catholics; and we admire their
forethought, and sagacity.

On our left is Terni,—the birth-place of Tacitus; and Narni, where the Emperor Nerva, and Pope John XIII., were born.  And before us, like an earthly paradise, the magnificent valley of the Nerva appears.  We are now whirling over a treeless, billowy, and barren plain.  The scene is cheerless, and desolate.  Can it be possible that we are approaching the city of Rome?  Surely, Æneas guided by the lovely Venus, would have chosen a more beautiful site, for the founding of such a city.  But yonder are the historic Sabine, and Alban mountains!  Behold the ruins that dot the plains!

> "The Niobe of nations! there she stands,
>   Childless and crownless, in her voiceless woe;
> An empty urn within her withered hands,
>   Whose holy dust was scatter'd long ago;
> The Scipio's tomb contains no ashes now;
>   The very sepulchres lie tenantless
> Of their heroic dwellers:"

Our polite and dark-eyed conductor shouts,— Roma!  And stepping upon Roman soil, we are warmly welcomed by a score of charioteers, who, with whip in hand, stand ready to do our bidding.

# CHAPTER XIII.

### ROME TO TURIN.

"Oh Rome! my country! city of the Soul!
The orphans of the heart must turn to thee,
Lone mother of dead Empires!
Alas, for Tully's voice, and Virgil's lay,
And Livy's pictured page! Come and see
The Cypress, hear the owl, and plod your way
O'er steps of broken thrones and temples;
The Goth, the Christian, time, war, flood, and fire,
Have dealt upon the seven-hill'd city's pride;
She saw her glories, star by star expire,
And up the steep, barbarian monarchs ride.
Alas! the lofty city! and alas
The trebly hundred triumphs! dost thou flow
Old Tiber! through a marble wilderness?
Rise, with thy yellow waves, and mantle her distress!"

AND is this the city of Romulus and Remus; Cæsar and Cicero? Is this the home of popes, and the scene of martyrdoms? It is difficult to realize, that before us, set in a frame-work of mountains—the Apennines, Sabine, and Alban, and the ridge of Soracte—and divided by the turbid Tiber, is the Rome of history, poetry, prophecy.

But this is the city, founded more than 700 years before the birth of Christ, to which, in the language of Virgil, universal empire—"imperium sine fine"—was promised by Jupiter,—the father of gods and men! This is the "Eternal City." These are the "Seven Hills;" and yonder glitters the shining dome, that crowns St. Peter's! With what inexpressible delight we take a seat in a Roman chariot, and roll past the Villa Albani, and through the Via Sistina, to the Piazza di Spagna!

Rome is situated—40° north latitude—in a billowy plain on the banks of the Tiber, 14 miles from its influx into the Mediterranean. This historic river, springing from the Apennines and rolling 200 miles southward, enters Rome sweeping round the base of Mount Pincio; and, after describing three curves, flows onward to the sea, quitting Rome as it glides past Mont Aventino. On the left bank rise the famous "Hills;"—Celio (125 feet), Aventino (155 feet), Capitolino (161 feet), Palatino (170 feet), Viminale (170 feet), Exquilino (188 feet), and the Quirinale (141 feet). On the right bank, are Mts. Vaticano and Gianicolo, (260 feet). The river is spanned by five bridges, the Ponte S. Angelo—leading to the tomb of Hadrian, the Vatican, and St Peter's, on the right bank—being built by Hadrian in the year 136.

Rome is surrounded by a wall 12 miles long, and 50 feet high. This brick wall was built by the Emperor Aurelian, about the year 270. The city is entered by twelve gates. The population of ancient Rome was—according to some writers —about three millions; that of Rome to-day is estimated at 220,000. Hence, the area covered or occupied by modern Rome, is not co-extensive with that of ancient Rome. Ancient Rome climbed the far-famed "hills;" but these hills are to day, to a great extent, uninhabited. Here and there along these depopulated and deserted heights, stand majestic ruins pointing backward to the time, when millions crowded through the 423 streets, and 37 gates, of the imperial city. Some few of the streets are wide and straight; but the larger number are narrow, and—very obligingly—run in every possible direction.

In appearance, Rome differs from all the cities thus far visited. The ancient and modern are here brought face to face. The monuments of the past confront the structures of the present. The Theatres, Baths, and Colosseums, of two thousand years ago, representing the wealth of nations, and pride of kings, stand over against the edifices of recent erection, and of less imposing dimensions. Crowning the desolate hills, and spanning the ancient thoroughfares, are triumphal arches, which, in massive grandeur and beauty of ornamentation, outrival all modern competitors. Lofty columns decorated with exquisitely sculptured figures, and designed to perpetuate the memory of pagan conquerors, are now crowned with effigies of the Apostles, and cast their shadows upon miserable dwellings, tenanted by the ignoble and the base. Obelisks, chiseled thousands of years ago on the banks of the Nile, and dedicated to Egyptian heroes, decorate either the public market-place, or adorn fountains of quite modern construction. Marble pillars that once upheld temples consecrated to heathen gods, stand lonely and yet grandly, sentinel-like, along the public highways. Public buildings, and private residences, are erected upon the sites and foundations of ancient palaces.

But nowhere are the contrasts so striking, as in the sacred edifices. Here, the ancient and the modern, the pagan and the Christian, clasp hands and unite in friendly fellowship. Pillars and porches that once adorned the temples of heathen divinities, now decorate the Roman Catholic churches. Occasionally, the union is productive of most happy results; but frequently presents the most singular incongruities. These decorations, borrowed or stolen from heathenism, instead of adding beauty to the Christian edifice, mar the symmetry of the structure. This varied scene— of the ancient and the modern, pagan and Christian, beauty and deformity, in such close proximity, —makes Rome, as seen from one of the "Seven Hills," the most picturesque city in Europe.

But for a closer inspection and a better appreciation of these ruins, churches, and palaces, let us wander leisurely along these streets, and over those "Hills."

*Monuments. Ruins.* In the Piazza Colonna, adjoining the Corso—the Chestnut street of Rome —stands the "*Column* of *Marcus Aurelius.*" This was erected to commemorate victories over the Germans, and is beautifully embellished with "reliefs," and crowned by a statue of St. Paul. *Trajan's Column*, in the Forum of Trajan, is 158 feet high, and 36 feet in circumference. This was erected to celebrate the conquest and submission of the Dacians. It is most elaborately ornamented. In addition to the representations of machines, and figures of animals, there are more than 2500 human effigies, each averaging two feet in height. These march spirally around the column from the base to the summit. And this singular and sculptured stony procession of victorious Romans, and vanquished Dacians, is "headed" by no less a

Site of the Roman Forum.

personage, than the peaceful St. Peter! This
monument was formerly surmounted by a statue
of Trajan, but is now crowned by a shining effigy
of the crucified Apostle.

Passing through the Via di Araceli, we climb
the *Capitolino*. On the right is the "*Tarpeian
Rock*," from which in ancient times the condemned
were hurled. Before us is the *Forum Romanum*.
In the days of Rome's supremacy, the Forum
presented a busy scene. In this place, the popular
assemblies were harangued by Roman orators;
and judicial proceedings conducted by distinguished lawyers. And here are magnificent monuments, pointing to those ages of imperial sway.
Eight granite columns belonging to the *Temple of
Saturn*, erected 491 B. C., three columns from the
*Temple of Castor and Pollux*, erected 496 B. C.,
the Colonnade of the twelve gods, and the
Triumphal Arch of Septimius Severus, erected to
commemorate victories over the Parthians and
Arabians, greet the eye.

And here is the *Rostra*, or orators' tribune.
How many political and patriotic speeches were
delivered from this tribune, by distinguished orators, to delighted crowds of enthusiastic Romans!
But how changed the scene to-day. If Cicero
were to reappear this afternoon, and again ascend
this "Rostra," with what emphasis would he re-

peat the words—O tempora, O mores—thundered in the ears of Catiline, and in the presence of the Roman senate. How the "times and customs" have changed, since in the Temple of Jupiter Stator on yonder Palatino, this matchless orator confronted the bold conspirators! Columns, temples, palaces, are alike in ruins. And the present shiftless and lazy frequenters of this historic place, what "degenerate sons of noble sires"!

To the left, along the Sacra Via, are the three colossal arches of the Basilica of Constantine. These arches are of vast span, and served as models in the construction of the vaulting of St. Peter's. We now pass beneath the "Arch of Titus." This was erected to commemorate the victory over the Jews, and the destruction of Jerusalem, in 72. It is embellished with some fine sculptures,—representations of sacrificial and triumphal processions, the table with showbread, and a seven-branched candelabrum. The sculptured figures of captive Jews, and the Roman conqueror crowned with victory, are quite conspicuous. Climbing the slopes of the Esquilino, we visit the Thermæ of Titus, and the golden palace of Nero. An attendant with lighted torch, conducts us through a number of gloomy apartments once fitted up in the most costly and luxurious style. And in the flickering light of this Roman candle, we catch

The Roman Forum, Restored.

glimpses of those beautiful frescoes and paintings, that served as models for Raphael more than 300 years ago, and that have decorated this once royal mansion for nearly 2000 years.

But here is the *Colosseum*. What a magnificent structure! How completely it overshadows the numerous arches, and temple ruins, by which it is surrounded! By dropping a few soldi into the open hand of the watchman, we enter, climb some 100 steps, clamber over huge blocks of stone held together by iron clamps, and after reaching the summit, enjoy the finest possible view of the ruins, and one of the grandest views of ancient Rome. The Colosseum is elliptical in shape, a third of a mile in circumference, and over 200 feet high. The building, when completed, was inaugurated by gladiatorial combats, and the most cruel and bloody exhibitions. 100 days were devoted to these services of dedication, and 5,000 wild animals were slaughtered for the amusement of the 87,000 guests, invited to this feast of blood. The 1000th anniversary of the foundation of Rome, was here celebrated with great pomp by the Emperor Philip, in 248.

Yonder, is the gateway through which the royal chariot thundered. Here, are the tiers of " reserved " seats, along which jewels flashed, and from which proud matrons cheered the struggling gladiators. And far below, is the broad pavement so often stained with blood of martyrs, when Roman Christians were torn to pieces by wild and ravenous beasts.

> "His faithful heart, a bloody sacrifice,
> Torn from his breast, to glut the tyrant's eyes."

We shudder as in the light of history we look down upon this arena,—this place where murder was applauded in the very presence of the Emperor.

> "And here the buzz of eager nations ran,
> In murmur'd pity, or loud roared applause,
> As man was slaughtered by his fellow-man."

Descending, we visit the regions beneath the amphitheatre,—now being excavated. The stones used in the erection of the substructure are of immense size, and the foundations are like those of the "everlasting mountains." Some of the finest palaces in Rome, have been constructed from materials furnished by the "quarry" of the Colosseum.

> "A ruin—yet what ruins! from its mass
> Walls, palaces, half cities have been rear'd."

And the travertine-stone in the ruin now before us—only a third of the original structure—has been valued at $2,500,000, for, simply, building purposes! Pope Benedict XIV. by consecrating the interior of the building to the "Passion of Christ," in memory of the martyrs slain upon the arena, prevented any further thefts, on the part of Roman "contractors." The Colosseum is by no means destitute of vegetable life. An industrious botanist, has collected no less than 423 species of plants among the ruins. At all times and seasons, this symbol of Roman greatness appears grand;—

> "But when the rising moon begins to climb
> Its topmost arch, and gently pauses there;
> When the stars twinkle through the loops of time,
> And the low night-breeze waves along the air
> The garland forest, which the gray walls wear,
> Like laurels on the bald first Cæsar's head;
> When the light shines serene, but doth not glare,
> Then in this magic circle raise the dead;
> Heroes have trod this spot—'tis on their dust ye tread."

Turning slowly away from this majestic pile, we wander along the Via di S. Gregorio, passing under the *Triumphal Arch of Constantine*. This was erected to commemorate the victory over Maxentius in 312. The battle was fought at Saxa Rubra, a few miles distant from Rome; and by the defeat of Maxentius, Constantine became sole ruler in the West. It was while marching to this scene of mortal strife, that Constantine is said to have beheld in the sky, the brilliant form of a cross, inscribed with the blazing legend—Hoc Signo Vinces—By This Sign Conquer. He won the battle; accepted Christianity; promulgated the Edict of Milan in favor of religious toleration; and became the first Christian Emperor. The arch is ornamented with sculptures taken from a triumphal arch of Trajan.

Turning to the right, we gain admittance to the Palatine Hill. This is the site of the ancient city of Rome. Here Romulus dwelt. On this "Hill," Cicero and Mark Anthony resided; and along those sunny heights, the costly and magnificent palaces of Tiberius and Caligula were erected. Recent excavations have revealed many of the ancient landmarks, and resurrected several of the entombed imperial edifices. This is the wall built by Romulus,—perhaps 2500 years ago! Here are marble mosaic pavements, marble balustrades, and broken fountains that once adorned the palaces of the Cæsars. And before us are the ruins of the temple of Jupiter Stator, in which Cicero delivered those flaming speeches against Catiline. Descending to the "Domus Tiberiana," excavated in 1869, we find the walls of the house decorated with the most beautiful paintings. These mural paintings represent sacrificial scenes, landscapes, heathen divinities, glass vases, fruits, &c. Some of the walls are painted in three different colors,—brown, red, and green.  Wandering along the west slope of the hills, we enter the "Pædagogium."  The walls of this "school-house" are covered with the scribblings of ambitious, or indolent pupils, who doubtless blunted the point of many a "stylus," in thus defacing the old school-room.  And the whittling and scribbling boy is not dead yet.  Palaces may crumble and kings die, but this boy never dies.  He still whittles at desks and benches; carves his profile in blocks, to show what a block-head he is; scribbles his name on chamber walls, railroad cars, pillars and posts, bibles and hymn books.  Times and customs change, but that big, lazy, ambitious whittler and scribbler, never changes.

Here is an altar dedicated to the unknown God; and yonder is a grotto, where the wolf found shelter, after suckling those historic, or legendary twins,—Romulus and Remus.  This marble altar is adorned with figures of the *Lares*, or Roman house-hold gods!  We enter the throne room; and inspect the apartment where the Emperor's decisions were announced to the waiting assemblies.  Some writers and antiquarians declare, that in this once magnificent chamber, the Apostle Paul stood in the presence of the Emperor.  Probably from this very apartment, then adorned with the purest marbles, and most brilliant paintings, that heroic man went forth to martyrdom.

Retracing our steps, we wander leisurely along the celebrated "Via Appia," in the direction of the *Thermæ of Caracalla*. On the right is the *Cloaca Maxima*. This was built more than 2000 years ago, for the purpose of draining the Forum. In the construction of this great "sewer," the "arch" first made its appearance in Roman architecture. On the left near the Porta S. Sebastiano is the *Tomb* of the *Scipios*. Here, in a sarcophagus of peperine-stone, the bones of L. C. Scipio were found, 2000 years after that distinguished Roman had been buried. What a brave battle with the tomb! The Baths of Caracalla, are among the finest of the Roman ruins. Within these towering walls, once resplendent with shining marbles and beautiful statues, 1600 bathers were furnished with apartments fitted up in a style of royal magnificence. Here are the rooms, in which 1600 years ago proud Romans enjoyed the luxuries of a *tepidarium* and *frigidarium*,—a hot and cold bath. And here are beautiful mosaic pavements, from which we find it difficult to extract a small marble memorial of this afternoon's visit. Certainly, the pavers who laid this flooring in the days of imperial Rome, might well be imitated by "contractors" in some republican cities.

Returning from this suburban excursion, we visit the "Theatre of Marcellus"! Is there any harm in attending the Theatre? If a church member may visit such a place, why may not a preacher? Who are the particular "stars" shining through the "scenes," and shedding light from the "boards" upon a benighted audience? Ah, what a change for the better, both in the "actors" and "spectators"! Sturdy blacksmiths swing the hammer over red hot iron; and scores of busy Romans shut their eyes against the shooting sparks. This building was erected by Augustus, 13 B. C., and could accommodate 20,000 people. The arches are now tenanted by industrious blacksmiths; and the "scene" before us is much purer than those demoralizing "spectacles," that so hastened the destruction of Rome, by corrupting the hearts of its citizens. Would that all the theatres on the face of the globe were transformed into smitheries, and all the roving bands of "fancy," perfumed "artists," employed in swinging the sledge, or hammering iron!

*Palaces. Museums.* The Capitol museum contains many novelties, and numerous relics of past ages. Climbing the ornamented asphalt-stairway, we reach the famous Piazza del Campidoglio. This piazza, with its varied and elaborate ornamentation, was designed by Michael Angelo. Here are the statues of Marcus Aurelius, and Constantine; the groups of Castor and Pollux; the Senatorial

palace; palace of the Conservatori; and Capitoline
Museum.   In the Conservatori, occupying a conspicuous position are statues of Romulus and
Remus; here also, is the bronze " *Capitoline Wolf.*"
The bronze was thus shaped 2200 years ago.   In
the museum we find the famous statue of the
" Dying Gladiator."   How the struggle between
life and death, is represented in that chiselled
form !

> " I see before me the gladiator lie;
> He leans upon his hand—his manly brow
> Consents to death, but conquers agony,
> And his droop'd head sinks gradually low—
> And through his side the last drops ebbing slow
> From the red gash, fall heavy, one by one,
> Like the first of a thunder shower;"

Here also, are statues and busts of the  emperors
and philosophers.   How *character* is discovered
even in marble faces.   And what demons incarnate
some of the emperors must have been, if these
imperial effigies are " striking" portraits.   What
savage cruelty is disclosed in this stony face of
Caracalla !   Certainly the beautiful face of the
" Capitoline Venus," upon which we now gaze, is
much more attractive than this ugly portrait bust
of that cruel emperor.

*The Palace of the Vatican.  Paintings.  Statuary.*
The  palace of the popes, communicating with the

Basilica di S. Pietro, is the most extensive palace
in the world. It is 1277 feet long; has 20 courts,
and 11,000 apartments. Having secured a card of
admission to this magnificent residence of Pius IX.,
we hasten over the Ponte S. Angelo, past the
Mauseleo di Adriano, and through the Borgo
Nuovo, and Piazza Rusticucci. At the extremity
of the colonnade, we are confronted by the Swiss
guards. These brilliantly costumed zouaves politely bow to the "permit" we present, and point out
the Scala Regia, by which we may ascend to the
*Sixtine Chapel.* This edifice was erected by Pope
Sixtus IV. in 1473. It is 132 feet long, 45 feet
wide, and is adorned with most magnificent paintings by Michael Angelo, and other distinguished
"masters." The walls are decorated with scriptural scenes. One of these is "The Baptism
of Christ," by Perugino. In this painting, the
artist represents the Saviour as standing upon dry
ground. Certainly, Raphael's master was not a
good baptist. The ceiling was painted by Michael
Angelo. The artist, by these numerous paintings,
seeks to represent the preparation for the coming of
the Messiah. We have, in sections appropriately
grouped, representations of the successive scenes in
the creative work; the leading events recorded in
the O. Testament; the prophets Jeremiah, Eze-
kiel, Isaiah, Daniel, Jonah ; and various histo-

rical characters alluded to in the Bible.  What a magnificent procession of events and illustrious personages is thus pictured along the ceiling of this famous chapel !

The altar wall, is adorned with the celebrated painting of the " *Last Judgment.*"   It is 64 feet wide, and covers 900 square feet of canvas.  In the execution of this painting, Michael Angelo spent eight years, and when it was completed in 1541, the artist was just sixty years of age. Both in the figures, and the grouping, it resembles that " largest painting in the world,"—*Tintoretto's Paradise*, in the Doge's palace, Venice.  These distinguished artists teach the Roman theology. And the peculiar doctrines of this ancient church, are most brilliantly pictured upon the glowing canvas.  While gazing upon these beautiful creations of one, who was truly great as " architect, sculptor, and painter," we are suddenly startled by the quick tramping of feet, and the loudest and most joyous laughter.  What does it mean? Nearer and nearer come those strange foot-falls, and louder and louder grow these commingling and somewhat discordant sounds.  " Is it a pilgrim band " hastening to kiss the toe of " his holiness," and lay rich treasures at the feet of Peter's successor?  Certainly not.  Pilgrims, would march with slow and solemn step into the presence of

the only "infallible" mortal.  And these laughing
voices are those of females!  Can it be that some
of the numerous nunneries are enjoying a holiday,
and that the "sisters" are rushing from their prison
houses, to the beautiful and fragrant "Il Boscareccio," to enjoy an "audience" with the Pope?
This cannot be.  Pious and reverential nuns would
neither step so hastily, nor laugh so loudly within
the sacred precincts of the Vatican.

But here they come—all the way from New
England—some twenty merry Yankee maidens!
Through the ornate portals of the famous "Sixtine,"
they rush as wildly, as if it were the rustic gateway leading to some rural playground.  This is
"Young America" abroad,—independent, inquisitive, not excessively reverential, and somewhat
indifferent to the traditions of the past.  And
never did this venerable edifice shadow such a
joyous, happy, mirthful band, as is now marching
up and down beneath its gorgeously decorated
ceiling.  And how delighted these maidens
appear to be, at the scenes before them.  And
this spectacle is novel.  Such a company of angels, and cherubs, as decorate these walls, can only
be seen in the Sixtine chapel.  And to what expressions of admiration, and delight do we listen:—
"O what a beautiful angel"!  "See the dear little
cherub"!  "What a nice little head"!  "How

14

cunning"!  "Charming creature"!  "What a sweet little fellow"!  All those epithets, that so enrich the school girl's vocabulary, and adorn the compositions of these poetic maidens, are most lavishly and lovingly applied to those creations of Michael Angelo.  And if those lovely forms were not so long—for 300 years—*attached* to the consecrated walls, we should expect to see them leap to the floor, and respond to these affectionate salutations. But these happy tourists, under the guidance of a lady of uncertain years, pass from our presence, and we continue our rambles "solitary and alone."

Passing from this chapel where popes are elected, and some of the most gorgeous ceremonies of the Roman church celebrated, we proceed to the Loggie and Stanze of Raphael.  Here in the "Loggie," is Raphael's Bible,—a series of fifty-two paintings representing O. and N. Testament subjects.  In the "Stanze," we find the ceilings and walls ornamented with paintings and frescoes, representing Biblical and mythological scenes.  The school of Athens, in which the artist seeks to represent the various schools of ancient philosophy, and their distinguished representatives, is a most admirable painting.  Pythagoras, Anaxagoras, Democritus, Socrates, Plato, and Aristotle, are placed upon the canvas in company with Zoroaster, Ptolemies, and

Archimedes.   In this "school," we also find paintings of both Raphael and his master, Perugino. This is the only portrait of Raphael that we have seen thus far in our wanderings.

In the *Stanze S. Eliodoro*, are beautiful paintings of Moses at the burning bush; Jacob's vision; the Sacrifice of Isaac; and the liberation of Peter. In the picture gallery is exhibited the far-famed "Transfiguration," the Madonna of Foligno, and coronation of the virgin,—by Raphael. How beautiful are the portraits painted by this "master." Truly, we take no note of time, while gazing upon these marvelous creations of this inimitable artist. Some of Raphael's most brilliant works were executed at the age of 25. He died April 6th, 1483, at the early age of 37; and found a last resting place in the church consecrated to the martyrs—the Roman Pantheon.

*The Vatican Museum.*   This, in its collection of sculptures in marble, and celebrated antiques, is the finest in the world.   We wander leisurely and inquisitively through a corridor 39 feet wide, and 2263 feet long.   A good beginning is it not? And after surveying the thousands of objects that adorn this lengthy corridor, we walk through another apartment 530 feet long.   How beautiful are the frescoes that shine along these walls; and what an array of busts stare at us from stately pedestals!

But another door springs open, and another gallery 320 feet in length, invites us to continue our " wanderings." Stimulated by the somewhat pleasing reflection, that possibly the last "collection" is now before us, we carefully inspect the various objects, that are so tastefully arranged along this marble highway. What fineness of material, beauty of form, exquisite workmanship, and elaborate ornamentation are here exhibited ! But another saloon—only however 238 feet long—beckons us forward, and we continue our march. Our pencil now needs sharpening, and the white pages of our note book, are rapidly diminishing.

In the museums visited, are statues and busts of emperors, poets, warriors, heathen gods and goddesses, in black and red granite, green basalt, and purest Parian marble ; beautiful marble basins ; dancing satyrs in porphyry ; charming marble flower baskets; brilliant sculptured triumphal processions; marble fiery steeds attached to glittering marble chariots; curious and costly mosaics ; statues by Praxiteles ; a gilded bronze statue of Hercules 12 feet high ; the sarcophagus of Scipio, in which the bones of that distinguished Roman were found in 1780 ; sarcophagus of Constantia, daughter of Constantine, beautifully decorated with vintage scenes ; silver goblets and golden ornaments ; chains, rings, and wreaths, exhibiting the most

ingenious and exquisite workmanship—found in
ancient Etruscan tombs; terra cotta sarcophagi,
with life-size figures of the deceased chiseled on
the covers; and alabaster cinerary urns, where the
ashes of cremated heroes were, doubtless, once deposited.

> "His scattered limbs with my dead body *burn*,
> And once more join us in the pious *urn*."

But the doors of a dozen other galleries are
swung open! We are bewildered in the presence
of such treasures of art; and our heads grow
heavy, in attempting to carry so many marble statues in remembrance. How many miles we have
travelled since entering the museum we know not,
but, wearied and fatigued, we seek a temporary relief in gazing upon the 'Il Boscareccio, or garden
of the Vatican. What, if we should see the Pope
granting an audience to some pious pilgrims!
Might he not interpret our wistful look, as a desire to return to the dear old " mother church "?
And would he not immediately dispatch a red
hatted cardinal to welcome us to the " fold " of which
he is the only and true shepherd? And his love
for the great republic of the west, so pure, and un-
selfish, would it not incline him to grant us " abso-
lution " for the past, and, for the present, a " special
indulgence " to remain in the museum for the pur-

pose of more carefully and critically inspecting these marvels of art?  But the *Pius* old man is not to be seen; we are not favored with a glance of his "twinkling eye;" we are not dazzled with a glimpse of the shining tiara; and the soft, sweet, odorous breeze, that fans our cheek, does not convey to our open and willing ears the faintest jingle of the keys of St. Peter.

Somewhat disappointed, but exceedingly refreshed, we enter the Cortile di Belvedere.  Here is the famous *Laocoon* group.  What an exciting marble picture is this, of the "father and his two sons entwined by the snakes"!  Michael Angelo regarded it as a "marvel of art."

> "Go see
> Laocoon's torture, dignifying pain—
> A father's love and mortal's agony
> With an immortal's patience blending; vain
> The struggle; vain, against the coiling strain
> And gripe, and deepening of the dragon's grasp,
> The old man's clench!"

A little further along we find the *Apollo Belvedere.*  What beauty, dignity, and majesty in this statue of Carrara marble!  If the Pope's limbs were as shapely and shining as those of this marble divinity, that dear old man would not so frequently sigh for "a new pair of legs."  In this graceful statue we may deliberately

> " View the lord of the unerring bow,
> The god of life, and poesy, and light—
> The sun in human limbs array'd, and brow
> All radiant from his triumph in the fight."

*Churches and Catacombs.* There are in the city of Rome 300 church edifices. The population is about 225,000. Church accommodation in Rome is far in advance of the population. Spiritual guides are quite numerous. There are 6,000 clergymen, and 5,000 nuns. As the "sisters" are diligent promoters of the spiritual interests of the people, they may, properly, be classed as guides, instructors. Then, for the spiritual guidance of every twenty-one individuals—men, women, and children—within the limits of the Eternal City, there is either a priest or a nun! And these willing priests, and faithful nuns, perform their labors, and discharge their duties, under the eye of an infallible pope! What a magnificent army : what an able commander ! With these hundreds of churches, ornamented with purest marbles, and embellished with the loveliest Madonnas; with these thousands of carefully-trained and thoroughly devoted nuns and priests; and with this most experienced and infallible leader, the church in Rome should be most successful in turning men from sin to holiness. And yet, if the truth be told, the millenium has not even dawned upon this historic city. Of the 300 churches, a few may be named, and briefly described.

S. Prassede, was dedicated 1000 years ago, to the daughter of St. Pudens, with whom Peter lodged when at Rome (?). S. Maria in Trastevere, is erected where an oil spring welled forth when the Saviour was born (?). S. Maria Sopra Minerva, is erected on the ruins of a temple dedicated by Pompey to Minerva. This is said to be the only Gothic church in Rome. The paintings, frescoes, and monuments in this church are very fine. Here, we find magnificent monuments erected to the memory of Leo X. and Clement VII.—the two Medicis. S. Maria in Araceli, is erected on the site of a heathen temple, and is famous for its Christmas services. In one of the chapels, a manger is fitted up at Christmas. In this manger, a brilliantly-decorated image of the Infant Jesus —il santo bambino —is exhibited. And during Christmas week, children assemble in this chapel for the purpose of praying to this image! S. Pudenziana, is a comparatively small edifice. It is said to be the most ancient church in Rome, and is erected on the spot where once stood the house of Pudens, with whom Peter lodged. We look upon this old edifice with feelings akin to veneration. Peter, if he ever visited Rome, may have accepted the hospitalities of the excellent

Pudens, and enjoyed the pleasant society of the maidens, Praxedis and Pudentiana. After preaching the gospel to the unconverted, and when wearied by excessive labors, he may have slowly climbed the Viminale, and quietly rested in the home of these kind friends. S. Croce in Jerusalemme, was erected by S. Helena. There are numerous relics carefully preserved in this church; and conspicuous among these sacred treasures are " the Inscriptions on the Cross," brought from Jerusalem by St. Helena. S. Maria Maggiore, is 360 feet long, and 150 feet wide. It occupies a conspicuous position, and presents an imposing appearance. The nave is supported by 36 marble pillars; and the paintings and frescoes are beautiful. Here, are bronze statues designed by Angelo, and the splendid monuments of Popes and Cardinals. The relics are numerous. The remains of St. Matthew, and five boards from " the manger," are the most highly prized. We look wistfully into the Chapel del Crocefisso, but the " boards " are not exposed to vulgar sight. In the piazza, a singular scene is witnessed from January 17th. to January 23d. In front of the little church of S. Antonio, domestic animals of all kinds are sprinkled with holy water, and blessed! Even the Pope's horses are baptized!

Passing the Colosseum, and walking a considerable distance along the Via di S. Giovanni, we visit the famous *S. Giovanni in Laterano.* This was once the principal church of Rome. Until the removal of the Papacy to Avignon, in 1305, the popes resided in a palace adjoining this church. This edifice is 408 feet long; the nave is guarded, by colossal statues of the twelve apostles; the transept is decorated with brilliant frescoes; four columns of gilded bronze adorn the great altar; and the tribune is embellished with beautiful mosaics. The relics in this church are certainly remarkable—a wooden table once used by St. Peter; and the heads of the apostles Peter and Paul. In close proximity to the Lateran is the *Scala Santa.* This stairway consists of 28 marble steps. It was brought from Pilate's palace at Jerusalem to Rome by the Empress Helena, in 326. Those wishing to climb it may do so, but only on the knees. The Pantheon is now visited. This building was erected 27 B. C., and presents a most imposing appearance. The portico consists of 16 granite columns; the edifice is circular in form, and the roof is a semi circular dome, 144 feet in diameter. There are no windows; the interior is illuminated by an aperture in the centre of the dome. The floor is of different colored marbles. This strangely formed, and peculiarly enlightened, ancient edifice, was, as its name indicates, dedicated to all the gods; and these niches where altars now stand, were once occupied by statues of heathen divinities. In 610, it was consecrated to the Virgin Mary and all the Martyrs, by Pope Boniface IV. And in commemoration of this notable event, the festival of "All Saints" was instituted. It is known as the Church of Santa Maria Rotonda. It is,

> "Simple, erect, severe, austere, sublime—
>    Shrine of all saints, and temple of all gods,
>      *   *   *   * spared and blest by time;
>    Looking tranquility, while falls or nods
>    Arch, empire, each thing round thee, and man plods
>      His way to thorns, to ashes—glorious dome!
>    Shalt thou not last? Time's scythe and tyrants' rods
>      Shiver upon thee—sanctuary and home
>      Of art and piety—Pantheon! pride of Rome!"

Here is Raphael's tomb. It is not quite as costly and imposing a monument as that of Michael Angelo, in Santa Croce, Florence. The S. Pietro, in Vinculi, contains the statue of "David," by Michael Angelo, and the chains which bound St. Peter. The *chains* are annually exhibited to the "pious," on the 1st day of August. This being the day, the church presents a very attractive appearance. The monks show excellent taste in decorating the church; but their efforts to dazzle the "pious" are poorly appreciated. Few are present. Advancing to the altar, we "lay hands" upon the chains exhibited. They are certainly strong enough to bind any saint; but that Peter was "bound" by these "two chains," we cannot affirm.   S. Iguazia in Gesu—the principal church of the Jesuits—is gorgeously decorated.   The walls are covered with polished marbles; the ceilings adorned with beautiful frescoes; and the altars glitter with lapis lazuli and gilded bronze. Beneath the altar of S. Ignatius, repose the remains of Loyola, the founder of the order of the Jesuits, to whom this church is dedicated.   A memorial service is annually held in honor of this most remarkable man.   We attend this celebration, and witness a most brilliant church pageant.   The edifice is crowded with the better class of Romans clad in holiday attire; twenty-one glass chandeliers, each holding ten lighted candles, illuminate the building; 290 wax-candles blaze upon and around the highly ornamented altar; a "picked" choir of some twenty famous Italian singers, assisted by a splendid organ and well trained band, furnish the grandest music; red-robed, youthful friars march through the building in solemn procession; and dignified ecclesiastical functionaries, with heads closely shaven, long, beardless faces, and richly embroidered, glittering garments, bow the knee and swing the censer. The scene is impressive, grand.   What a forcible appeal to the senses, and the imagination, yea, even to the heart! In this church there is a beautiful monument to Cardinal Bellarmino, the celebrated Roman Catholic theologian.

The S. Pietro Vaticano adjoins the Palace of the Vatican. The piazza in front of the church is 1000 feet long, and 625 feet broad. In the centre of this piazza stands the great obelisk—weighing nearly a million pounds—brought to Rome by Caligula, while on either side rise the imposing semi-circular colonnades, formed by 88 buttresses, 284 columns, and surrounded by 126 colossal statues of departed saints. The façade is 379 feet long, 152 feet high, and ornamented with statues—19 feet high—of Christ and the Apostles. The portico is 236 feet long, 42 feet wide, 68 feet high, and guarded by statues of Constantine and Charlemagne. The interior of the building is 628 feet long and 209 feet wide; the dome rises 318 feet above the roof, and is 652 feet in circumference; and the cross surmounting the dome is 465 feet from the pavement. The edifice covers an area of 212,321 square feet; has 46 altars, 290 windows, 370 statues, and 748 columns. The interior of the dome is embellished with figures of the four Evangelists, in mosaic. These are of large dimensions—the pen held by St. Luke is 7 feet in length! Beneath the dome is the bronze canopy, over 100 feet high; under the canopy is the richly decorated high altar, and under the high altar the "Tomb of St. Peter." A beautiful statue of Pius VI.—in the attitude of prayer—guards the sacred enclosure where 89 ever-burning lamps shed a "dim religious light" upon the Apostle's tomb. The aisles, transepts and chapels contain splendid monuments erected to the popes; the floors and walls are of purest marble; the ceilings are gorgeously gilded, and the largest and most brilliant mosaics beautify the altars and the dome. We wander through the "hall of the Ecumenical Council," where the Pope was declared infallible; gaze upon "Mary with the dead body of Christ upon her knees," one of Michael Angelo's celebrated sculptures; pay a visit to the tomb of Gregory the Great; inspect the monument of Palestrina, author of the "Miserere;" and stand amazed in presence of the bronze statue of St. Peter. The right foot of this statue is almost worn away by the pious kissings of enthusiastic devotees! What a humiliating spectacle in this noble, grand, majestic edifice! Above us, in shining mosaic, we read, "Tu es Petrus et super hanc petram aedificabo ecclesiam meam et tibi dabo claves regni caelorum." This is the Latin Vulgate translation of the Greek, in Matthew, 16th. chap., 18th. and part of the 19th. verses. But was Peter ever at Rome? Upon this question the authorities are about equally divided.  And until these historians and controversialists shed more light upon the subject, we will continue believing that Peter visited this city.  As no other locality claims him, and as the traditions crucify him on the site of the church S. Pietro in Montorio, we accept, for the present, the "traditions."  But if Peter were to reappear this afternoon, with what sorrowful surprise would he gaze upon this *brazen face*; and how quickly would he order the Pope—his pretended successor—to cast out this relic of paganism, and inscribe Exodus 20th. ch. 4th. and 5th. vs., upon the doors and walls of this most magnificent temple.  St. Peter's, was completed in 1614; cost $60,000,000; and will accommodate 50,000 people. The annual expense is $30.000.  Here, popes are crowned, and saints canonized.  And what brilliant processions of gorgeously robed ecclesiastics have marched through yonder brazen doors, along those broad aisles, over this smooth marble pavement, under the lofty dome, and around this glittering shrine of the patron saint!  And what thrilling music has resounded through these lofty arches, when the grand pealing organ, and the trained papal choir, have united in the tender and pathetic "Miserere"!  This church was, in a measure, the cause of the Reformation.  When Tetzel, preached and peddled his shameless "indulgences" for the purpose of raising money to erect the church, Luther protested; and Luther's protest convulsed Europe, and emancipated millions from the papal yoke. This was the noblest service St. Peter's ever rendered the church of Christ.

*Catacombs.* We had read of these underground abodes of the early Christians, where centuries ago, in the dark days of persecution, the living found a refuge in the homes of the dead. We select the Catacombs of St. Calixtus. Here, a number of the popes were buried, and under the auspices of Pius IX., many important discoveries have recently been made. These grounds are on the celebrated *Via Appia*, several miles beyond the walls of the city. A wave of the hand summons a Roman cab, and having described the route to the dark-eyed driver, we are off at a gallop. Our chariot rolls through the Piazza of St. Peter, along the western bank of the Tiber, over the Ponte Sisto, and onward to the Porta Sebastiano. On either side rise the majestic ruins of ancient Rome.

We have now passed beyond the walls, and are rolling over the Campagna. The scenery is grand, inspiring. The billowy Campagna stretches away toward the blue Mediterranean. Here and there, lonely arches of ancient aqueducts, and hoary ruins of tombs and temples greet the eye. In the distance rise the Sabine and Alban mountains, so frequently mentioned in the annals of Ancient Rome. Historic memories are being rapidly revived, when suddenly our coachman halts, and in pleasing Italian, points out the catacombs of St. Calixtus. A few sad-looking cypresses, and a small brick building mark the entrance to this sacred place. The keeper, who is present, conducts us to the gloomy stairway by which the descent is made. Just at this point our courage is tested. We are alone; our guide is an utter stranger; the tombs are—said to be—sixty feet beneath the surface. And to see them, we must descend with this guide—our pathway illuminated by the flickering light of a wax taper! What, if this tiny torch should expire? What, if the guide should prove treacherous when we reach those subterranean labyrinths? Such thoughts trouble us for a moment, but the martyr spirit prevails, and we slowly and cautiously descend. The descent safely effected, our explorations are begun. The galleries or passages are from three to five feet wide, seven or eight feet high, and run, apparently, in all directions. In the sides of these galleries small recesses are excavated; these served as tombs, and rise tier above tier, like berths in a ship. In one of these galleries we count five or six successive tiers of graves. When the interment took place the grave was covered with a marble slab, on which was inscribed the name of the deceased. Our guide leads us backward and forward through quite an extent of these intricate and involved subterranean passages; and many interesting places are pointed out, and historical facts stated. Here is a chamber of considerable size, containing the tomb of Sixtus II., who died a martyr in 258. Yonder is a marble slab inscribed, "Cornelius, Martyr." Passing through another gallery, we enter an apartment in which there are a few good frescoes, and some very fine mosaics. Here is a well-preserved likeness of Cyprian, looking mournfully down upon the inquisitive tourist, and seemingly charging us to remember our latter end. In another chamber, quite large, and evidently intended as a place of worship, are tombs, elaborate inscriptions, and numerous symbolical representations.

As we wander through these tortuous galleries, looking upon these tombs, and reading those inscriptions, we experience strange emotions. The silence so profound; the darkness so intense; and the memories so exciting! We feel as if standing upon holy ground. Here the oppressed and persecuted saints fled for refuge; here they sang the praises of their newly-found Redeemer; and here they rested when their earthly pilgrimage ended —perhaps 1,600 or 1,700 years ago!

There are more than a score of these catacombs in the vicinity of Rome; and if all these winding and intricate chambers were placed in a straight line, they would extend nearly 600 miles. Some writers estimate the number of interments in these catacombs as high as 6,000,000. From the inscriptions and representations upon the walls and tombs in the catacombs, many suggestive truths respecting the early Christians are learned. Peter's primacy is not asserted. Mass for the dead is not mentioned. Celibacy is not enjoined. Divine honors to the Virgin Mary are not prescribed. " Resting in Peace," is everywhere symbolized.

But the usual circuit has been made, and allotted time spent, and we return to the light of day. Our guide is well-informed, affable, patient. He listens to all our inquiries, and explains with great fullness. A slight addition to the usual compensation lights up his sombre countenance, and with a cheerful smile and graceful wave of the hand, he bids us farewell.

We return to the city by the Via di St. Paolo. On this road, quite a distance beyond the walls, and in the most unhealthy suburb of Rome, is erected the magnificent church dedicated to the Apostle Paul. On this precise spot, according to tradition, the Apostle was buried. The church is superbly decorated. It is paved with pure, polished marble; and, above the columns, we count 173 portrait medallions of the popes. These are in mosaic, each five feet in diameter. Two colossal marble statues of Paul and Peter guard the transepts. On the roadside, further along, a little chapel indicates the place where Paul and Peter bade each other a last farewell. On our left is the Protestant cemetery, and the pyramid of Cestius, 117 feet high. We pass through the gate of St. Paul, under the very arch, we presume, that shaded the heroic martyr.

The *Carcer Mamertinus* was used as a prison in ancient times. Here Jugurtha and Catiline's confederates perished. Some twenty poor and ignorant Romans, are kneeling inside the entrance. The custodian, with lighted torch, conducts us down to the lower chamber. The place is well suited for a prison, and our guide points out the narrow, dark cell, where many a condemned criminal awaited the axe of the executioner. But in this low, dark, underground chamber Peter and Paul were, it is said, imprisoned. Here is a well which Peter caused to flow, in order to baptize the converted jailor; on the wall is a bronze relief, representing Paul praying and Peter baptizing; close to the stairway is a stone, against which Peter leaned, and on which he left the impress of his cheek! At that time Peter must either have had a very "hard cheek," or this stone must have been very soft.  We wander through the Ghetto, where the Jews have lived for centuries.  What a foul and filthy place!  How very much like the "five points" in New York city; and yet what remarkably beautiful faces have these little ragged sons and daughters of Abraham.  Marching past the colossal "Horse Tamers" in marble, we knock at the gate of the Quirinal Palace, but the "Roman soldier" will not allow us to enter.  King Victor Emanuel, and Prince Humbert, have occupied the building since September 20th, 1870.  Passing the church of S. Maria del Popolo, erected on the very spot where the cruel Nero was buried, we ascend by a winding roadway, Monte Pincio.  This little park —formerly the celebrated gardens of Lucullus— situated at the extreme north-western part of the city, and beautified by shady trees, and shining busts, commands a most magnificent view of Rome and the surrounding country.  Here, the plebs and patricians promenade.  It is the "Hyde Park" of Rome.  Through the Corso, up the winding road ornamented on either side with beautiful statues, and sparkling fountains, the carriages move to the Pincio in grand procession.  The brilliant circle of costly equipages, the splendidly robed and princely ecclesiastics, the richly dressed and haughty Roman matrons, the brotherhood of Dominican and Franciscan friars, clad in garments of singular shape and different colors, the tastily attired, and stately "Roman citizen," proud of his Sabine ancestry, and crowds of picturesquely costumed peasants, pass before us in review. If you wish to see the Rome of to-day, you must climb the Pincio, when the sinking sun sets the domes on fire, and Victor Emanuel's trained band discourses patriotic music, in the presence of " free and united " Italy.

The Sabbath-day in Rome, is quiet. There is little traffic. The people go to church, and then go promenading. The band plays in the evening at the Pincio, and the Piazza Colonna; and hither thousands flock to sip wine, and listen to the music. The churches are by no means crowded. From what we have seen, we fully believe that the Roman catholic churches are better attended the farther they are removed from the Eternal City. The pope's influence is more potent with the Irish, than with the people of Rome. Distance, does certainly in this case "lend enchantment to the view," taken of his holiness.

But the vesper bells are sweetly ringing; and " when in Rome," we must " do as the Romans." Passing the Collegio di Propaganda Fide, in which students representing different nationalities are educated as missionaries, and the monument erected by Pius IX., in commemoration of the doctrine of the "immaculate conception," crowned with a bronze statue of the Virgin Mary, we climb the "Spanish staircase," and enter the church of S. Trinita de' Monti. Some sixty "sisters" and young maidens, wearing long white veils, march in solemn procession to the pews in front of the altar. A nun presides at the sweet-toned organ.

> "Her face was veiled; yet to my fancied sight,
> Love, sweetness, goodness, in her person shined."

The choral service is performed by the "sisters;" and the singing is, without exception, the sweetest of the kind to which we have ever listened.

But, thanks to the battalions led by Garibaldi, and to the presence of King Victor, there are other church services than Roman, within the gates. In the afternoon we visited the English church, outside the Porta del Popolo; and now from the Trinita, we proceed to make a tour of the Protestant churches. A young Englishman, the Rome correspondent of several London journals, leads the way. It is now dark, and through the narrow, crooked by-ways we wander in search of the saints. In the vicolo soderini, we find the Waldensian church. Matteo Proche is the pastor. There are thirty persons in attendance. They are well dressed, and look quite intelligent. Old and young *stand* while prayer is being offered, and at the close, every voice repeats distinctly and emphatically the *Amen.* This we believe is apostolic. The Italian Free church occupies a nice room—third floor back. This is Rev. (Father) Gavazzi's church. There are seventy present. At the service in the English Weselyan Methodist church, there are between sixty and seventy in attendance. The preacher Sciarelli—a converted monk—is a noble-looking Roman, and a splendid speaker. In a little room, in a side street, we find fourteen persons attending a " branch " of the Waldensian church. Prochet and Gavazzi are both absent. This is the season for " summer vacation." Possibly they are " recruiting " along the breezy heights of Soracte, or " recuperating " on the Sabine or Alban mountains. Their congregations, considering the localities of the churches, and the summer heat, are respectable in size. Both preachers and people are converts from the Roman church. And it is said that multitudes are awaiting a favorable opportunity to join the ranks of the protestants. To be successful in the work of evangelizing Rome and Italy, there must be unity among those who labor. Italy, to-day, is politically united; the Roman Catholic church is, ecclesiastically united ; and these Roman converts cannot comprehend why there should be such division and disunion among their newly found friends.  Money given to sustain purely sectarian missions is partly thrown away.

*Naples* is distant from Rome about 164 miles. The train rolls southward through the Nuova Porta, and onward over the Campagna.  The desert plain is dotted with tombs, and broken arches of ancient aqueducts.  On our left rise the Alban hills, and on the right the Volscian mountains. Along the valley of the Sacco, past Segni, Frosinone, Ceprano, and through the broad and fertile Liris we are rapidly whirled.  The mountains climb on either side to a height of 4,000 feet. Yonder is Aquino, the birth-place of Juvenal and Thomas Aquinas.  Beyond Germano, on a lofty eminence commanding a charming view of the fertile valley, is the celebrated monastery of *Monte Casino*.  This institution was established by St. Benedict, the founder of the Benedictines, in 529, on the site of a temple dedicated to Apollo.  The library is said to be rich in rare manuscripts,— some of these Mss., dating as early as the 6th century.  At the station, where we halt for a few minutes, the scene is exceedingly grotesque and amusing.  Men with sandaled feet, swathed legs, red neck-ties, and blue girdles ; women robed in gaudiest garments, with pink, orange, and purple colored head-dress, stare at us wonderingly, and inquisitively.  Mountaineers with flowing grey mantles,

15

leathern leggings, felt hats, long "raven locks," and piercing black eyes, come galloping through the glens on spirited ponies. In form, movement, and dress, these Italian rustics closely resemble the Irishman of Connemara. They look like brigands, or banditti.

And as the mountain region surrounding us is infested with robbers, doubtless these very horsemen belong to the fraternity of freebooters. The place, and the people, suggest those beautiful lines in Dante, descriptive of the pious labors of the sainted Benedict:—

> " In old days,
> That mountain, at whose side Cassino rests,
> Was, on its height, frequented by a race
> Deceived and ill-disposed : and I it was,
> Who thither carried first the name of Him,
> Who brought the soul-subliming truth to man."

Along the route, towns and villages climb the sloping hillside, and castles and churches crown the shining heights. Men are threshing in the open air; and horses attached to central posts are marching around a circular track, treading out the corn. These fields are most fertile and luxuriant. Two crops of grain, and one of fodder, may be gathered in a single season. Through Capua, where Spartacus marshalled the gladiators 73, B. C., and Caserta, with its palaces, beautiful gardens and sparkling fountains, our train thunders, when lo, the smoking summit of Vesuvius looms up grandly in the East, and before us the magnificent bay of Naples glitters in the golden sunlight!

*Naples,* has a population of 500,000. The situation is beautiful. The city, built on sloping ground, along the N. side of the somewhat semi-circular bay, assumes an amphitheatre-like form. It extends east and west three miles, and north and south two and a quarter miles. The view from *Castel S. Elmo*—erected in 1343, and 900 feet above sea level—is magnificent. Eastward, with Herculaneum and Pompeii at its base, rises *Mt. Vesuvius;* along the south-east, Monte Santangelo, 5000 feet high, shelters the towns of Lubrense, Castellamare, and Sorrento ; westward, M. Posilipo, Capo di Miseno, and the island of Ischia greet the eye ; while in front, guarded by the shining isle of Capri, is the far-famed bay of Naples. The houses are high ; the streets, excepting a few wide avenues, are narrow and without sidewalks. The Strada di Roma—the Chestnut street of Naples—is the most crowded street we have seen since leaving London. The activity of these Neapolitans is surprising. Carriages roll rapidly through the streets, the drivers cracking their whips in search of passengers ; light wagons whirl along bearing fruit and vegetables to market ; donkeys, burdened with heavy loads of purple

grapes and juicy lemons, march in files led by picturesquely costumed peasants; barefooted peddlers,
pace the streets advertising their wares with loudest shouts and liveliest gestures; beggars with
outstretched hand, and piteous plea, pursue their
fleeing victims, and never halt until the soldi
jingle upon the pavement. Along the narrow
lanes, amid braying donkeys, blatant hawkers,and
ragged urchins, men and women are cooking and
eating!  In some respects these scenes remind us
of the " colored" quarter in Philadelphia; but the
jovial Ethiopian must yield the palm to the
hilarious Neapolitan.  The procession along the
" Chiaja," in the afternoon and evening, is quite
brilliant.  This road skirts the sea, and is the
favorite " fashionable " drive.  We have not seen
so many, nor such costly equipages since leaving
Hyde Park, London.

As we approach *Virgil's Tomb*, daylight disappears; and in turning toward the city, the scene,
in the twilight hour, is both beautiful and grand.
Yonder, emitting sulphureous smoke, is the dreaded
Mt. Vesuvius: along the eastern coast rise the
lofty Santangelo, while at its base, the fires of Castellamare and Sorrento are being kindled; around
the shelving, curving shore, quickly flash the
blazing lamps; and suddenly, a crescent of spark-
ing jets encircles the beautiful bay, from Messino

to Herculaneum!   And now, the full orbed moon climbing above the mountains shines upon the waters; tiny craft, freighted with joyous, happy youth, flit phantom-like over the silvery wave; while tender melodies, sung by sweet Italian voices, are wafted over the rippling tide by evening zephyrs, and greet the ear, like music from "that other shore."   Entering the park, ornamented with shady trees and shining statues, we find two splendid bands, alternately playing; hundreds of handsomely dressed men and women promenading; and cafés, brilliantly illuminated, crowded with men and women sipping coffee and light wines, enjoying sweet "ices," and "Neapolitan cream."   Here, are all classes, all sexes, including friars black, and friars gray—a merry, joyous crowd.

> "Ring Victor in.   The land sits free
> And happy by the summer sea,
> And Bourbon Naples now is Italy!
> A new life breathes among her vines
> And olives, like the breath of pines
> Blown downward from the breezy Apennines."

*The Museum*, exhibits bronzes, mural paintings, and papyri discovered in the ruins of Herculaneum and Pompeii.   These paintings are very beautiful; and the papyri reveal the methods of book making, with bark, 2000 years ago.   And here is a loaf

found at Pompeii and stamped with the baker's
name—Q. Cranius. How few loaves have lived
through seventeen centuries! But we must see
this resurrected city. A ticket is purchased, and
the train rolls along the coast. The road is cut,
in some places, through lava streams 40 feet thick
and 200 feet wide! On our left is smoking Vesuvius, on the right is the shining bay. We stop at
Resina. Beneath us—119 feet—are the ruins of
Herculaneum. This Hercules-worshipping city
was destroyed by the eruption of 79. It was discovered in 1719; and in one of the disentombed
houses, a papyrus library of 3000 rolls was found.
Our train sweeps onward and halts at Pompeii.
Having paid an admission fee of 40 cents, we are
conducted leisurely through this resurrected city,
by an intelligent guide. Along the street of the
Tombs, through the Forum, and temple of Venus,
we wander. Here, is the residence of the tragic
poet; and this is the house of Sallust; and now we
enter the villa of Diomedes. In this building, 17
bodies were found. The streets are paved with
blocks of lava; the houses are built of brick and
stone; the rooms are small, have no glass windows,
but the walls are decorated with paintings in most
brilliant colors. Our excursion takes us through
barber-shops, taverns, bake-houses and various re-
tail establishments. In the museum, four bodies

found in 1863, are exhibited in glass-cases. One of these is that of a girl, with a ring on her finger—worn 1700 years! About 600 bodies have been taken, thus far, from the ruins. These were found in various localities, and in striking and suggestive attitudes. Some were attempting to carry off their treasures; others just locked the doors, and fell with keys in hand; and the Roman soldier—brave man—stood petrified at his post! What fear and anguish seized the hearts of men; what cries for help were heard along these streets; what mortal agonies endured within these courts, when the loud thunder startled the air, the vivid lightnings illuminated the sky, and the burning lava billows rolled down the quaking mount, and over this wicked and devoted city! The heat to day is intense, terrible. Affrighted tourists have fled northward weeks ago, and we will wander no further south. After dining at the hotel Diomede, the north bound train comes thundering from Salerno, and with ticket in hand, we "step on board" homeward bound! The distance from Pompeii to Pisa is 380 miles; the route lies through Rome, Civita Vecchia, and along the shores of the blue Mediterranean. The ride for 200 miles in sight of these shining waters is delightful and refreshing. Elba, Napoleon's island prison, is visible. The towns of Follonica and Cecina are

passed, and our train halts at the city of the leaning tower.

*Pisa*, is situated on the river Arno, six miles
from the sea. The marble Cathedral, with its
sixty-five ancient Greek and Roman columns,
richly gilded ceiling, bronze angels, exquisitely
carved stalls, shining mosaics, and beautiful altar-
paintings, is a stately edifice. In the nave swinging from the ceiling, we find " Galileo's bronze
lamp." The swaying of this lamp is said to have
suggested to Galileo the idea of the pendulum.
The marble *Baptistery*, is a circular structure 100
feet in diameter, and crowned by a dome 190 feet
high. It has an hexagonal pulpit and octagonal
font, both beautifully ornamented. The *Leaning
Tower*—13 feet out of the perpendicular—completed in 1350, rises in eight stories to the height of
179 feet. 294 steps climb to the summit, where
seven bells—the heaviest weighing six tons—startle the air by their pealings. The *Campo Santo*,
founded in 1200, is quite a unique burying-ground.
It was formed of earth—53 ship loads—brought
from Mt. Calvary. Inclosing this grave-yard is
a structure, 138 yards long, 57 yards wide, and 48
feet high. In the interior, surrounding the green
quadrangle, is a large hall. This hall has beautifully arched windows; the walls are decorated with
numerous paintings; the pavement is formed of

tombstones; and numerous monuments are erected to the memory of illustrious personages.   Here is a most beautiful monument to Angelica Catalari. An angel figure unrolls a marble scroll, on which is traced the inscription " Eleemosynæ tuæ comme- moratæ sunt."   Alas, how many die, and leave no kind deeds to be remembered !   In returning to the railroad station we visit the market place, and quay.   Scores of sturdy men are lazily lounging along the Lung 'Arno, and the old city—once the rival of Venice and Genoa, and the conqueror of the Saracens at Tunis and Palermo—is as quiet as if it never ruled the Mediterranean.

> " Not a shout from gladsome children, or the clatter of a
>     wheel.
> Nor the spinner in the suburb, winding his discordant reel.
> Nor the stroke upon the pavement of a hoof nor of a heel:
> Even the slumberers, in the church yard of the Campo
>     Santo seemed
> Scarce more quiet than the living world that underneath
>     us dreamed."

But a sail upon the Mediterranean is on the pro- gramme, and we hasten to *Leghorn* to charter a steamer.   This city has a population of 100,000 ; the squares are large and the streets well paved. In the evenings, the principal thoroughfares present a scene of great animation; and in the early morning, our slumbers are disturbed by the musical shoutings of venders of macaroni.   The

15*

distance from Leghorn to Genoa is about one hundred miles. Our vessel proudly steams through the Porto Nuovo, and we joyously float on the waveless waters. The sunset is gorgeous. Signal fires blaze along the shore. The lights of Carrara, Spezzia, and Chiavari brightly burn. In the clear blue sky, the stars shine with wondrous brilliancy. How beautiful is this night upon the Mediterranean! We pace the deck, gazing upon sea, sky and shore. Our enjoyment is complete. Suddenly, a light from the tower—520 feet high—flashes over the harbor, and rising from the sea, the city of marble palaces greets us through a veil of mist.

> " Rise Genoa, rise in beauty from the sea,
>     Rise peerless in thy beauty!  What remains
>   Of thy old glory is enough for me,
>     And breathe, ye orange groves, along her plains,
>   Ye fountains, sparkle through her  marble fanes."

*Genoa*, is the chief commercial city of Italy. It has a population of 130,000; and the situation is most charming. There are a number of wide thoroughfares, flanked by massive and imposing structures. These marble palaces beautifully ornamented with statues, paintings, and mosaics; those blooming gardens, sparkling fountains, and perfume breathing bowers; the orange groves waving along the sunny heights; and the shining sea flecked with spreading sail, compel us to look and linger. In this pretty piazza stands the marble monument to Columbus. It was erected in 1862, and is crowned by a statue of the immortal mariner. And yonder is the palace once occupied by the discoverer of America. The church of S. Lorenzo is crowded this morning. Thirty glass candelabra, holding 480 burning candles, shine upon a motley crowd. Peddlers, crouching beggars, and richly dressed, stylish Genoese, bow side by side before the blazing altar. This feature of Romanism we admire. We find no " reserved seats" for the man " with a gold ring in goodly attire." When will Protestants cease pushing the poor into the dark corners and dusty galleries? The remains of John the Baptist, brought from Palestine by the crusaders, are said to be preserved in one of the chapels.

At Genoa, we take the cars for Turin—distant about one hundred miles. Up along the mountain to a height of 1200 feet, through wild, rocky ravines and eleven smoky tunnels, over noisy mountain streams, in sight of crumbling castles and flashing cascades, we are safely borne. The fertile plains of Lombardy are before us. Our train rolls past Alessandria, near the battle field of Marengo, and enters the former capital of Italy, as the dinner bells are merrily ringing.

*Turin,* is situated in a beautiful plain, on the

banks of the Po. This northern Italian city has a population of 208,000; and in the uniformly wide and straight streets—running at right angles —reminds us of Philadelphia. Bronze and marble statues adorn the public squares. Here is a beautiful monument, erected in 1873, to Count Cavour. This distinguished statesman was born in Turin.

The Cathedral contains the burial chapel of the Dukes of Savoy, and the handsome monument of Maria Adelaide, Queen of Victor Emmanuel. In the Academia della Scienze, we find the celebrated papyrus with the annals of Manetho, discovered by Champollion. The university boasts of 1500 students; and the library contains over 200,000 volumes.

We visit the church of the Waldenses. It is a beautiful building; and the first erected since the establishment of religious toleration. There are no statues, no paintings. The pulpits and pews are of black walnut; and on the pulpit lamps are inscribed the suggestive words, *Lux lucet in tenebris.*

In the eleventh century the Waldenses separated from the "Mother Church." Excommunicated by Popes, condemned by Councils, they have survived the bitter persecutions of their enemies, and, in the lovely Piedmont valleys, worship God with Apostolic simplicity. In the erection of this beautiful

Protestant edifice, may we not see an answer to Milton's prayer:

> "Avenge, O Lord, thy slaughtered saints, whose bones
> Lie scattered on the Alpine mountains cold."

In the evening, the citizens of Turin march either to some public piazza or garden, and sit for hours sipping and smoking. We have seen no drunkenness in Italy. There are few purple cheeks or scarlet noses. Coffee houses are numerous; and good coffee, with or without milk, is sold cheaply. How much better is coffee than old Monongahela, or " Jersey lightning." Why cannot American temperance philanthropists engage in the coffee business? Railroad and hotel charges are about the same in Italy, as in Germany; and the social habits of the people are somewhat similar. At Turin we take the train for Paris. Away in the distance towers the Col. de Frejus, 8338 feet high. Our train winds along the valley of the Dorsa, rolls through the wildest gorges, and climbs the mountain to a height of 4163 feet. We halt at the entrance to the *Mt. Cenis* Tunnel. This tunnel is eight miles long. It was completed Dec., 1870, and cost $15,000,000. The height in the centre, is 4245 feet above sea level, and 4093 feet below the surface of the mountain. Bidding farewell to the sunny land of Italy, we enter the gloomy passage, 26 feet wide, 19 feet high, dimly illuminated by lighted lanterns.

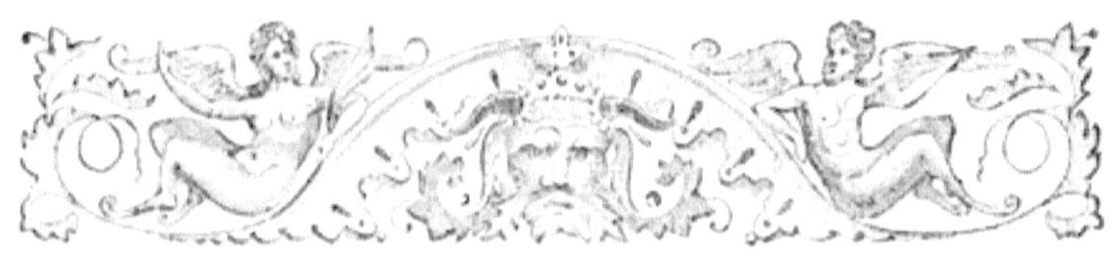

# CHAPTER XIV.



In passing through the tunnel, we have passed into France. At Modane, our innocent baggage is closely inspected by the French custom-house authorities; and even passports are demanded! We inform this official in very vigorous French, that we belong to the "land of the free, and the home of the brave," and never carry such documents. He shakes his head, shrugs his shoulders, "chalks" our luggage—nearly red, white and blue—and points to the waiting train. "On to Paris!" is the watchword, and we sweep joyously over rapid rivers, through lovely valleys around the Savoy mountains, and past Chambery, Caloz, and Amberieux. Here is Macon, beautifully situated on the river Saone. From Chalon to Dijon, the sunny slopes of the Côte d'Or are covered with smiling vineyards. The best Burgundy wines are produced in this district. Dijon was formerly the capitol of the Duchy of Burgundy, and in this town the famous Dukes resided.

358

The scenery through the valley of the Ouche is beautiful and picturesque.    Here is Montbard, the birthplace of Buffon, the great naturalist.    Tonnerre, is charmingly situated on the Armançon. The broad and beautiful valley of the Yonne opens before us.    And this is Fontainebleau !    The forest is 60 miles in circumference, and covers an area of 50,000 acres.    What charming scenery !    Look at those shining cottages crowning the sunny heights !    France may with propriety be called "beautiful."    But the capital is in sight ; the train halts ; and 100 cabs are waiting to whirl us to the Rue St. Honore.

*Paris* is France,—so says Victor Hugo ; Paris is the place to which "all good Americans go when they die,"—so says the oracle.    Whether this be so, or not, Paris is certainly the Mecca of pleasure-seeking pilgrims ; the rendezvous of all travellers and tourists ; and the gayest and most brilliant of European capitals.    The topography, buildings, and boulevards of this fair and wicked city, are too well known to require any lengthy or elaborate description.    Its parks and palaces, street scenes and social pleasures, are familiar to all readers of "foreign correspondence," and students of illustrated monthlies.    We may therefore dispense with the preparation, and presentation, of any lengthy catalogue of the "attractions" of this metropolis of fashion and of folly. Still it must not be ignored. Our "wanderings" would be incomplete without some reference to the "scenes," and "sights," that render it so attractive. Paris —in 1873—had a population of 1,851,792. The city is 21 miles in circumference; and its area nearly 25 square miles. The streets are wide and clean. The "boulevards" are the very broad thoroughfares. These have a macadamized asphalt pavement, are shaded by stately trees, and flanked with the most brilliant shops. Many of the streets and boulevards radiate from so-called "Places;" and the view from some of these focus-es, along twelve diverging streets, is commanding and beautiful. The houses are high— three to five stories—and the public buildings are stately structures. Paris differs from London in its uniformly wide streets, and "magnificent distances." In Paris, the streets, houses, parks, shops, are so constructed and adorned, as to present an attractive scene, and produce a pleasing impression. Indeed, the city appears to be always *on exhibition*. Even the men and women, however humble their employment, are tastily attired, and seem conscious of citizenship in the metropolis of fashion. The very market women—large and cumbrous though they be—might sit for photographs of the latest styles. Would that all the slovenly and greasy venders of meats and vegetables, were like unto these tidy and neatly dressed Parisian provision dealers! And the market-places—in the classification of merchandize, cleanliness, and freedom from putrescent smells—are models. The articles for sale in the meat, vegetable, and fruit departments, are arranged as artistically as if the scene was about to be photographed. The flower markets are worthy of a visit. Here are rows of little cottage-like structures resting on iron posts, and covered with metallic roofs. Hither come the rich and poor to purchase sweet odors, and brilliant colors. Artists are busily engaged in selecting and arranging the flowers, and quick-footed messengers are carrying off blooming bouquets.

Cafés and restaurants are found in every part of the city. They are beautifully ornamented, and in the evening, brilliantly illuminated. The coffee sold in these cafés is strong, and of excellent flavor. The "café au lait" is a popular and most refreshing beverage. At the restaurants, " viands of various kinds allure the taste." It is a positive pleasure to dine at one of these, truly, Parisian institutions. The table cloth so clean and white; knives and forks so bright and shining; food so carefully cooked; and the waiters so prompt and polite. Then the shops are brilliant. The stores along the boulevards, the Rue de Rivoli, and Palais Royal are exceedingly attractive; and in the evening when illuminated, present a scene of beauty that fairly dazzles. These French shop-keepers are genuine artists.

The boulevards, from the Madeleine to the Place de la Bastille, are crowded in the afternoons; 24,000 vehicles roll over the smooth pavement in a single day. Here, tourists from all climes meet and mingle, and here the " exquisites " and "fashionables " promenade, clad in finest garb. In the afternoon, a military band discourses excellent music at the garden of the Tuileries. In the evening, the Champ Elysées—with its sparkling fountains, winding and flower-bordered paths,perfume breathing bowers, brilliant procession of carriages and pedestrians returning from the Bois de Boulogne, —is like a fairy land. And then, those wide and well lighted streets are alive with omnibus and cab. 6,600 cabs roll through Paris, and 32 different lines of omnibusses tempt us to ride at a very low fare. These omnibus lines are controlled by one company, furnish exchange tickets, and charge six cents (inside), and three cents (outside). Just think of being whirled through the brilliant and crowded boulevards of Paris for the small sum of three cents !

The parks, galleries of art, monuments, and public buildings, are in some respects, unrivaled.

*The Colonne Vendôme*, recently re erected, is 144 feet in height, and 13 feet in diameter. The metal of 1200 cannon, captured by Napoleon I. in the wars with Russia and Austria, was employed in its construction. Around this column, in a spiral procession 300 yards in length, march bronze effigies of both victors and vanquished. It reminds us of Trajan's column at Rome. *The Tomb of Napoleon* I., is in the Dôme des Invalides. It is an open circular crypt 20 feet in depth, and 36 feet in diameter. The sarcophagus—$6\frac{1}{2}$ feet wide and $14\frac{1}{2}$ feet high—consists of a single block of reddish-brown sandstone, weighing 60 tons. It was brought from Finland at an expense of $30,000. Above the crypt, rises the lofty gilded dome crowned by a shining cross, the summit of which is 330 feet from the pavement. *The Palais Royal*, was erected by Cardinal Richelieu. The garden inclosed by this extensive pile of buildings, is 257 yards in length, and 110 yards in breadth. It is shaded by limes and elms, adorned with statues, and illuminated by 200 lamps. In the evening, a band discourses delightful music, in the presence of thousands of gaily dressed Frenchmen and foreigners. *The Bibliothèque Nationale*, is the most extensive in the world. This library contains 8,000 vols., engravings, 150,000 Mss., 300,000 maps, and 3,000,000 books! The reading-room is by no means as pleasantly situated as that of the British Museum. *The Champ de Mars*, is a large open space surrounded by rows of trees. It is 1000 yards in length, and 500 yards in breadth. Here, the military are reviewed; and over this smooth, level parade ground 30,000 men can be easily manœuvered. *The Hotel des Invalides*, is the home of disabled soldiers. It is approached from the left bank of the Seine by an esplanade 540 yards in length, and 270 yards in width. The ornamented façade of this magnificent structure is 220 yards long; and an area of nearly 30 acres is covered by the establishment. Here are collected numerous trophies of war, and numberless models of death-dealing instruments. *The Jardin des Plantes*, is on the left bank of the Seine, and covers an area of 75 acres. Here, we find a botanical and zoological garden, laboratory and library. The trees, plants, flowers, and buildings are most admirably arranged. And the bears are quite merry this afternoon, grinning and growling for the amusement of delighted visitors. Buffon, the celebrated naturalist, was director of these gardens, and died here in 1788. *The Palais du Luxembourgh*, is a handsome edifice, and most beautifully ornamented. Within these palace walls are collected the finest modern paintings. The palace garden, intersected by winding flower-bordered paths, ornamented with flower-beds, shady trees and sparkling fountains, and guarded by shining statues, is much frequented by the citizens on the left bank of the Seine.

*The Bourse*—225 feet long, 135 feet wide, and 100 feet high—is a stately structure. It is surrounded by a colonnade of sixty-four Corinthian columns—each column being thirty-five feet high. Climbing to the gallery, we look down upon a lively crowd of apparently frantic Frenchmen. What wranglings, shoutings, and excited gesticulations! No tourist should fail to see those writhing, frenzied, Parisian stock-jobbers. *The Palais du Corps Législatif*, is quite conspicuous on the left bank of the Seine. It is an imposing and costly edifice. Here, the Duchess of Orleans appeared, with her two sons, before the National Assembly in 1848. To how many a stormy debate did these palace walls listen, during the sessions of the Chamber of Deputies! How frequently the "right" attacked the "left," and the "left" the "right," and both "moved" on the "centre"! The scene, to-day, is less turbulent. The patriotic Alsacians, galled by the yoke of the victorious German, are desirous of emigrating to Algeria; and a "loan exhibition" is being held for the purpose of assisting the emigrants. The spacious saloons are decorated in the most sump-

tuous style.   Gobelin tapestries, beautiful paintings, sparkling gems, and ornaments in gold and
bronze presented by noble and aristocratic Parisians, are here exhibited.   And before us are the
autographs of Luther, Calvin, Pascal, Cromwell,
Queen Elizabeth, Peter of Russia, and Charles
XII. of Sweden.   For good writing, we put
Queen "Bess" at the head of the class.

This "loan exhibition" is really a "fashionable" reception.   A brilliant company is in attendance.   Through these shining halls march the
*élite* of the metropolis.   *The Palais de l'Industrie*
—in the Champ Elysées—is 810 feet in length,
354 feet in width, and 114 feet in height.   In this
building, the great exhibition of 1855 was held.
It is crowned with a glass roof, through which the
sun shines upon a gravel floor.   Here are exhibited modern paintings, novel inventions, and
various kinds of manufactures—tables, chairs,
lamps, stoves, etc.   In some respects it reminds
us of Kensington Museum, London.   This afternoon, the building is crowded with thousands of
happy exhibitors and joyous pleasure seekers.
How fond of exhibitions are these fickle Frenchmen.   *St. Cloud*, is a few miles down the river.
The fare is ten cents, and the little steamer carries
us thither at a good rate of speed.   At St. Cloud,
in Nov. 1799, Bonaparte dispersed the council of

five hundred: here, in July 1815, Blucher's head-quarters were established, and the capitulation of Paris was signed: and during the siege of 1870-1, the Germans occupied the town.  The palace of St. Cloud was the principal summer residence of Napoleon III., but it is now a ruin.  It was burned during the German occupation.  The view from the terrace in front of the palace is magnificent.  The Park reminds us of Windsor.

*The Bois de Bologne* covers an area of 2250 acres.  It was formerly one of the crown domains, and a favorite hunting-ground.  It is now city property, and the pride of the Parisians.  This afternoon, we walk from St. Cloud to the Champ Elysées through this once royal park.  The lakes, islands, and cascades are pretty; the roads broad and smooth; and the procession of carriages brilliant.  But it cannot boast of a winding, silvery Schuylkill, or shady and romantic Wissahickon.  In the centre of the city, on the right bank of the Seine, are the palaces of the *Louvre*, and *Tuileries*.  These buildings are of vast extent, covering an area of twenty-four acres.  We must visit the Louvre.  Passing between winged bulls, chiseled thousands of years ago on the banks of the Euphrates, and sphinxes, sculptured along the Nile when the Hebrews were in bondage, we climb to the spacious galleries, and wander through saloons

a quarter of a mile in length!  With what sculptures, gold and silver ornaments, frescoes and
paintings are those royal apartments adorned!
The picture galleries, if united, would extend
three-quarters of a mile!  Here is the "Marriage
at Cana"—32 feet long and 21 feet high—by
Paolo Veronese.  And yonder is a "Madonna
and Child," painted on wood, by Perugino, for
which $11.000 was paid.  And this is the paint-
ing of the "Conception of the Virgin" by Murillo.
This picture cost $125,000!  The Tuileries—
348 yards in length and 36 yards in width—is
in ruins.  It was set on fire by the communists in
May 1870.  The *Garden*—780 yards in length,
and 347 yards in width—with its flower-beds
most artistically arranged, velvety lawns, sparkling fountains, and shady bowers, is the children's
paradise.  The *Place de La Concord*—390 yards
in length, and 235 yards in width—is the largest,
and the most beautifully ornamented "square" in
Paris.  In the centre, stands the *Obelisk of Luxor*.
This is a monolith of reddish granite.  It weighs
500,000 lbs., and is 75 feet in height.  The inscriptions, in hieroglyphics, indicate that it is
3200 years old.  In this *place*, Louis XVI.,
Queen Marie Antoinette, the Duke of Orleans,
and Robespierre, were executed. More than 2800
perished by the guillotine in this square, in  1793-

1795. The *Champ Elysées*, forms a magnificent avenue, one mile in length. It is shaded with elms and limes, and flanked with stately edifices. Through this broad and beautiful thoroughfare the carriages roll in going to, and returning from, the Bois de Bolougne. On a slight eminence, at the termination of the grand avenue, stands the *Arc de Triomphe*. This was erected by Louis Philippe, to commemorate the victories of the French armies. It is 160 feet in height, 146 feet in width, 72 feet in depth, and cost $2,000,000. The triumphal arch is two miles distant from the Rue du Louvre; and the entire intervening space is occupied by the Louvre, Tuileries and Gardens, Place de Concord, and Champ Elysées. These costly palaces, beautiful gardens, wide and shady avenues form an uninterrupted succession of "magnificent distances." In *Père Lachaise*, France buries her illustrious dead. This cemetery covers an area of 107 acres. The "lots" are small—only about twenty square feet. There are 18,000 monuments; and in the erection and ornamentation of these "memorials," $40,000,000 have been expended. Here is the tomb of *Abelard and Heloise*. Beneath a gothic canopy rests the sarcophagus, adorned with recumbent effigies of those erring, ill-fated lovers. In this city of the dead, we find the tombs of Champollion, Laplace, and

16

Cousin. Many of these monuments are decorated with wreaths formed of black and white beads. *Notre Dame*, and the *Madeleine*, are the two most "popular churches." In the erection and decoration of the Madeleine $3,000,000 were expended. 300 insurgents fled for refuge to this church in May 1871; but they were pursued by the troops, and butchered in the very shadow of the high altar! Paris does not remember the "Sabbath day to keep it holy." Theatres and concert rooms are open: dog markets are held; saloons are crowded with men and women drinking and gambling; "Punch and Judy" exhibitions are given in the Champ Elysées: both sexes and all ages seem to be possessed with—well—evil spirits. God grant that our American cities may never be cursed with a Parisian Sabbath!

Having purchased an "express" ticket for London, and selected a comfortable seat, we are whirled at a rapid rate through northwestern France. Here is Amiens the capital of Picardy. The beautiful valley of the Somme opens before us. The railroad now skirts the English Channel for forty miles. We halt at Boulogne; exchange the cars for a steamboat; and bidding farewell to France and the Continent, steer across the stormy "Straits," with prow pointed toward the snow-white cliffs of Albion.

WE are safely landed at Folkestone.    Liverpool
is distant about 250 miles.    The route lies through
London and Birmingham.    And what shining
cottages, blooming gardens, and sparkling lawns
greet the eye on every side!    A day is spent in
Wales—stopping at Holywell, Bangor, and Holy-
head.    The scenery along the Welsh coast, in
view of the Irish sea, Mount Snowdon, and
the old castle of Conway, is exceedingly beautiful.    These Welshmen are descendants of the
ancient Britons.    They are the true natives—
the Englishman is only a foreigner.    And
the Welshwomen, proud of their ancestry, wear
high, sugar loaf-shaped hats!    The port of *Liverpool* is crowded with shipping, and a forest of
masts shadow the Mersey.    But yonder is the
"Java," and the passengers are going on board.
The noble vessel steams through St. George's
Channel, and along the Irish coast.    The land
suddenly disappears; and the wide, western
ocean is now before us.    The passengers—the
majority of whom are tourists—appear delighted
at the prospect of a smooth sea, and swift passage.
But how fickle is the wind; how treacherous the
sea!    The sky darkens; and a violent wind
sweeps the ocean.    For three days, neither sun, nor
star appears.    The ship pitches and plunges;
passengers are sick; decks are deserted; women

cry for help; trunks break loose and roll through
the cabins; and plates and dishes, leaping from
the table, go whirling through the dining-room.
Clinging to the swaying mast, we gaze upon the
"elemental strife."  The rush and roar of wind
and wave, is terrible.  Over the quivering ship,
the billows leap like racers.  At night, the scene
is wild and grand.  The angry waters are illumined by phosphorescent flashes; and the dashing
spray sparkles like gems.  But, there is a calm.
Passengers now pace the deck, and look with
pleasure upon a sunny sky, and smiling sea.
Laughter is heard in the cabin; and the steward's
bell—how musically it sounds!  Propelled by
wind and steam, the "jumping Java" carries us
homeward with rapid motion.  But that lonely
craft, flitting phantom-like over the waters—what
is it?  It is the pilot boat!  Yonder are the
"Highlands"!  We sweep joyously through the
"Narrows."  The shining bay is before us: and
"Softly we drift on its bright silver tide."

> "Glory to God! all our dangers are o'er,
> Glory to God! we will shout evermore,
> We're home at last."

9 783337 194185